STRIPPED AWAY

STEPHANIE K CLEMENS

To everyone that struggles with something others can't see.

CONTENT WARNING

This book contains moments of ableism, off-the-page familicide, fighting, sex, & kidnapping

Kingdom
Longmore Forest
Bellecote
The Dragon
and
Unicorn
The Rare Quill
Tahra's
Cabin
The Pilgrim's
Respite
Dradon
The Five Sisters
Wreswel
Dalcastar

Maurasus
brooke
Faerie Glen
Barrel
Aleria
Slotuslands
rg
Southwark

CHAPTER ONE

"Eljin, are you ever going to learn how to put books back properly? You've been working here at the university library longer than I have, and I swear you haven't figured out the difference between historical treatises and famous plays. Not to mention, you refuse to alphabetize by last name." Kennara grabbed books off the shelf, carefully using her cane to balance as she stood on the tiptoes of her left foot.

"I know how much you love redoing my hard work. If I did it perfectly, what would you do all day? Sit around looking like the Queen of the Library on your throne, that's what. And I know you would rather be shelving books." Eljin's dark eyes glistened as he smiled at Kennara. His smile always melted away her ire.

It's like he tries to get under my skin, and then smiles, just to see what he can get away with, Kennara thought as she limped across the room, roaming from shelf to shelf to put the books in the correct spot, not wherever Eljin felt the right spot was for the day. She sighed. Her right leg was dragging, which meant she was going to need help meeting up with her twin sister, Kellesha. She hated when her cane wasn't enough to get her around. It meant having someone push her in her chair at least for the next day or so.

"Looks like you're going to have to skip training today. Your right leg is already dragging," Eljin said.

"Tell me something I don't know," she said, sitting down with a huff.

All Kennara wanted was to find a healer so she never had to use a cane or chair ever again. Her sister thought she was irrational for wanting such a change, but her sister didn't live with her ailment and the fear that came along with it.

Having escaped the Quickening when it went through their hometown, she and her sister were hiding from the king and his men because they still possessed their magic. Kennara's biggest fear was that she would be the reason the king's enforcers caught her sister because she couldn't move fast enough unless she was strapped to a horse—then, she flew like the wind.

Kennara shook her head to clear the fear. The fear was constant, but it normally lived in the back of her mind. That's where she preferred it; when it came to the forefront, it could be overwhelming.

"Come on, Kenna, let's get you in your chair. I'll take you over to where Kellesha and Cas are training. We can watch them beat up on each other before you head home."

"Thanks, Eljin, I can walk." She stubbornly pushed herself out of the chair and grabbed her cane. Kennara knew she was letting pride rule her actions. She even knew walking down to the practice yard meant depending on others to wheel her around even longer than she wanted. It didn't matter though; it felt necessary to prove she could walk across town on her own. Even though the thud of her cane followed by the sound of her leg dragging indicated a different reality. Kennara bit her lip as her eyes filled with water. She wiped away the tears with her left hand as she continued to hobble out of the library.

"Kenna, stop. You're causing yourself more pain than necessary. Let me help you. Please." The catch in his voice as he said those last words had Kennara stopping mid-step, or mid-drag, if she was being accurate.

She turned to him. His brown eyes were pleading with her to be reasonable, to accept his help. When he looked at her like that, she didn't know how to say no. Plus, sweat was already dripping down her back and forehead after her bout of defiance. She blew a strand of her strawberry-blonde hair out of her eyes. "Fine, I will allow you to help me today. If it will make you feel better."

Her sea-green eyes met his brown ones. She looked away as a smile lit his face. "It will, Kenna, it honestly will. Now, your chariot awaits." Eljin gestured to her wheeled chair with a grand bow.

A giggle escaped despite herself as Kennara watched his antics. Putting on a stern face as she sat, she said, "Let's go. You know how Kellesha gets when I'm late."

With Eljin pushing her down the streets of Wreswell, it felt like mere moments before they were at the practice fields. It would have taken her three times as long to walk the distance, causing her sister to worry, halt practice, and come looking for her. Kennara would never admit it, but she was thankful for Eljin's pleading eyes insisting on her using her chair.

Kennara watched Casaworon and her sister finish their weapons' training. Kellesha swung her practice sword at Cas, the muscles in her arms and shoulders rippling as she moved from one pattern to the next in quick succession, causing the hulking Cas to retreat. Kellesha's auburn braid whipped around as she spun, sweeping her leg out and taking Cas to the ground. Kennara clapped as her sister stood over their friend grinning from ear to ear.

Her sister looked like a warrior in that moment, with her hair braided in the style of the northern tribes, her muscles defined under a sheen of sweat, and her foe lying before her vanquished on the ground. Kennara sighed, she would never be a warrior like her sister, no matter how good she was with a bow and arrow or how well she could ride a horse. She would always be the person everyone needed to protect, whether she liked it or not. At least, that's how she constantly felt that way. Her sister took steps to protect her, something about a promise to their mother five years ago when they escaped the Quickening. They were only thirteen years old at the time. Somehow they made it out of town and hid among a group of travelers on a pilgrimage to Dradon. The holy site was a day's walk from the university town of Wreswell. Their companion suggested they stay in Wreswell because of the university. Her sister fought her at first, wanting to go somewhere more isolated, but their companiion had prevailed, arguing the constant change of town occupants was a boon. No one would have the desire to get to know them because everyone would assume they wouldn't be around for long. That was, until Eljin and his friend, Casaworon, insisted on befriending them. Those two had weaseled their way into the twins' life despite their resistance.

Kennara blinked and saw the sparring had stopped. Cas stepped to the side, grabbing a towel to wipe the sweat from his eyes. Kellesha stood next to him, at least a head shorter and swiped the towel from him. Kennara watched as Cas just shrugged, causing his muscles to dance down his back. She swore Cas's muscles had muscles. He ran his hand through his shoulder-length dark hair before turning to where she sat with Eljin.

"I see you've decided to skip out on training again," Cas said as he walked over.

"You know me, anything to get out of working out." Kennara tried to make a joke of it, but she didn't think she had fooled anyone, especially Cas.

"You could still work with your bow and arrow," her sister said, rubbing Kennara's shoulder the same way her mother did whenever she was feeling down on herself.

"What do you mean, Kelle? How can I practice archery?" she asked, curious and somewhat hopeful.

"Well Kenna, you need to be able to shoot even when your leg is acting up. You can learn how to balance and build strength not only in your core but also in your left leg," Kellesha suggested.

"That's a great idea," Eljin said. "I can help you while Cas and Kellesha spar."

"Do you really think it's possible?" she asked, sitting taller in her chair.

"Of course. Where's your bow? We'll start today." Eljin winked at Kellesha and took off to grab her bow and quiver.

CHAPTER TWO

"There's my favorite couple," Quade said as he pushed his wares to the daily market.

Kennara looked over at Eljin, eyebrow raised. "How many times do we have to tell you, old friend? We are not a couple. I'm more likely to run off with you than I am this fool here." She gestured to Eljin, who managed to take over Quade's burden. Eljin insisted they walk by Quade on the way to the library every morning so he could help the old man truck his produce to the market. Kennara thought it was very sweet of Elgin. Not that she would ever tell him.

"It isn't true love between us, Kennara, just your love of my moonberries, especially my moonberry tarts," Quade teased.

"I do love your moonberry tarts—you wouldn't happen to have an extra one, or maybe even two, with you this morning?" Kennara made a show of glancing into the cart Eljin was pushing.

Quade paused, stroking his gray beard as if he was deep in thought. Kennara knew better: this was part of the game they played most mornings on the way to the market. She saw the twinkle in Quade's wizened eyes right before he pulled out two tarts from his knapsack. Kennara clapped her hands with joy as they continued to the market.

"I couldn't let my two helpers go hungry, especially when my moonberry harvest is plentiful this year."

"Thank you, Quade, but you know it's not necessary to feed us," Eljin said.

"Speak for yourself." Kennara jabbed her friend with her elbow. " I happen to need these tarts. Without them, I wouldn't be able to focus all day, just thinking about the sweet and tart berries sitting in the flakey, buttery perfection of crust." Kennara's mouth salivated just thinking about it. "If I didn't have one, the thought of it would be a constant distraction."

The three of them arrived at the market. Eljin and Kennara unpacked Quade's cart, arranging the fresh fruits and vegetables in an inviting array of colors. On the other side of the booth, Quade displayed his baked goods. He had an assortment of delicious sweet tarts as well as scrumptious savory hand pies.

"Thank you so much for all your help. It makes my mornings so much easier. These old bones would have had to retire if it weren't for your help." Quade lowered himself into the rocking chair he kept at his booth.

He would be at the market until the end of the day unless he sold out of his wares. On those days he left early, sometimes straight for home, other times he came to the library and told stories of the old king while Eljin and Kennara worked. Those were her favorite days, however Eljin was always irritable, and he never told her why. Kennara hoped Quade would stop by today; it had been forever since he had come around to talk of the past.

The old king sounded so much better than his brother,

the current king. King Hedrek never hunted down women with magic and stripped them of their powers; instead, he had given every womn the choice to decide what happened to their magic. If King Hedrek was still on the throne instead of his younger brother, Sheamus, Kennara and her sister wouldn't be in hiding.

"I hope we see you later today." Kennara took her tart from Quade.

With a quick wave goodbye, she and Eljin made their way to the library for another day of work.

THE HEAD LIBRARIAN PUT KENNARA AND ELJIN AT THE FRONT OF the library. It was Kennara's least favorite place to work because it involved interacting with the public. She would rather shelve books in the back or have a new research task than sit all day in the front of the library, answering questions from the public, and directing them to different parts of the library to find what they were looking for, but never actually touching the books. She couldn't slip away and read anything when she was assigned here.

Eljin's company helped. He loved it up in the front. Kennara watched him interact with everyone who came in. He was so easygoing and natural with the patrons. He would smile at chem, and they would leave happy, even if they left without the information they wanted.

"Quade!" Kennara exclaimed, happy for anything that interrupted her day. Even watching Eljin charm everyone in town bored her after a while. "Are you here to tell us stories?"

"Unfortunately, no. I've come to warn you." Quade's eyes darted around the foyer of the library.

Kennara felt her heart drop into her stomach. Today. It was happening today. She started throwing everything of hers into a bag, not waiting for Quade to continue.

Quade ran his hand through his graying hair, and his eyes filled with concern as he watched her pack. She didn't know how he knew—Kennara and her sister never used their magic—but Quade's demeanor conveyed his knowledge. Just him being here to warn her meant he knew. And knowing that put him in danger.

"The king's men. They're on their way. A scout arrived not that long ago. Viggo and Maeryn are about a day behind. You must leave now. There's no time to delay."

"I know, Quade. Can't you see I'm hurrying?" Throwing her bag over her shoulder she grabbed her cane, ready to warn Kellesha of the impending danger.

"You are. But he's not." Quade gestured towards Eljin, who was standing there as if he had seen a ghost.

She looked back at Quade and then Eljin, confused. Why did Eljin need to run? He'd been here forever, as far as she knew. What did the king's arrival have to do with him?

Kennara placed her hand on his shoulder. "Eljin?"

He shook his head. "Fine, I'll go. I would rather stay here and fight, but . . ." Eljin looked at Quade and then Kennara. "It seems now is not the time to stand my ground."

"You'll come with us, won't you, Quade? I don't know if you'll be safe here," Kennara asked.

"I'll be fine, Kennara. Just keep Eljin here safe; he won't admit it, but he needs you." With that mysterious statement, Quade left the library.

Kennara had thought the warning was only for her and

her sister, but after the last sentence, she was confused. She glanced over at Eljin, wondering who he was that he needed her help, and not the other way around.

"Let's go, Kenna. We need to tell Kellesha and Cas it's time for us to leave." Eljin grabbed her hand and pulled her across the room.

"I know, Eljin! I'm walking as fast as I can. Dragging me along isn't going to help us get there any quicker."

"I'm sorry, Kenna; I just want to get to them before the scout starts asking around."

"Who are you? And why are you running from the king?"

CHAPTER THREE

"Come on, Gallagher. We have to hurry if we're going to stop them," Abria said, sword in one hand, dagger in the other. She was ready for the inevitable. Too many women were sedated, waiting, to have their powers ripped from their bodies and stored in a talisman, a talisman that the law said could only be used by men. It had happened to her and her entire village five years ago when King Sheamus had taken the throne after murdering his older brother, Hedrek, and his nephews. Some people insisted that Prince Bryok lived and would one day save the kingdom from Sheamus, but Abria was not about to wait for a man that may or may not be alive to save the kingdom. So she traveled around the country, stopping the Quickening from happening anywhere she could.

Abria had believed winning these fights would be easy. How could she be overpowered by men, soldiers lacking in magic, when she was fighting to free a village full of women with elemental magic? It was never as easy as she thought it would be. First, many of the soldiers had talismans but no idea how to harness its power. Due to their inability to control the magic, the soldiers caused so much damage that it was hard to attack them without risking the very people she was trying to save.

Second, some women wanted the Quickening. They didn't care about all the women who didn't and would even use their powers to ensure that it happened. Abria didn't understand it, couldn't understand it, why women would willingly gave up their magic so that men could protect them. While she didn't understand that thinking at all, she really didn't understand why *those* women thought it was right to force the women who wanted to keep their powers to give them up. Why didn't they want women to have a choice on what to do with their magic?

It was one of those women that held Abria down while the traitor king's servant stole her magic. Abria was still haunted by nightmares, her screams for mercy echoing in her head as her life was stolen.

The third and final reason it was difficult is that the unwilling women were drugged, sedating them so they could not draw upon their magic. Whatever was used acted like a dampener of sorts

"What's our plan this time, Abria? Please tell me it's something different from all the other times. Storming in screaming with weapons drawn is so risky. One of us is going to get hurt, and you're so reckless it's probably going to be you." Gallagher grabbed his bow.

"Do you have a better plan? Cause I don't. I would love one, but if we wait to come up with one, it'll be too late."

"Dear gods, please let this end well," Gallagher prayed before notching an arrow in his bow. "I'll take out as many as I can. Can you try to get at least some of the women to safety before . . ."

"Fine, Gallagher, I'll try," Abria said before disappearing

around the building. She stuck to the shadows as she moved, weapons at the ready in case she came across a guard unexpectedly. She heard the whiz of the wind as an arrow went by her, followed by the thud of it hitting the center mass of a body. *One down, who knows how many more to go? I really should start planning these things better,* Abria thought.

She heard another body go down as she arrived at the end of the line.

"Damn!" She muttered under her breath.

The king's men must have been told to prepare for her: for the first time, the women were tied together with rope. This was an unwelcome development that added time she didn't have to the rescue.

Thud—this time followed by a scream. There went their cover. She had planned on trying her hand at subtle, but that was out the window now. Abria charged forward, her battle cry echoing off the buildings. She was looking to fight anyone guarding the women.

What she saw instead was a young soldier cutting the women loose and shooing them away into the woods. *What in the gods' names was happening here?* The young soldier looked up and shouted something at her, but it was too late. She felt a blade slice into her leg, followed by a body falling on top of her.

"You couldn't have shot him a moment sooner," she groaned as the waves of pain caused her to lose consciousness.

Abria awoke to a burning sensation that lanced through her leg like a fiery brand. She tried to escape the tortuous feeling but found she could not move. She opened her eyes to see a young woman hovering over her leg. The woman's straight black hair was pushed to the side and hanging over one shoulder. The young woman looked over to see Abria staring at her.

"Well, it's unfortunate that you woke up. Healing of this sort is much easier to do when the patient is unconscious. They move less." The woman's deep brown eyes belied a kindness that her tone did not. "Zayden, I'm going to need you to hold her down. I can't have her jerking away as I close the wound."

The young soldier that had distracted Abria earlier approached. On closer inspection, it was clear he was not a soldier at all. His uniform was ill-fitting, too narrow across the shoulders; his pants were baggy and almost dragged on the ground. King Sheamus would never allow one of his men to walk around looking so sloppy. Abria wondered who he had stolen the uniform from, and why he was releasing women. Gallagher was the only man she had ever been able to convince to help her, and sometimes he seemed to do it just because he was bored.

"This is going to hurt," the woman said.

Abria looked down expecting to see something in her hands, like a needle and thread or a hot poker to cauterize the wound. But there was nothing: her hands were empty. The woman closed her eyes and pain ripped through Abria's leg. It was all she could do not to scream, but as she watched the woman and her leg, she saw her body knit itself back together until all that was left was a minor scar. She had never seen a true healer at work. Having experienced it for the first time, she could not understand why the king would take away such magic. This was so much better than the lengthy process the body normally took to heal.

"Your leg may look fine, but it will take a few days to regain strength. Although that's not really the right word." The woman grabbed a wet towel and wiped her hands. "My work is fragile for a few days; put too much strain on it, you'll rip it open. If it rips open, you will most likely die of blood loss. So don't let that happen. I don't like wasting my time."

"Of course," Abria said.

"When was the last time you listened to a healer? Never, that's when," Gallagher interjected.

"Shut up, Gallagher. I'll be careful." Abria turned to look back at the woman. "Who are you and how did you . . . ?"

CHAPTER FOUR

"I could ask you the same thing." Eljin grabbed Kennara's right hand. She watched as he wrapped it around his waist and then snaked his arm around hers becoming her crutch. "Now's not the time to be sharing secrets. Lean on me so we can get to Cas and Kellesha."

"Fine, but don't think this conversation is over." Kennara didn't like it when people kept secrets from her. Was that hypocritical of her? Maybe a little, but Eljin's secret could put her and her sister in danger. That was unacceptable.

"You're right, this conversation isn't over. But we have bigger things to worry about right now. We'll hash everything out later when we have a second to breathe."

Kennara's feet barely touched the ground as Eljin lifted her the entire walk to where Kellesha and Cas trained. In moments, she was standing outside the practice fields like she did every day. She watched them spar. It was surreal. She had stood here every day watching them, today felt the same, but it was the last time she would ever be here, in this spot, doing something she had done for so long.

She waved to get her sister's attention.

"Kenna, Eljin, what are you doing here so early?" Kellesha ran over to the gate.

"They're coming." That was all Kennara had to say. Her sister's blue eyes widened her and sweat beaded on her forehead. That's when the wind picked up, leaves and dust swirled around their feet. "Kellesha, you have to stay calm." Kennara glanced pointedly at the leaves.

Kellesha looked down and took a deep breath. The breeze settled, and the leaves fell to the ground.

"We have to go now. How's your leg?" Her sister looked her up and down, taking in the fact that all her weight was on her left leg. "Never mind, I can see how it is. You've been pushing yourself too hard, like always."

"I haven't been pushing myself. I've been working and training like you suggested. Stop treating me like I can't take care of myself. After all, I'm the one who's lived like this my entire life."

"I know, Kenna." Kellesha wiped the sweat from her forehead. "I'm just concerned now about leaving. You haven't rested your leg, and we can't stay here any longer or we'll be caught."

"I appreciate you pointing out my flaws. Maybe you should leave without me. That way, at least one of us will be safe." Kennara crossed her arms and turned away from her sister. This wasn't the first time they'd had this fight, and it would not be the last. Kennara was sick of her sister constantly telling her she did things wrong. Especially when Kellesha didn't have to live with a body she couldn't trust to do what she wanted . . . or needed it to.

"I'm sure she didn't mean anything by it, Kenna." Eljin put his arm around her shoulders. She looked at him. He smiled at her with the one smile that always made her forget herself for just a moment.

"I'm sorry, Kelle, I'm just worried I'm going to hold you back. I don't want to be the reason you get caught. It's on my mind every single day." She turned back to her sister, grabbing her hand.

"We don't have time for this. We have to go now." Kellesha withdrew her hand as she went about packing up her belongings at the practice field.

Kennara sighed. It was always like this when she mentioned her feelings, her fears. Whenever she opened up, Kellesha walked away and ignored her. Kennara watched her sister throw things into her bag.

"Eljin, can you take me back to my house? I need to pack my stuff. And yes, I'm actually asking for help to get around."

Eljin stood there; Kennara followed his gaze and watched as Cas stepped up next to Kellesha, nudged her, then tossed his things into his bag.

"Eljin, I can pack our bags. You help Kennara," Cas said.

"Are you sure?" Eljin asked.

"Of course, I'm capable of packing a couple of bags. This isn't the first time we've had to leave in a hurry."

Kennara took in their quick conversation, and it raised more questions in her head. It definitely didn't provide any answers. It was strange for her to think of Eljin and Cas being on the run as well. She was used to looking around corners and into the shadows scared; she never thought men lived that way.

"Are you ready?" she asked Eljin.

"Yes, we'll meet you on the south side of town." He threw a bag of coins to Cas. "See if you can get some horses for the journey. For now, let's join those on their pilgrimage. And when we can we'll break off from them."

"You don't have to come with us," Kellesha said, her eyes betraying just how confused she had been over the past few moments.

Cas grabbed his bag. "It's not safe for you to know why, but we have to leave if the king's men are coming. We might as well stay together." He handed Kellesha her staff. "Let's find some horses. We'll travel faster."

Kennara turned away from her sister and Cas. She knew Kellesha enjoyed having a plan, but more than that, she liked being in charge of the plan. Kennara wasn't sure if her sister was going to accept the help Eljin and Cas were offering, but Kennara was. She hoped having assistance on this journey would help Kellesha. Right now, she knew her sister was a bundle of nerves.

Eljin and Kennara waved as they made their way back to her home. It wasn't a large home but a cottage not too far from the library and the market. Eljin insisted they keep a leisurely pace as they walked from stall to stall. She tried to stroll and look at some of the wares, unsuccessful until she saw a navy-blue cloak. Kennara didn't recognize the merchant, but her clothing was like nothing she had ever seen before. The wools were fluid and luxurious to the touch.

"You like it?" the woman running the shop asked Kennara.

"I do. The fabric is so . . ."

"It's yours, then." The woman pushed the navy cloak and a second forest-green one into Kennara's arms.

"I can't; I don't have anything for you."

"Take them. They're for you and your sister."

"How do you know I have a sister?" she asked, looking up from the fabric piled in her arms. She turned in a circle. The shopkeeper was gone.

CHAPTER FIVE

"Come on, Eljin, we don't have much time." Kennara was grabbing everything she could get her hands on and shoving it into her leather bag.

Eljin grabbed her by the shoulders and turned her towards him. "I know we're in a hurry, but if we take a moment to pack thoughtfully, we'll be better prepared. We'll have a better chance of actually escaping."

Kennara stared at him, annoyed he was preventing her from packing. However, she was still able to acknowledge he was right. She looked around the home she had shared with her sister for the past five years. Instead of grabbing everything in sight, Kennara planned.

"Grab as much food as you can. I'll pack some clothes for Kellesha and me." Kennara limped into her room. She gathered a couple of chemises, her two favorite wool dresses, and a pair of leather leggings. She picked clothes for her sister as well, more leggings, fewer dresses, but enough that they wouldn't have to wear the same thing every day.

When she left the room, Eljin was waiting with a bag

full of food over his shoulder. Kennara threw the green cloak the shopkeeper gave her over her shoulder. She made eye contact with Eljin and her lips trembled as she offered him a smile.

"Let's go. It's time to leave." Eljin held the door open for her. She walked through, using Kellesha's extra staff to take the pressure off her leg.

The two of them walked through town like there was no rush, pretending everything was normal and they weren't running for their lives. That is, until they saw old man Quade. He looked at them, and then past them, and his eyes went wide. Kennara glanced back to see the black-and-silver livery of the king's men behind them. She felt Eljin grab her clammy hand, and her heart raced at just the thought of being this close to someone they had been hiding from for so long.

"Go, get your sister and Cas, and get out of here as fast as you can," Quade whispered as he passed, his smile never leaving his face. "My good men, what brings you to our humble town?"

Eljin's arm wrapped around her like before. She used his strength to carry her to the stables as fast as they could go without raising suspicion. Kellesha was leading out a beautiful chestnut mare right as she and Eljin arrived at the stables. Cas followed her out with a dappled gray already loaded down with bags.

"Kennara, the chestnut is for you. Let me help you on and strap your leg in." Kellesha meant well, even when it made Kennara feel helpless.

"Won't it look suspicious if I'm the only one riding a horse? I think it would be better if we all walked out of town," Kennara said as she threw her bag on the chestnut.

"Let's talk about this, I really think . . .," her sister started, but Kennara held up her hand to stop her.

"I want us to get out of town. That's not going to happen if you treat me like, well how you always treat me. I am able to make decisions that can help us escape."

"Kennara, I'm just thinking of you."

Instead of continuing to argue, Kennara walked away. She was tired of having this conversation. Especially since the outcome never changed. She petted the chestnut, and the horse nuzzled her back. Eljin came up behind her, placing a hand on her shoulder.

"She likes you," he said.

"What's her name?"

"Whiskey, and this girl is Shadow," Eljin said, pointing to the gray. "I think your plan to walk out of town is smart. I'm here to help in any way you want me to."

Kennara wiped her hair out of her eyes and looked at the man who had just said the words she wanted to hear from her sister. "What would help me right now is if you can give this cloak to Kellesha. I need a moment before we head out." She handed the blue material to Eljin.

She continued to strap down the bags on Whiskey, taking time to pull the ties tight ensuring everything was secure. Sweat dripped down her forehead as she finished packing. As a reward, she fed Whiskey a carrot, patting the gorgeous equine as she did so. The nuzzle Whiskey gave her made Kennara feel appreciated. The horse whinnied as she led her over to the others.

"Ready to go?" Kellesha asked. She took the blue cloak Eljin had given her and put it on before grabbing her staff.

The four of them made their way towards the edge of town, passing everything that had become familiar to her over the past five years. It was unreal to think that she might never see any of Wreswell again, especially the library where she had found sanctuary since escaping all those years ago. And here they were, on the run again. Kennara wondered if she would be running for the rest of her life.

"Halt!" A man in the king's livery stepped out in front of them.

Kennara's good leg almost gave out on her as her heart dropped to her stomach. She looked around wildly; there was a scryer standing just off the side of the road. There was no way she and her sister would make it this time. Scryers used an opalescent stone that glowed red whenever someone with magic was close. It was going to glow as soon as it was near her and Kellesha. Kennara glanced over at her sister, panic in her eyes. Kellesha's knuckles were white, gripping the staff she held. Kennara shook her head no, her eyes pleading for her sister not to do anything rash.

"By the king's orders, our scryer must search everyone leaving town," the man announced.

Kennara held her breath as the cloaked scryer approached, the fear-inducing stone part of this elaborate scepter was already pointed in their direction. All of Kennara's concerns about leaving town seemed like nothing now that it would take a miracle for them not to be caught.

CHAPTER SIX

"You don't seem the type to waste time asking questions you already know the answer to." The woman tossed her long black braid over her shoulder.

"I'm sorry, I don't know what you mean." Abria watched as the woman that healed her leg moved about the room, packing all of her things into a small bag.

"Asking how I did what I did—you know how I healed your leg. Why bother asking something you already know the answer to?" the healer repeated, buckling her bag closed.

"I don't know who you are, and I can only guess as to what you are, or what skills you possess." Abria rubbed her leg. It was almost unnerving to look at her healed leg; there was only a small white line where the soldier's blade had inflicted its damage. She knew the woman in front of her was a healer who still possessed her magic. And her magic was the element of heart.

"I'm not going to tell you anything about me until I know it's safe to do so. You get to answer my questions first.

Starting with who in the name of Ened are you and why are you here threatening my safety? I can't believe Zayden dragged you inside." The woman shifted from glaring at Abria to glaring at the young man sitting in the corner.

"I don't mean you any harm at all. My name is Abria, and I'm here to stop the king and his atrocious Quickenings." She pushed herself up to stand, but sat back down as pain shot through her injured leg.

"I told you to take it slow. It may look completely healed, but it takes a few days for the body to cooperate completely with the, shall we say, assisted healing process," she said. "And going up against the king? You're a danger to yourself, me, and anyone who decides to help you out."

"We should leave. I don't want to cause you any trouble. People need healers. I would never intentionally put you, or any healer, at risk of being discovered."

The healer sighed and sat on a stool next to a heavy wooden table in what appeared to be a kitchen. She brushed a few loose strands of her hair away from her dark brown eyes and looked at Abria from beneath hooded lids. Abria could tell that the healer was deciding whether or not to trust her. She hoped the skilled woman would and maybe even . . .

"I'm Reilynne." She brushed her hands down the front of the apron covering her long maroon dress. "I'm lucky that my special skill is one the people need. The folks here hide me whenever the king's men come around."

"Special skill," Abria scoffed. "You mean m—"

"Shut your mouth. Someone might hear you. You're determined to get me caught," Reilynne said.

Gallagher walked across the room, nonchalantly pouring a glass of water from a jug on the table. "Abria is like that, constantly speaking without thinking. Who am I kidding? She acts without thinking too. And has the audacity to say she has a plan." He winked at Reilynne. Gallagher had a way with people. It always surprised Abria how quickly they warmed up to him.

Abria took Gallagher's comments in stride. She could be mad at him, but he was right about her. She had always leapt before looking, and so far in life, it had served her well. Even if her closest friend didn't always agree with her.

"Just because you're more methodical than me doesn't mean my methods are wrong. They're different and they're mine." She glared at Gallagher. "In fact, I think Reilynne and Zayden should join us. It would be nice to have a healer on our team," She turned towards Reilynne. "You could be part of stopping the king's atrocities."

"What makes you think I want my life to be any different? I have a good life here." Reilynne stood. She scurried around the kitchen, organizing the already organized room.

"A good life? You're in hiding, relying on the kindness of others to keep you safe. Or worse, relying on the fact others need you to keep you safe. One bad healing and they would hand you over to the authorities. How is that a good life?"

Reilynne dropped a teacup, the clattering sound illustrating the effect of Abria's words. She could see the woman's hands tremble, but wasn't sure if it was in anger or fear. Either way it seemed she had hit a sore spot. It made sense. Abria couldn't imagine how frightening it would be to rely on others to maintain a secret so integral to one's existence. She would never want to live that way. It was better to risk her life, risk getting caught, than depend on others to keep her safe, but she had already lost her magic. There wasn't much more she could lose. Reilynne had so much to lose. When a person still had the magic she was born with, it defined who she was and what she did with her life.

"You know nothing of my life. How dare you come in here and question how I live it."

Abria watched as Reilynne banged around the kitchen, finishing her outraged statement by throwing a towel across the table.

"I should say I'm sorry, but it would be a lie. I know not everyone can do what I'm doing. But I lost everything because of the king. My element was earth, and they held me down as it was ripped out of my body. This happened after I watched them do the same thing to my mother. Her identity was so tied to her magic she couldn't handle not having it. The bakery we owned started to fail because my mother didn't believe in herself without her magic. Before long, no one was coming to the bakery, and my mother never left her room until she died." This time, when Abria stood, her leg supported her. She paced as memories of the past filled her mind. Emotions swirled within her. "Gallagher, we need to leave. I don't want to impose on Reilynne and Zayden any longer."

Zayden stood, for the first time since Reilynne finished the healing process. Abria watched as he approached Reilynne. The two of them spoke in hushed tones, gesticulating wildly throughout the conversation. It actually looked more like an argument.

"Fine." Reilynne smacked the table. "We'll do it your way." Reilynne sighed before turning toward the door where Abria stood. "Abria. Wait."

CHAPTER SEVEN

The scryer approached their little traveling group with the scepter pointed directly at the twins. Kennara grabbed Eljin's hand, the telltale sign of her panic clear in the viselike grip. He didn't let go or wince as they continued to walk. The woman stopped them, passing the scepter in front of each of them. The stone never changed color, it never turned red, nothing happened.

Kennara looked over at Kellesha to see color return to her sister's knuckles as her grip loosened around her staff. Kennara let out the breath she was holding. For some reason, the stone hadn't picked up their magic. It made no sense, but Kennara was not one to question their luck.

"What was that about?" Eljin asked, glancing down at his hand, which was still entwined with hers.

Kennara dropped his hand as if it had burned her. "Now is not the time. We need to keep moving," She uttered through clenched teeth. But once we are clear of Wreswell, the four of us need to sit down and talk. There are things you don't know about my sister and me, and things I don't know about you and Cas. I would rather each of us know exactly what we are getting into by traveling together before we are on the road too long to change our minds."

Eljin nodded slowly. Kennara couldn't tell what was going on in his mind, but he didn't seem to be opposed to her suggestion.

"Tonight, when we are clear of Wreswell," he said, leaving her by herself as they walked the rest of the way out of town.

As they walked, the stone buildings of the town became interspersed with trees. First, it was trees with giant leaves that changed colors with the seasons that appeared to be planted by the building owners. Then, as they continued on their journey, trees soon outnumbered the houses. And the variety of trees grew—they were still the gorgeous giant leaves, but near them were copses of trees with white bark and small green flowers that turned gold in the fall. And last, there were the enormous pine trees that seemed to have existed for hundreds of years as they towered over everything, maintaining their deep green year-round. The way the light trickled through the breaks in the foliage changed as they continued on their journey. Every now and then, a critter would dart across the road, startling Kennara. She wondered where the creatures were going, and suddenly, she heard it. The musical sounds of rushing water.

Thirst overcame her at the thought of cold water from a stream. Hours had passed since they had left the city walls, and Kennara was tired, her leg was tired, and the staff had become more of a hindrance than a help because it was so heavy after carrying it for hours. It wasn't even a weapon she could use if their group had to fight. She wondered if it was possible to use her bow as a cane instead of the staff.

"Let's take a break. Fill up our water pouches. Sit for a little bit." She headed towards the sound of the water without a glance back. Kennara knew if she stopped on the road, her sister would debate whether it was wise to do so. She also knew her sister would never let her walk into the woods alone if Kellesha thought there could be danger.

"Kenna, wait for me," Eljin hollered after her.

She stopped at the sound of his voice. Unfortunately, all her weight was on her bad leg, and it gave out as pain shot from her ankle to her hip. She gasped, as she braced herself for a sudden impact with the dirt. However, the impact never came. Instead, she felt an arm wrap around her waist. She came into contact with the length of Eljin's body instead of the ground. They stood there for a moment, barely breathing. At least, she was barely breathing.

"Um, thank you," Kennara said. She awkwardly patted Eljin's shoulder before carefully taking a step back. The pain was still present, but she managed to stay on her feet this time.

"Are you okay?" Concern filled Eljin's eyes. It was hard for her to ignore, even if she wasn't sure he was worried or if it was actually pity she saw and not concern. She didn't want him to feel sorry for her; however, she didn't mind if he cared about her well-being just a little.

"I'm fine."

"You can tell me the truth; you don't have to be fine around me." Eljin took her arm and helped her make it to the stream.

"I'm not fine. My leg is tired and in pain. But we need to keep moving. It's too early for us to stop for the night. It's only been a few hours since we've seen the last building at the edge of town. If I'm not fine, I'm going to make it worse for everyone. Endanger everyone."

"That's a lot to put on yourself. I don't know what the best thing to say to you is because I don't know what it,s like to be you. So, if what I'm about to say is wrong, tell me. I think we will be safer if we work within your limits. The more you let yourself rest, the stronger you are. It could make all the difference in a moment when we need you to be your strongest."

Kennara took in Eljin's words. When had he become so smart? What he said made sense. She had just never thought of it that way. She was always trying to push herself to be more like everyone else, instead of just being her.

"Would you mind suggesting that we stop for the night? I want to stay here and rest for a bit."

"Of course, I'll be right back."

Kennara heard the rustling of leaves and the thud of Eljin's steps on the ground. She took a deep breath, inhaling the pine scent of the forest. It had been a long time since she had just sat somewhere and let herself be. She hoped it would help her be honest with herself and those around her on this surprise journey.

She heard the rustling of the leaves behind her. "Elj . . . Oh, it's you, Kellesha." Kennara turned back to the stream, not looking forward to the conversation she was sure was going to happen.

"Kennara, how are you?" her sister asked.

"Not great: my leg is hurting, and I think we should stop for the night," she said in one long exhale. Then she waited. She waited for her sister to say something discouraging and upsetting. It was what Kellesha did. Kennara didn't expect that to change right now, but maybe, someday it would.

"Kennara, you should have been on the horse; it would have been better for your leg."

"But it wouldn't have been better for the group; it could have hindered our escape out of town. And I can't have that guilt on me. Kelle, I need you to listen to me and trust me when I say I can do something. I feel like you're always telling me what I should do, but what you think I should do is nothing. I'm more capable than you believe."

"I'm just looking out for you."

"I know that's what you think you're doing. But I feel like you have no belief that I can handle myself. And I can. Maybe not like you, but despite being twins, I'm not like you. I've taken all this worry that I'm going to be the cause of our capture. I think about it every day. But maybe, if I listen to my limits and I learn to be better at the things within my limits, I can help and not be a burden; and, Kelle, I almost always feel like a burden when you're looking out for me."

"You're not—"

"Just say you'll try. That you'll try to listen and hear me *before* trying to take care of me. Like right now, I need help. I'm asking you, Eljin, and Cas to help me. I can't go farther, and I don't think I will be much assistance in setting up camp. But tomorrow is a new day, and maybe if I rest tonight, I can walk more tomorrow. And if I can't, I,ll let you know, and we,ll figure out how to make my riding less suspicious. So, can you try?" Kennara looked at her sister. She wasn't sure where her words were coming from, but she knew she had needed to say them for a long time. And maybe they could actually start being the sisters their mother wanted them to be, instead of being always at odds with each other.

"Yes, Kennara, I will try."

CHAPTER EIGHT

Kennara sat by the campfire watching their food cook while everyone else was moving around. Kellesha was out gathering more firewood and refilling water flasks for the journey. Eljin and Cas were setting up their tents. All Kennara was doing was sitting there, stirring a pot of vegetables every now and then, and making sure the meat Eljin had put on a makeshift spit didn't burn.

Did she need to be sitting? Yes, her leg hurt and it was swollen from all the walking they had done today. But it was times like these, when she was left alone with her own thoughts, that she questioned her value. She felt like she wasn't helping their little group enough, letting everyone else do the work while she sat and rested. In these moments, the concern that was always in the back of her mind pushed its way forward, and all she could think about was how they were going to get caught and it was going to be her fault. If she wasn't careful, she would start imagining different scenarios with great detail, illustrating how she was going to fail her sister.

She leaned in to stir the vegetables and flip the meat, when the small fire Eljin had built went out. Kennara had started to tell him he was placing the logs wrong but stopped herself as the fire lit. She had been worried it would go out before long, but he had looked so pleased with himself that she didn't want to dampen his spirit.

Kennara looked around to ensure everyone was busy with their tasks and not watching her. She held her hand out in front of her, palm up, until a small flame hovered over her skin. Carefully, she moved closer to the firepit and placed her flame under the logs. She did this a few more times until there was a continually burning flame under all sides of the base of the log structure Eljin had created. She then encouraged the flames to keep burning each of the logs they caught. Needless to say, the fire was going strong as everyone finished up with their tasks and found a piece of ground to sit around the fire. Eljin looked at the flickering flames proudly. Kennara looked away hiding a knowing smile.

Kellesha sat next to her and took her hand. It had been a long time since they had shared a moment that wasn't controlled by an unaddressed tension between them. It felt like their earlier talk had helped. There would probably be rough patches between them in the future, but right now, in this moment, it was nice to feel like they were sisters that got along instead of constantly being at each other's throats. Kellesha looked at Kennara and nodded. It was time to tell their friends the secret they had been hiding for five years. Especially if Eljin and Cas were going to risk their lives by traveling with them.

"We need to share something with the two of you," Kellesha said. Uncertainty seemed to radiate off her.

"You know you can tell us anything," Cas said.

Kellesha tossed her braid over her shoulder as she responded, "You might regret saying that."

"Stop stalling." Kennara made sure everyone was focused on her before she continued, "My sister and I have been on the run for years. Our mother helped us escape when the king sent his men to our hometown. King Hedrek had been dead for five years. Prince Magnus and Prince Bryok was assumed dead. But there were rumors that one of them had escaped, at least that's what everyone hoped." Kennara paused when she mentioned the young princes. "Anyway, the king's new policy was in full effect, and our mother wanted to save us from it. So, she told us to run, to find somewhere safe to live. So we did and we stayed there for five years, happy. We felt safe. We were wrong."

"Wait, are you saying that the two of you have . . .," Eljin started.

"Magic. Yes, that's what I'm saying."

"That's so exciting. What are your powers? How do they work? What's it like to have magic?" Eljin was more excited than a dog with a new bone.

Kellesha swiped her hand in front of her. A breeze rushed through the campsite, causing leaves to tumble through. The fire flickered like it was going out. Kennara stuck her hand out as the flames roared to life.

"Well, I guess that answered one of my questions. Kellesha, your element is air, and Kennara, yours is fire."

"We rarely use our magic, though. It's too risky. But it's not something we want to be taken from us. My magic is part of me, and no one else should get to have it without my permission." Kennara wiped her hair from her eyes.

"I couldn't have it any other way. I don't understand what the king is doing by stripping away power from all women. It's wrong." Eljin shook his head in disgust.

"It is wrong, but traveling with us puts you in danger. I have no idea how we made it out of town. The scryer should have caught us. The longer you're with us, the more likely you'll be captured."

"I understand your concern. And I appreciate you thinking of our well-being. But I think Eljin and I can decide what risks we want to take," Cas said.

"I actually don't know why you left with us? Why are you on the run?" Kennara asked.

"They're on the run too? I thought they had just decided to come with us; I didn't know they were escaping the city." Kellesha's blue eyes were wide with shock.

"Quade came to warn Eljin and me about the king's men. Looking back, part of me wonders if he was warning both of us, or if he was really just warning Eljin. I assumed it was me he was talking to because Quade always seemed to know things, but I could have been wrong." Kennara leaned forward, her eyes affixed on Eljin. "So, are you going to let us know what's going on? Whom are you running from and why?"

Eljin pushed his fingers through his hair. "We're running from the king's men as well. But I think it's safer for everyone if you don't know why."

"Plausible denial. You can't tell anyone what you don't know," Cas added.

Kennara's eyes widened. Was he really going to keep his secret from her after she had shared her secret? She glared at him and her eyes narrowed. "It seems like you don't trust us with your truth, but expect us to tell you ours. Seems unfair."

"We just want to protect you," Cas said.

"Since when do I need protection from you?" Kellesha

jumped up from her seat, almost knocking over the makeshift spit.

"Wait, Kellesha, the food is ready," she called after her sister's retreating body.

"I'm not hungry," she yelled back as she bent and laid down in the tent.

"Well, everyone else should dig in. We have more travel tomorrow, and we need to stay rested and nourished," Kennara said as she made herself a plate of food.

CHAPTER NINE

It took longer than Abria wanted for Reilynne to pack for the journey. She was the type of person who always had a bag ready to grab and run if necessary. Reilynne was not, which surprised her. It seemed like a dangerous way to live when a person was hiding from those in power. Who wouldn't be ready to go in an instant? But Reilynne would not be ready to go in a second; she did not have a bag packed in case of an emergency; instead, she was the slowest packer Abria had ever met. This did not bode well for traveling together.

Abria sat down and drummed her fingers on Reilynne's dining room table.

"Gallagher." Abria motioned for her companion to come sit.

Gallagher sauntered over. "What do you want now?" he asked, leaning on the table.

She looked at him and smiled. Gallagher was always giving her trouble, but it kept her on her toes. He was like a brother to her, and she was pretty sure he felt the same way, especially since he was always talking back to her.

"I need you to contact your source in the castle. This was the last Quickening she told us about, but you know it won't stop here. He's at least going to send his men to the coastal region, or so I would assume."

"Aye, aye captain. Anything else I can do for you?" Gallagher grabbed his bag and walked to the door, pausing a moment before leaving.

"Yeah, stay alive," Abria said.

"Always my plan, captain." Gallagher saluted and walked out.

She rolled her eyes after he left and began drumming her fingers on the table once again.

IT FELT LIKE WEEKS, BUT WAS ONLY A COUPLE OF DAYS BEFORE Reilynne was ready to leave. Zayden had decided to stay back to ensure the town had a healer. He may not have magic, but Reilynne had taught him the basics of healing, such as how to set a leg and what herbal remedies to use for specific illnesses. Abria could see tears glistening in the healer's eyes as she took one last walk around her cottage.

"It must be hard to leave your home." Abria tried to be sympathetic. It was a struggle because it was not in her nature since she never truly felt that she had a home. The last time she called a place home was where her magic was taken. She no longer used the term to describe that place. "But at least you're leaving your home with someone you trust."

"I know you won't like the delay, but I have to go into the village and say goodbye. It would cause suspicion if I just left. And I fear it would bring more of the king's men our way if I treated this trip like something other than normal. Not that this is in the realm of normal, but for now, I can pretend," Reilynne said.

"If you must, but let's get to it." Abria stood, causing the chair to scrape against the floor, the raucous noise at odds with the solemn moment.

Reilynne made her way to the front door, caressing pieces of furniture as she walked by, picking up an item as if she was going to pack it, but instead putting it down right where she took it from and straightening it until it was just so before moving on.

Abria stood in the doorway watching Reilynne's progress, Zayden following behind her a bit like a puppy following its owner, nudging Reilynne on any time it felt like she was going to change her mind and stay.

Abria shifted her weight, her hand clenching the hilt of the sword that hung at her waist. She didn't want to rush what was clearly a hard moment for the healer, but the urge to run was creeping up on her. She wasn't sure if it was because of the emotions she could feel emanating off Reilynne or the need to move on and find where the king was going to strike next. Maybe it was a combination of both things, but her skin seemed to itch with her need to be gone.

Reilynne closed and locked the door to her home, resting her forehead on the wooden frame for a brief moment, saying her final goodbye to the only life she had ever known before turning around. She pasted a smile on her face. Abria noted that the smile did not come anywhere near Reilynne's deep brown eyes. Zayden threw an arm across her shoulder and whispered something in her ear. It caused Reilynne to sigh as she moved one foot in front of the other, heading into town to say her goodbyes, Zayden continuing to follow her.

It didn't take long for Reilynne to say her farewells in town. With Zayden staying to watch her home there wasn't anything left for her to do but leave. Abria watched as the healer gave directions to Zayden on how to mix and prescribe her herbal remedies, even though he had done it himself a hundred times. Abria sat there waiting, the thought that she wanted to have this type of connection somewhere making its way into her conscience. She tried to shoo it away with a shake of her head, but it was there and would continue to live there for who knew how long.

"I need to stop somewhere that's on the outskirts of town. It won't take long," Abria said. She made her way through the town's cobblestone streets as if she had lived there all her life. It was her first time in this specific place, but one of her unexplainable skills was this innate knowledge of how a place was laid out, whether it was a small town like this, a city like the capital, or the wild areas inbetween. Abria could follow her instincts and find her way to any destination.

"Does she even know where she's going?" Reilynne muttered as she followed Abria.

"I've never seen someone walk with as much of a purpose as she is and not know where they're going," Zayden replied with a shrug. "You might as well follow her. The worst that will happen is she'll ask for directions when she doesn't find where she's looking for."

Overhearing the pair, Abria waited as Reilynne hugged Zayden one final goodbye and ran to catch up to her.

Abria stopped in front of the pigeon post door. "Here we are. I need to talk to the pigeoneer before we head out." She opened the door and stepped inside, leaving Reilynne outside, staring at where she last stood in wonder.

"Hello, how can I help you?" the pigeoneer asked, running his hand over his gray beard.

"I was wondering if you had a message for either an Abria or a Gallagher?"

"I believe something just came in, let me check. I'll be but a moment." The old man loped away, his movements reminding Abria of someone much younger.

She stood there, listening to the cooing of the messenger pigeons and the shuffling of papers, tapping her fingers on the table in front of her.

"Ah, yes, I thought so." The pigeoneer's voice could be heard from the back room. A door scraped on the wood floor, and the man entered with the same fluid movements he had when he left. "I believe this is what you,re looking for."

Abria took the small paper he held out. She carefully unrolled it, then read the words she had dreaded seeing. The king had sent his men to Wreswell for the first time in over a decade. Abria threw a coin on the table and rushed out of the building, leaving the paper lying there.

CHAPTER TEN

Kennara sat astride Whiskey, her body in rhythm with the horse's gait. She loved riding; it was one of the few times she felt completely capable, even if the only reason she sat atop the mare was that her leg couldn't take another day of trudging through the forest. The battle in her head of whether riding was a sign of weakness or something she excelled at was constant, but she pushed those thoughts away so she could enjoy the time she spent astride the mare.

At least, she tried to enjoy the time. Their little merry band was anything but merry after the revelations of the other night. For what seemed like weeks but had only been two days, they had traveled in silence. Someone needed to break the silence, but Kennara refused. Eljin and Cas insisted on keeping their reasons for running a secret. It was wrong, no matter what their reasons were. How could Eljin support her need and ability to take care of herself in one moment, then tell her he was keeping secrets for her protection in the next? If he listened to himself, he would see that his very words were contradictory. Her fists clenched, causing the horse to shift sideways.

"Are you okay, Kenna? Do you need to take a break?" Eljin looked over, his hand reaching towards the reins.

"What I need is the truth, a little trust in my capabilities —oh, and for you to help and protect me when I ask, not when you happen to think I need it." She squeezed her knees together and clicked her tongue, encouraging her horse to move faster.

She let Whiskey continue to trot ahead of the group. She was tired of the tension, the secrets, and the fear. If she could outrun all of it, she would. Right now, on the back of Whiskey, she could get away for just a little bit. So that was what she did. She sank into the rhythm of the trotting horse. The trees passed by, light filtered through the branches, and everything felt quiet, peaceful. It didn't feel like she was on the run, or like she had spent most of her life in hiding. For once, she just felt good on her own, surrounded by nature.

Out of nowhere, Whiskey stopped. Kennara tried every-thing to get her moving again, but the horse refused. Her eyes darted around her. Turned out the peace she felt on her own was because she was truly on her own. The merry band she was traveling with was out of sight. She slid off the horse, intending to drag Whiskey back to wherever her sister and the other annoying traveling companions were.

But then the rustling of leaves alerted her to the pres-ence of someone or something else. Kennara took a step back to shield herself from whatever was making the noise. She grabbed at her bow slung over her shoulder in an effort to reassure herself. The bow was still there, but it offered her little reassurance as her horse stomped, whinnied, then ran, ripping the reins out of her hand. Completely exposed to whatever was making the noise, Kennara stood there, balanced on her good leg, her bow now in her hand, with an arrow notched and ready to go.

"Damn my stubbornness," she muttered. "I wouldn't mind a little help now, but I had to prove a point."

There was a thud to her right, then one to her left. Next, she heard something behind her. She was about to turn and run, when a man stepped out from behind the trees.

He smirked. "Well, what do we have here?"

Kennara stood there silent, not sure what to say, or if she should say anything. Her eyes swept over the road she had been traveling. No one was there except for the four men surrounding her.

"I asked you a question. It's considered bad manners not to respond." The man moved to stand in front of her, tapping his dagger on his leather-clad thigh. His hair, dirty and stringy, shrouded his face. He stared.

"I'm on my way to Dradon. I'm, um, on my pilgrimage." Her eyes darted from one man to the next. Each one looked like more trouble than the last. Kennara tried to determine her next move. One that would get her out of this situation safely.

That's when she saw the amulet around the leader's neck. She wasn't just dealing with brigands; she was dealing with men wielding stolen magic. The bow slipped in her hand as her palms started to sweat. She wasn't a fighter, and she didn't know how to fight someone using magic, especially someone who was most likely using it poorly.

"Looks like that bow is more than you can handle, darling." The leader swiped his hair out of his eyes, staring at her coldly. "Why don't you put that down and come on over here?"

"I would prefer to stay here," Kennara said. She braced herself for whatever was going to happen next.

The leader laughed like she had said the funniest thing he had ever heard. He nodded at the man to her left. Kennara sent a burst of flame up in the air with one hand. She hoped Kellesha saw the fire and realized it was a cry for help. The man to her left lunged and Kennara slammed her bow into his torso, then swung the other end around, striking his face. The man crumpled. Shocked, Kennara stared at the man on the ground, unable to comprehend that she had bested him. She jerked back to the present as something whistled by her ear, turning her focus to the other threats surrounding her.

The leader kneeled, placing one hand on the ground. Kennara felt the ground beneath her start to rumble. Panic set in. She was already unsteady on her feet; if the ground moved, she was screwed. For a moment, the bow helped her balance. Kennara focused on the leader, which was the only reason she saw him lose his balance momentarily.

She looked up to see Kellesha come crashing out of the forest on Shadow. Her hand swiped out, and the leader fell to the ground. The other two men circled Kennara, focusing on the one they believed they could control the easiest. Kennara grabbed an arrow from her quiver, lighting it on fire as she notched it. She fired at one man's feet, lighting fallen leaves and pinecones as she grabbed another arrow to light and shoot at the other man. Before she could, Kellesha knocked the man off his feet with wind from one hand, using the other hand to manipulate the air and yank the amulet from the leader's neck. It landed at Kennara's feet. She raised her bow and smashed the amulet into dozens of pieces. A green mist rose from what was left of the amulet and dissipated into the air.

The leader looked around. Kennara assumed he saw two women with weapons, panting, red hair swirling as the wind blew all around, fire burning behind them. At least she believed it was that image that had all three of them running away, dragging their friend with them.

Eljin and Cas came running up the road, Whiskey with them.

"What happened?" Cas asked.

"Are you okay?" Eljin looked around until his eyes made contact with Kennara's.

"We just proved we don't need protecting," Kellesha said with an air of defiance.

"And that we know when to ask for help when it's needed," Kennara added.

CHAPTER ELEVEN

The four of them continued to travel the pilgrimage road. It provided their group with the cover they needed to pass by watchful eyes. Kennara watched as they passed the pilgrims and the pilgrims passed them. That's when she noticed the same people walking one way in the morning and then in the opposite direction in the afternoon. She didn't say anything the first few times it happened. But after the third day, she knew she needed to say something.

Kennara slowed Whiskey down to walk next to her sister. "Kellesha, have you noticed anything strange about some of the others on this trek?"

"What do you mean?" Kellesha glanced around her.

"Over to the left, the man with the gray beard, I saw him traveling the other way yesterday evening. And the day before that, we passed him going this way. Same with the burly man over there. I've seen them both multiple times a day for the last few days."

Kennara watched as her sister glanced at each man she'd pointed to. Kellesha nodded before making her way over to Cas and Eljin. Kennara watched her sister tell their companions about the two men. Each one of them surreptitiously glanced at the suspicious men. Eljin and Cas looked over at each other, then back at her. Cas nodded to the side of the road before he made his way through the crowd. Kennara reined Whiskey back and followed Cas. Once they reached the edge of the road, they ducked among the trees, continuing to move forward until Kellesha and Eljin caught up with them.

"They are part of the king's guard," Eljin said the minute they were all together.

"We need to find an alternate path; we can't continue on this one any longer. What if they have a scryer with them?" Panic laced Kennara's voice.

"I agree, and I think I know where we can go," Cas said.

Eljin's head snapped to look at Cas. "Are you sure?"

"We're running out of options." Cas sighed. "I know that you were told to go there and speak to her only as a last resort. What would you call this?" He gestured as if he was pointing to all the things that had happened.

"You're right, but getting there is challenging."

"That's putting it nicely. It can be straight-up dangerous. I don't think we have a choice though."

Listening to Eljin and Cas, Kennara had serious thoughts about turning around. She was already afraid; she and her sister had been in hiding almost their entire lives, but their lives had been stable. Intellectually, she knew she was on the run, but once they found Wreswell, she never really felt like anyone was after them. Now, she felt hunted, and Eljin and Cas were talking about the dangers just to get to a single location. She feared she couldn't handle whatever was coming next.

"Who is this person, why should we go speak to them,

and what do we have to do to get there?" Kellesha went straight to the point.

"When I was left in Wreswell, I was told to seek this woman who lives on her own by the sea if I ever found myself in danger of getting caught. She was a dear friend of my mother's and has lived a solitary life on the coast for decades. It is supposed to be a safe haven for me if I can't return home. As for the danger, the coast has inclement weather most of the year," Eljin explained.

The weather didn't sound that troublesome to Kennara, and a safe haven made putting up with a little rain worth it. She was longing to feel safe, even if it was just for a moment.

"I say we go; we need to get off this road. And I could use a moment to feel safe and catch my breath," Kennara said. "Which way do we go from here?"

It didn't take long for the weather to change. The blue skies darkened as heavy gray clouds covered them. Kennara's hair whipped around as the winds picked up around them. It was so strong she was practically lying on Whiskey's back as she clung to her saddle, her knuckles white, the fear of falling off at the forefront of her thoughts. The farther they trudged along, the more concerned Kennara was that she wasn't strong enough to stay on her horse. The clouds gave out and water pelted them from every angle as the wind continued to whip around them. She felt her grip slipping as water filtered through her fingers. That's when a gust of wind picked up her cloak, tugging on it so hard it seemed inevitable she was going to fly away. The more Kennara tried to hold on, the more it felt like she was going to lose the battle.

Suddenly, the wind stopped and she felt safe even as the rain continued to soak her. She looked up to see Kellesha gesturing in movements so small that unless you knew her well, they were imperceptible. Leave it to her sister and her power to help make the trip safer for a moment.

"She won't be able to hold it back for long. We need to find shelter while she's controlling the wind. It's exhausting with weather this bad, so we need to hurry." Kennara pushed the men to move faster instead of standing there gaping at the lack of wind.

Eljin and Cas both looked at her, confusion clear on their faces until they looked over at Kellesha deep in concentration with her hands carefully positioned. It was then that they realized she was keeping the wind away. Suddenly everyone was moving with a purpose.

Cas turned into the forest, taking the group towards a rock circle interspersed with tall pines that helped block the wind and rain. Kellesha continued to hold the wind back while the others set up camp and made dinner.

When everyone was done with the chores for the night, Kennara watched her sister let go. She immediately fell to the ground, exhaustion overtaking her. Kennara ran to her sister's prone body, her uneven gait belied her own exhaustion. She tried to lift Kellesha into a sitting position so she could eat. Nourishment was necessary to build her strength after so much magic was used, but her own arms were too tired from clinging to Whiskey.

Cas was by her side in an instant, holding Kellesha up and feeding her the stew he had made. He gestured for her to go and eat, that he had it under control. Kennara didn't want to leave her sister's side, but she was of no help until she took care of herself. Reluctantly, she made her way back to the food.

She lifted one foot after the other to ensure her feet cleared any obstacles. Tree roots and buried rocks were the worst tripping hazards. It was the presence of a small rock that did her in; she didn't clear the protrusion. Before she could even think, she was plummeting towards the ground, then she stopped as she hit a hard surface that was not the cold ground. She felt the warmth of arms wrap around her. She looked up to see Eljin staring down at her. His eyes were filled with both warmth and concern. Kennara stayed there for a moment longer than necessary, taking comfort from this man she had called a friend for the last five years. She pushed herself away slowly and felt his arms fall.

"Are you okay?" he asked while looking into her eyes.

"I'm fine. Kellesha is the one that needs help." She pulled her eyes away from his.

"As long as you're okay." He reached for her.

"I am," she said. She pushed herself farther from him and walked away frustrated that she was incapable of putting one foot in front of another without losing her balance.

Kennara continued walking, leaving the safety of the rocks and trees behind. The wind pushed her as she made her way up the hill. She refused to stop though, after that miniscule rock felled her. She needed to prove to herself that she was still capable. Water blinded her as it rained sideways instead of falling gently from the sky. She pushed her wet hair out of her face and persevered until she stood on a cliff overlooking the tumultuous ocean below. Out in the distance, surrounded by fog, were the Five Sisters: rocks protruding from the sea that stood tall as wave after wave tried to batter them down. The waters churned between them and below the cliff face. Everything was wild and untamed, including Kennara; her hair and cloak whipped around as gusts of wind blew off the ocean and up against the cliffside. She shivered as she watched the waves crash on top of each other, the pushing and swirling in different directions mimicked all her emotions.

CHAPTER TWELVE

Abria sat back on her horse as the university village came into sight. It had been a long, hard ride, and Reilynne was not happy with her. The healer's grumpiness made her miss Gallagher's smug sarcasm. She hoped Gallagher received her message in time so he could join her soon. In fact, she was hoping he was already in the village below and had convinced the twins to trust him. Abria's promise from five years ago rang in her head. If those girls weren't safe, she didn't know what she was going to do. She should have never left them, but how could she fight against the king if she had stayed and watched over the two girls? And was it really fair of their mother to give her that duty? She wasn't much older than the twins and had a life of her own she wanted to, needed to live. Which included stopping, or at least trying to stop, the Quickenings from ever happening again. Something she failed at all too often.

Reilynne stopped beside her. She had barely kept up during the journey, and now she had to warn Reilynne about what was happening in the town below.

Abria sighed. "The king's men were here not too long ago, searching for women who have escaped the Quickening. They still could be down there. I'm not sure if you want to go into town or stay here on the outskirts. I fear both choices have their dangers."

"Have we come this far for you to get me captured? I trusted you to take us to safe places." Reilynne pushed her hair out of her face.

"I know, but there are two people here that I've promised to protect. At least, I hope they're still here." Abria swung off her horse.

"There are others you're worried you failed? How were you protecting them by bringing so much notice to yourself? With all those battles?" Reilynne asked.

"It's complicated. All I can say is that I thought they were safe. Turns out, the king is getting desperate." Abria rubbed the side of her horse, not facing Reilynne. She turned. "I'm worried there will be scryers in town, but they could have moved on. The only way to know is to go into town. What do you want to do?"

"Turning around's not really an option now, is it?" Sarcasm dripped from Reilynne's voice. "Might as well go into town."

Abria walked beside her horse, concerned she had dragged the healer into her mission without fully assessing all the dangers. Especially now that she needed to protect the twins, running headfirst into known danger with Reilynne, instead of letting the healer stay back where it was safe while she charged into battle.

The pounding of hoofs on the ground drew Abria's attention to the present. Two riders approached. She gestured for Reilynne to hold back, then swung up on her horse to meet them eye to eye. As she got closer, she recognized her friend, Gallagher. Next to him was an elderly man she did not know.

"Abria, good to see you again," Gallagher called out.

"I'm surprised you made it here before me. Did you even get my last missive?" Abria asked.

"I didn't, but as soon as I heard where the king was sending his men, I knew you would head here immediately. I've been here a few days," Gallagher explained.

"I'm relieved you're here." Abria glanced over towards the old man, a questioning look on her face.

"This is Quade. He's one of us." Gallagher nodded, his way of letting her know he had vetted Quade.

Recognition set in. "Oh, it's you, Quade, I didn't recognize you after all these years. It must be the beard. I'm glad Gallagher brought you here, do you have any information for us?" Abria leaned forward on her horse.

"I've been keeping my eyes on a handful of people who needed protecting. Your twins, and two others, to be exact. When the king's men came, I told the four of them to get out of town. Which they did, following the pilgrimage road. I'm not sure how, but they made it past the scryer. And should be safe for now."

Abria dismounted. "That's some news, at least. Doesn't mean they're actually safe, or that the king doesn't have spies along the pilgrimage road. If they do, do you have any idea where they might head?"

"I don't know if they would risk it, but Eljin and his guard were told to go to a lone cabin near the Five Sisters and ask for the woman who lives there. It's a dangerous journey." Quade's brow furrowed. "I'm worried about them. The pass is always treacherous, and I haven't heard from the woman in ages."

"It appears we need directions and supplies. How far ahead are they? Are the king's men still in town?"

Abria and Quade talked as they walked into town. He caught her up on all the important details since the arrival of the king's men. Engrossed in the old man's news, she barely took the time to make sure the others followed them.

DAYS AFTER RIDING INTO TOWN WITH QUADE, ABRIA AND THE others trudged along the pilgrimage road before turning onto a path that led into the forest and eventually to the cliffs above the ocean. The closer they got to the cliffs, the more the wind whipped around them. The gusts so strong Abria feared one of them would lose their seat and be knocked to the ground. She gestured for everyone to dismount as the wind picked up her cloak and tugged so hard she went with it, only stopped by her tense grip on the pummel of the saddle.

Abria breathed a sigh of relief as her feet hit the ground. She looked around to see the others were also safe. Then the sky opened up and buckets of water came pouring down on them. The wind blew so hard, and rain pelted them from every direction, making it hard for her to see the trail in front of them. There was no way they could continue in this weather. Gallagher waved, then pointed towards a circle of rocks. She clung to the reins as she followed him to the rock circle; Reilynne wasn't far behind.

The rock circle acted like a safe haven from the storm. They worked together to set up camp for the night. Abria tripped, almost spilling her dinner. She bent over and picked up the protruding piece of stone. With a slight chuckle, she put the stone in her pocket before eating her stew.

Reilynne and Gallagher laughed as they sat around the campfire, but Abria's thoughts of the twins distracted her, making it impossible for her to take part. Instead, she walked up the cliff. She used her cloak to block the icy sting of water hitting her face. The wind pushed back as she took one step after another until she was standing at the edge, looking at the Five Sisters as the waves attempted to batter them down. But the rocks stood proud in the ocean, water swirling and crashing around them and onto the cliff. Abria took the rock from camp out of her pocket and tossed it into the turbulent depths below.

CHAPTER THIRTEEN

The next morning brought about more rain, but less wind. Kennara breathed a sigh of relief as she mounted Whiskey. If today was anything like the last bit of the journey, she might have quit, never left where they had slept last night, learned to live off the land. However, that was not to be. The sun was peeking through the clouds, forcing the day to look brighter even though water still fell from the sky. She rolled her shoulders back, clicked her tongue, and set off on the journey. She didn't look back to see if the others followed her since she knew they wouldn't be far behind.

Kennara looked out to the ocean and the Five Sisters rising above the waves. This morning they stood tall, like the beating of wind and water from the night before had not happened. It gave her hope, those rocks standing there, representing the magic powers women possessed, the same powers being stripped away from them. She sighed. Her magic was such a part of her, she couldn't imagine herself without it. Of course, she couldn't imagine leaving Wreswell, but here she was on a strange road, going who knew where, with friends that she didn't know as well as she thought.

Eljin and Cas still hadn't talked about why they were on the run. Even though Eljin was always there to support her, she didn't like the feeling that he didn't trust her enough to know the truth.

With a squeeze of her legs, Kennara encouraged Whiskey to move faster, distancing herself from those who refused to trust her. The need to be alone with her thoughts overcame her need to know where she was headed. At least there was only one road for her to follow.

Whiskey was surefooted as they made their way towards the sand dunes that lined the beach. She could just barely see the hills of sand below her through the rows of evergreen trees. She slowed to appreciate the light as it shimmered and danced through the needles and leaves of the trees. It was beautiful, and almost enough to make her smile, almost.

"Eljin said to go left once we clear the trees," Kellesha said.

Startled, Kennara tensed. Whiskey interpreted her involuntary movement as an encouragement to move faster, and lunged forward. She instantly pulled her horse back, regaining control in mere moments, but not before Kellesha reached out for the reins to stop Whiskey, once again undermining her abilities.

"I had it, Kelle. You should have trusted me to take care of myself."

"I know, but habits are hard to break. I'm used to looking out for you."

"Fine, but maybe try a little harder." Kennara took the reins back from her sister.

She clicked her tongue as the trees cleared to open

expanses of sand everywhere. She could hear and taste the ocean, but couldn't see it yet. The sand dunes blocked any view of the surf. Out in the open, she let Whiskey loose. The freedom was exhilarating. Her hair tumbled from her braids, flying behind her. The rhythm of the horse's hooves matched the beating of her heart as they flew down the beach until the ocean was before them. Kennara reined Whiskey in and dismounted. She quickly took off her boots and stockings so she could walk along the beach, feeling the cold water on her feet and the sand slip between her toes.

Kennara left Whiskey standing on the beach, the water called to her, the rhythmic crashing of the waves inviting her to wade further into the sea. She did just that, hiking her skirts above her knees as she walked further out, the water swirling first around her ankles, then her calves, and finally her knees. There she stood, she didn't know for how long, but the sand that was once beneath her feet now covered them, like the earth itself wanted to lock her in place and never let her leave this spot.

It didn't matter that her feet were buried because she had no intention of leaving anytime soon. Water had never soothed her before, but there was something here, about this spot that calmed her. Until she felt tendrils climb up and wrap around her leg. Her eyes widened, all she could do was stand there, looking up and down the deserted beach. Her friends were off in the distance, but if anything were to happen, there was no one near to save her. Nothing happened. She let out the breath she had been holding. She was clearly on edge, overreacting to every little thing.

The water's grip on her leg tightened. It felt like a hand had reached up from the waves, grabbed her, and its fingers were now digging into her calf. The water yanked her leg, sending her face-first into its depths. She felt her body twist, no longer able to sense which way was up. The grasp on her tightened more as she was dragged out to sea. Kennara tried everything to get free. She kicked her legs; she pulled through the water with her arms; she gasped for air every time she felt mist hit her face instead of the now oppressive feeling of the waves. She thought that she was done for in that moment. Everything she tried failed, and soon she would be out in the middle of the ocean with no way back.

Kennara refused to let the ocean win. She had not come this far, only to drown on the first leg of the journey. In her mind, she imagined the water splitting, so a path appeared before her. She wished for each of the fingers wrapped around her calf to let go one by one.

Wait, was she free? Kennara kicked her leg, the vicelike grip suddenly gone. Then, just like she had imagined it, the waters parted. She fell to her knees, no longer supported by the raging waves. She coughed up water, gasping for the air that had been denied from her. As much as she wanted to scramble to her feet and get out of this predicament, she needed to breathe, to fill her lungs with air instead of water. She pushed her sopping wet hair out of her face as she looked up.

At the very end of a tunnel, now formed by water, a woman stood on the beach. Her arms outstretched as if she was pushing the water apart with her two hands.

Kennara stumbled to her feet. She was afraid the tunnel would come crashing down on her, so in her mind she imagined it continuing to form the tunnel above her as she limped out. More than anything, she wanted to hurry, but her leg was already dragging after the terrifying ordeal. She cursed, annoyed by her own limitations. Glancing up, she saw the woman who had saved her, long white and black hair swirling around her body as her arms shook and her dark skin dulled from exhaustion. If she didn't hurry, the woman was going to collapse, taking the water tunnel with her.

"Kennara, are you okay?" Eljin ran into the tunnel and swept her into his arms, carrying her out like she was a delicate package. He was warm and dry and smelled of the forest, a stark contrast to her cold, wet state. She burrowed into his chest, soaking in the sense of security of his arms. Later, she would remember she was frustrated by his secrets, but for now, she let herself forget, let herself be saved, let herself feel protected.

As soon as they were safe, the woman dropped her arms. Water crashed to the ground and escaped back into the ocean. She teetered a bit before falling to her knees.

When she looked up at Kennara and Eljin, distrust shown in her eyes. "Who the hell are you? And what are you doing here?"

CHAPTER FOURTEEN

Kennara peeked out from where she had burrowed into Eljin's arms. She considered having him set her down as a show of her strength, but she didn't feel strong at the moment, and she needed the comfort being held by him brought her.

Eljin's arms tightened as he turned towards the unknown woman. Kennara felt tension course through his body. Clearly, this was not the welcome he was expecting.

"I'm Eljin, and these are my friends. I was told to come here to see Tahra if I was ever in need. I've avoided it until now, but circumstances are such that my friends and I need her help." The terse formality in his tone was so unfamiliar to Kennara, she almost looked back to see if it was really him speaking.

Instead, she watched the woman questioning them. She saw the woman's eyes go wide at the mention of Tahra. Kennara saw a single tear fall before the woman wiped it away. Something had happened, and it was recent. As much as the woman was trying to hide it, Kennara could sense her loss. Her grief was almost palpable.

"It seems you've made this journey for naught. Tahra is no longer here. She cannot help you." The woman turned away.

"What do you mean, no longer here?" Kennara asked. She tapped Eljin's shoulder to let him know he could put her down. He sighed but moved the arm that held up her legs. She slid down his body until her feet hit the ground, his other arm still wrapped around her, holding her so tight she felt his muscles tense through her wet gown.

The woman stopped mid-stride. "What does it matter to you what I mean? She's no longer here to help you. You might as well continue on your way."

"Surely she left some message for Eljin and Cas. They were told to specifically seek her out when . . ." Kennara paused. She looked up at Eljin, gesturing that he should continue, but he said nothing.

Cas stepped forward to explain. "We were told to seek her out after escaping the castle. It was a long time ago, and we've managed to stay safe until now. The current king sent men to the town where we have been hiding for the past ten years. Even worse, he has men searching for someone along the pilgrimage road."

"Wait, you escaped the castle?" The woman pushed her white and black hair off her face. "Did all four of you escape the castle or just some of you?"

"Does it matter?" Kellesha raised a questioning eyebrow.

"It does. It matters quite a bit actually," she responded.

"Why? Why does it matter?" Eljin glared at the woman, unwilling to budge.

"Eljin, there's no need to fight her." Cas took a step forward, physically inserting himself into the conversation. Something he rarely did.

Eljin gestured for Cas to continue. Kennara was pretty sure that if he wasn't holding her, he would walk away. Instead, he stayed solid and unmoving.

Cas glanced over at Eljin and shook his head ever so slightly, as if he was disappointed in him. "It was just the two of us that escaped the castle. We met the twins while we were hiding, and now we're all running from the king."

"You're him." The woman's jaw dropped as she stared at Cas.

"I'm not, but he is." He pointed to Eljin.

Kennara watched as the woman's head whipped from Cas to Eljin. Despite the fact that Kennara stood there, wrapped in the arms of the man everyone was talking about, she felt like she didn't belong. Whatever they were talking about was information she was not privy to, and it bothered her. She knew this had something to do with whatever Eljin was withholding to protect her. The fact that this stranger knew more than her hurt so much that it felt like a physical blow tearing through her chest. Angry, Kennara stepped back, away from Eljin, forcing him to let go of her. He looked at her intently before letting his arm drop. Kennara felt like he wanted to argue with her, to keep her close, but whatever he saw on her face told him now was not the time. She was not going to budge. Maybe it would convince him to talk to her instead of hiding who he was. Especially now that it would only confirm what she already guessed.

Kennara waited for the woman to speak again. Instead, the stranger just stared, mouth agape, like she was unsure of what to do next.

"Miss, are you going to explain why you needed that information, or are we going to stand here on this beach staring at each other forever?" Kennara was abrupt. The cold of the water had seeped into her bones, and she was losing the battle to not shiver. The day had taken a toll on her and her body, and she just wanted to be somewhere she could sit and forget it had ever happened.

"It would be nice to have an explanation." Kellesha crossed her arms across her chest.

"I'm sorry. I just wasn't expecting anyone, much less this. I guess I should start at the beginning. My name is Zenevieve. My mother was Tahra; she passed away about a year ago. I've been here, on my own, ever since," she said.

"I'm sorry. You've clearly had to deal with a lot," Cas said, his tone comforting.

"It's all worth it now that you're here. Come, let's go to my home. I have something for you and . . . your friend." Zenevieve turned and walked away from the group, towards the sand dunes. She climbed them like the ground was completely solid under her feet while Kennara felt like she went backward a foot for every two she went forward. The dunes constantly collapsed under her, making it impossible for her to climb them. She was already exhausted from the ocean trying to take her out to sea, and now her body felt like it could no longer move another step, her leg especially. Her muscles were tired, her foot ached, and pain shot up to her knee with every step. She fell to her hands, frustrated with everything, annoyed with her body for not being able to handle the task, angry that she was showing weakness to this new person already. Tears streamed down her face as she fisted her hands in the sand, the tiny rocks imprinting in her skin as her grip tightened. She wanted to scream, throw things, curl up into a ball, anything but continue on. Instead, she pushed herself back to her feet and called her sister over.

"I need help," she whispered, defeated. The sand dune was more than she could handle, and she hated it.

"Don't worry, I got you." Kellesha slipped her arm around Kennara's waist and lifted her up. Together they conquered the dune, Reaching the top only to see a small house at the bottom.

Kennara sighed. "Where's a sled when you need one?" She smiled, picturing them sitting and sliding to the base of the dune.

"I could see you doing it and loving every second. You were always the more daring of the two of us," Kellesha laughed.

"Me? Daring? I spend my days in the library dreaming of adventures. Now that I'm actually on one, I'm absolutely terrified of what's going to happen. Who's going to get hurt trying to protect me? What's going to happen to them because of me? It's nothing like I imagined."

"What you dreamed of probably didn't involve running from the king."

"No, it was more like reading a book on the beach while I stayed in a rustic but somehow still fun cabin."

"You might be on the adventure of your dreams, then." Kellesha pointed to the home in front of them. It looked worn from the weather on the outside, but a glimpse inside through the open door looked about as cozy as a home could get, filled with books, blankets, pillows, and over-stuffed furniture.

"You two, come here. I have something for you." Zenevieve gestured for Cas and Eljin to follow her, leaving Kennara and her sister standing in the living room with nowhere to go.

"Should we follow?" Kennara asked.

Kellesha laughed. "I know you want to, but it's probably not the best idea."

Kennara pushed her sister's arm away and plopped onto the sofa. "True . . ." The knock on the door was insistent. "I'm curious who else is around." Kennara stood and hobbled her way to the door, her sister close behind her. She yanked it open, standing on the other side was a warrior woman accompanied by two others.

"Abria?" Kellesha asked.

CHAPTER FIFTEEN

Abria stared at the two girls, now women, she had abandoned in Wreswell all those years ago. She could still hear their mother's voice making Abria promise to look after her girls, to make sure they were safe, to help them escape the Quickening. Which she did. Abria had made sure the twins were safe in Wreswell before leaving them there. She also still felt guilty for leaving them there, alone. But she had been called to fight, not babysit. So, she left the two girls on their own, and at the time, they really were just girls. Not the young women who stared back at her now.

"Kellesha, Kennara? Is it really you?" she asked.

"Of course it's us. Do you know any other red-headed twins?" Kellesha crossed her arms and turned away.

"Kellesha, who is this, and why are you acting like that?" Kennara hissed.

Abria guessed Kennara didn't want her to hear, but the space was small and the sound traveled.

Kellesha glared at Abria over her shoulder. "You don't remember her? Mother left us with her. She promised to keep us safe, and then she left us, alone, breaking her promise to us and our mother."

"Kellesha, it wasn't like that . . ." Abria reached out to pat Kellesha on the shoulder; instead, her arm fell to her side.

"Oh, really? What was it like then?" Kellesha turned back to her, a breeze whirling around her as she did so.

"I couldn't protect you like your mother needed me to. I was too young to have that much responsibility. So I found somewhere safe for you. And I made my own path. And every step of it has been formed by the promise I made to your mother," Abria said to Kellesha's back. She wanted to beg Kellesha to understand, even though she barely understood herself. All she knew was when their mother made her promise to protect them, she was only eighteen, and hollow. Her magic had just been stripped away from her. Some days she felt more dead than alive, and she was somehow responsible for two thirteen-year-old girls. Girls that weren't that much younger than she was, and still had their magic. Because of her protection, they escaped losing what she had lost. She tried, but she couldn't handle the strain, the jealousy, so she dropped the girls off somewhere she thought would be safe. She made connections to watch the twins and to alert her if anything changed regarding their safety. In her own way, she had kept her promise.

Kennara stepped forward. "Abria, why don't we go find a place where we can sit and talk?"

"I don't want to talk, Kennara. I want her to leave. Shouldn't be too hard. She's done it before, and she'll do it again." Kellesha stood with her back to the room, arms crossed.

Abria looked on as her former charges tried to figure out how to handle the situation.

"You don't have to come talk. I'll talk to Abria, and when you're ready to be reasonable, you can join us, or not. Whatever you decide." Kennara grabbed Abria's arm, steering her towards the door.

Once outside, Kennara turned towards her. "Look, I don't have the same memories of you that my sister has. I don't remember that you were supposed to watch over us or keep us safe. All I know is you got us somewhere safe, and it worked for a long time. What I want to know now is, why are you here?"

Abria stood there a moment. She took in the young woman in front of her. The thirteen-year-old girl she had left behind was barely noticeable. She turned towards the ocean, taking in a deep breath as she organized her thoughts.

"I have a network of people set up in Wreswell. I was to be alerted if anything happened that put you in danger. Which is exactly what happened."

"At least you didn't leave us to flounder on our own. We were only thirteen."

"And I was only eighteen, dealing with the loss of my magic and two young girls. It's not that I didn't want to protect you; I just couldn't do it in the way that was expected of me. I needed to be out there fighting, not sitting on the sidelines."

"Is that what you've been doing? You've been out there fighting?" Kennara shifted her weight off her weak leg.

"I've fought the last five years to stop the Quickenings in small villages. It isn't much, but I've had some success. I've also been searching for the missing prince. I want to believe he's alive, and the change that he could bring if it were true." Abria sat on the sand, still looking at the waves crashing on the shore.

Kennara followed Abria's lead and sat on the ground. Abria could feel the young woman's eyes on her, questioning everything she said.

"Sounds like you've had an interesting five years. Much more interesting than my time working in the library. Or Kellesha's time training every single day because she promised our mother to look after me, and she thought she had to do it on her own."

"I'm sorr—"

Kennara held up her hand. "I don't need your apology. My sister might, but I get it. You weren't much older than we were and had gone through your own traumatic experience. One my mother managed to save us from. So, no, I don't need your apology. I understand what you did and why you did it. Again, what I would like to know is why you are here now."

Abria looked over at Kennara for the first time during the conversation. "When I got the message that the king had sent men to Wreswell—that he was planning a Quickening there—I came to save you and your sister. But by the time I got there, you had already left. It wasn't enough for me to know you were gone. I needed to know you were safe."

"How did you know to come here? I didn't even know we were coming here."

"This was happenstance. I was coming here to regroup and then to search for you and your sister."

"Interesting."

They both turned their gaze back to the water. Abria thought of the two girls she left behind and what they were like today. So different, so much stronger in such different ways. Kellesha looked like a warrior. The time she spent training was visible in everything she did. Then there was quiet Kennara—or not so quiet anymore. Abria wouldn't have recognized her if it wasn't for her limp. The girl she had left behind had been afraid of everything. She had cried for days after leaving her mother. Once she stopped crying, she never spoke, only taking food and water from Kellesha. It was why Kennara didn't remember Abria (or so Abria assumed): the entire journey she was in a stupor, only interacting with her twin.

The pounding of someone running interrupted her thoughts. She jumped up to see a young man running towards them. She raised her fists, ready to defend herself and Kennara, who was still sitting on the ground, fighting a smile as her eyes locked with the intruder's.

"Eljin, what are you doing?" Kennara asked, stifling a laugh.

"You won't believe what I just read. Come look at this. I think . . . I . . ." Eljin stopped talking as he noticed Abria standing there, ready to fight.

"I'm sorry. Who are you?" he asked.

"I could ask you the same question," she responded.

"You could, but I have a feeling you weren't invited here, and I've made friends with the host." Eljin did not look pleased that a stranger had made their way to the cabin.

"Fine, I'm Abria. I'm here to find the twins." She didn't like the look of the man standing in front of her. There was something about him that brought up terrible memories.

"I'm Eljin. Kennara and I worked together at the library. Why are you looking for my friends?"

CHAPTER SIXTEEN

"Eljin," Kennara put her hand on his shoulder, "it's okay. I know her . . . That is, I used to know her."

Kennara looked over at Abria, unsure of what to say and how much she should tell him. He knew her secrets, but Abria's were not hers to tell. Abria shook her head almost imperceptibly.

Eljin looked at Kennara, then at Abria, and back at Kennara. "What do you mean, used to know her?" he asked, raising his eyebrow.

Kellesha returned just in time to hear Eljin's question. "What she means is Abria is the person who abandoned us. Left us to fend for ourselves in a strange place, away from everything and everyone we knew, and she's looking for us now because she's worried the king is close to finding us. She has suddenly remembered her obligation to our mother. Her promise to protect us. After five years of not caring."

Kennara could feel her sister's anger almost as if it was her own. While she knew it wasn't her emotions, the feeling was so strong it was almost impossible to ignore. Which was why when Abria reached out to Kellesha, she stopped her. Kellesha wasn't ready for physical contact and would probably turn it into a reason to fight Abria. A brawl might do the two of them some good, but Kennara would rather it happen when she wasn't around.

"Sounds like the two of you have some things to work out." Eljin's eyes darted between Abria and Kellesha. "Kenna, why don't we let them?"

"Wait, where are the others? I know they left while we talked. Where did they go?"

Abria moved closer to the door. "I'm sure they're on the beach, letting us have our little reunion. Especially since it was such an awkward one."

"And whose fault is that?" Kellesha asked, her sarcastic tone laced with anger.

"Why don't you go find your companions?" Eljin's clipped tones belayed his own suspicion. He turned to Kennara. "Come on, Kenna, I want to show you what I found." He grabbed her hand, pulling her with him just like he had done back at the library when he found a book he thought she would enjoy.

Abria grabbed Kennara's free arm. "Are you sure you should be alone with him?"

"Look, I'm willing to give you a chance because I don't have the same memory as Kellesha. That being said, I will continue to choose who I spend time with, especially when it's a friend who has been by my side for the past five years. You know, the five years you weren't around."

Abria dropped her arm. Kennara could tell the woman wanted to say more but realized she didn't have any authority to do so.

"Come on, Eljin, let's go. You can show me whatever it is that has you so excited." Kennara took his arm and led him inside, but not before she made eye contact with her sister. She looked over at Abria and back to Kellesha, letting her sister know she thought they should talk while she was with Eljin.

She leaned on Eljin as they walked. He didn't seem to notice or mind. His lack of concern allowed her to accept his help.

"What did you find?" she asked as they came to a flight of stairs. She groaned as she took in what felt like an insurmountable barrier at the moment. It had been a long day, and it was nowhere near over. How was it not later in the day? Her shoulders drooped at the thought of walking up the stairs.

She felt Eljin look down at her. He didn't answer her question; in fact, he didn't say anything at all. He bent down and slipped one arm beneath her legs, the other encircled her waist, and he lifted her. Before she could protest, he was climbing the stairs. She wrapped her arms around his neck and snuggled into his embrace. Part of her wanted to yell at him that she could have climbed the stairs, but she hadn't wanted to climb them. In fact, she was enjoying the warmth of his arms around her.

They reached the top of the stairs. The arm beneath her knees moved away. Her legs slid down the side of his body. She looked into his dark eyes before her gaze shifted lower, to his lips. She bit her lower lip before her arms dropped to her sides and she looked away.

"I could have walked up the stairs on my own," she said, stepping away from him.

She felt his eyes on her, but she couldn't look at him. It

felt like something was shifting between them, and she wasn't sure how to handle it.

"Of course you could have." He stepped aside, allowing Kennara to see more of the attic. "But how often do I get to play the hero and save a damsel in distress, even if I'm only saving her from her own stubbornness?"

Kennara quickly turned back towards him, too quickly for her tired right leg. She saw Eljin wink at her before either one of them realized she was falling. There was nothing there to stop her fall, or so she thought. He darted towards her, but wasn't quick enough to stop the fall. Instead, he somehow maneuvered his body under hers, so she landed on top of him and not on the hard floor.

"I guess you get to be a hero twice today," she said as she tried to push herself off him, but his viselike grip around her waist prevented her. "I'm fine. You can let go now."

"What if I don't want to let go of you?" he muttered.

The loud footsteps of someone wearing boots climbing the stairs interrupted whatever was happening between her and Eljin. His arms fell away. She rolled off him and sat up so she could see around the attic.

"What did you want to show me?"

He stood, offering her a hand. Once they were both on their feet, he pointed to a chest in the corner. "It was Zenevieve's mother's. She worked for the queen. Her journal is in there."

"What are you two doing up here?" Cas asked as he walked through the doorway.

Eljin glared at his friend for a moment. Cas shrugged it off. With a sigh, Eljin turned back to the chest.

"I was about to show Kenna the journal I found.

Zenevieve's mother was one of the queen's most trusted servants."

Kennara watched the two men in front of her. It was like they were having a conversation with their eyes. Whatever it was, it did not include her.

Cas threw up his arms in defeat. "Fine, tell her everything. Why don't you just tell everyone your secret?"

"They can keep a secret. And we both have always trusted them." Eljin said, turning towards her. "Here's the journal."

He held a worn leather-covered journal in his outstretched hand. Kennara hesitated before taking it. She wasn't sure she wanted the responsibility of knowing whatever the journal would tell her. She sat and opened it at the beginning and read of a young woman, Tahra, with a young child of her own, living through the turmoil of the old king's murder. How his brother, the new king, locked the two princes in a tower, forbidding anyone from going up there. The widowed queen, desperate to free her sons, turned to Tahra and tasked the woman with their escape. The queen gave Tahra an amulet with her magic and the love of her sons trapped in it. The amulet was supposed to protect her sons. But during the escape, they captured one boy. Tahra didn't know what to do. She feared if she went back, they would capture both. But if she left with only one, it would seal the other's fate—a certain death.

The words blurred as Kennara tried to read on. She wiped the tears falling from her eyes. This young woman was on the run with her daughter and one of the rightful heirs to the throne. It was so brave, but so sad.

Kennara continued to read. After hiding in the forest for a few days, Tahra realized they were being followed by the young boy who was supposed to become the prince's guard. If he could follow them, she figured the evil king could as well. She found a town that constantly had people coming and going. A university town where she hoped no one would notice the presence of two young boys. She left them there, but not before telling the young prince he couldn't use his real name, that he should go by something different, something like Eljin.

CHAPTER SEVENTEEN

"You're—the—missing—prince." Kennara spit out one word at a time. "That's what you've been hiding from me and my sister." She heard herself get louder with each word. "That you're the f . . ."

Eljin scrambled, covering her mouth before she could get out the last words.

"Yes, but right now, it needs to stay a secret. I don't trust Abria and whoever she's with." Eljin bent down, looking at her in a way she had never seen. There was no sparkle of laughter in his eyes. Instead, his dark eyes were darker. She could see and feel both his anger and fear. Not that either emotion was directed at her.

She licked his palm.

He jumped away as if she had bitten him. "Why did you do that?" His brow furrowed in disgust.

Kennara couldn't help herself. She burst out laughing. Both Eljin and Cas stared at her as if she had turned into a frog, or maybe a dog—some creature that did things like lick to get their way. Their faces only made her laugh more. She shook her head at their incredulous stares.

"You're the one that put your hand over my mouth. What else did you expect?" She raised an eyebrow. "I'm assuming this is the secret that had you running out of town with us?"

"Yes, its dangerous information to have. And—well—I want you to be safe." Eljin's eyes dropped to his hands. He stood there fiddling with his fingers while she took in what she was learning.

"So you're," she lowered her voice to a whisper, "the missing prince. What are you planning to do with your power?"

"Power? What power? It's more like a death sentence."

"Is that really how you see it? You have the ability to stop what is happening in this world—if you claimed what was rightfully yours." Kennara stopped. "Wait, where's the amulet? The one mentioned in the journal."

Eljin pulled on the leather strand circling his neck. There at the string's apex was a blue stone that glowed from within. "You mean this amulet? The one I wear every day to remind me of what I lost." He gulped, his eyes glistened with unshed tears.

"But you could get some of it back. Your home, your kingdom . . ." She trailed off as she watched this man she thought she knew become someone else. The happy, flirty individual she had spent the past five years with was gone, disappeared. The person who stood before her was angry, sad, and (she hated even thinking it) almost broken. When he carried her up here, this was not what she expected him to show her. She felt like it wasn't what he expected either.

She took his hand in hers. "You could do something. You could actually change the world we live in. I know you don't like what's happening any more than I do."

He slipped his hand out of hers and turned away. "You

don't get it. I lost everything. My home, my family, my place in this world. Gone. I can't change it now."

She stepped back, stumbling as she did so. "You lost everything. You did. But do you think you're the only one? My mother sacrificed herself to save me and my sister, just like your mother did. Abria lost the life she knew, her magic, and has been fighting the king since she left us in Wreswell. Zenevieve lost her home and her mother. She lives by herself on the edges of the earth to stay safe from your uncle. So yes, you lost everything. But so did my sister and I, and so many others in this world. And we all want it to change, you have the power to make that change happen. If you can get over yourself."

Kennara made her way to the stairs, trying not to let her right leg drag as she left. She heard Eljin turn towards her, but he said nothing. That didn't mean she couldn't feel his gaze boring holes in her back.

She needed to talk to her sister. Kellesha would know how to handle this information. Right now, she didn't know what to do with it. Her emotions were as tumultuous as the sea the day before. Crashing against her over and over again were waves of hurt, anger, and happiness. Kennara wished she had known Eljin's secrets for much longer than a few moments, but there was this light, almost giddy feeling below the hurt and anger, one that came from the knowledge that he trusted her with his life. He trusted her.

"Kellesha, I need to talk to you," Kennara said before

she looked around the room. Her sister was not alone. The rest of Abria's crew had made their way to the beach house and Zenevieve had welcomed them all. "Never mind, it can wait until later."

She turned to leave. Perhaps being alone with her thoughts would clear her head. She felt someone grab her arm. Turning back, she saw Kellesha had hold of her.

"Let me introduce you to everyone," Kellesha said.

Kennara looked around the room, now filled with people all staring at her. She pasted a smile on her face before nodding to her sister.

"You know Abria; her right-hand man is Gallagher; next to Gallagher is Reilynne. She has her own healing practice."

Her eyes darted from the stunning woman sitting in front of her to her sister. Did she just say "healing practice"? Kellesha nodded. This was what Kennara had been looking for. A healer with magic who could fix her leg. It would change everything. She took a step towards the healer, but stopped. This wasn't really the time to be asking for favors from strangers.

"Nice to meet everyone," she said, instead of begging the healer for help. She took a deep breath and slowly let it out.

Nobody spoke. She fidgeted as the silence overwhelmed her. She wanted more information about why these strangers were here, now, at the same time she was there. But she didn't know how to ask the question without sounding rude. Just the thought of being rude, and Kennara swore she could hear her mother's voice teaching her manners.

Kennara knew she said it could wait just moments ago, but she wouldn't be able to focus until she told her sister about Eljin. It was either that or blurt out that she needed a healer to fix her leg, and that seemed even more wrong than dragging her sister away with no explanation.

"I'm sorry to interrupt, but I need to talk to my sister." She stared at Kellesha, hoping there was a twin connection and it was working right now.

Kellesha stood, the chair scraping against the floor a cacophony of noise in the silence-filled room. Its disturbing sound somehow made the awkwardness caused by her interruption even worse.

Kennara nodded at the group she just met before taking her sister's arm and dragging her out of the cozy home. She tripped as she crossed the threshold of the door. Her sister's arm tightened around hers, preventing her from crashing to the floor.

"You need to be careful. I don't want you to hurt yourself," Kellesha scolded.

Kennara looked at her sister with a look only her sister would understand.

"I'm sorry. I know we talked about this. I'm trying, I really am," Kellesha said.

"It's fine." Kennara sat on the stairs leading up to the front door. "I have information that's more important."

Looks of concern and curiosity warred across Kellesha's features. Kennara waited until her sister sat next to her to tell her what she'd learned moments ago.

"What is it?" Kellesha took her hands.

"It's Eljin . . ."

"Is this about you finally realizing you have—"

"He's the missing prince."

"What?" Kellesha dropped her hands, standing with such speed it was as if someone lit a fire under her. Kennara watched her sister pace as she processed the information.

"It's unbelievable, but true. He escaped with

Zenevieve's mother. She left him in Wreswell to hide, just like we were left there."

Kellesha stopped. "More like we were abandoned there by someone that promised to protect us."

"You remember so much more than I do from that time. But, you should let it go. Abria was young, too young to have the responsibility of grieving twins." She grabbed her sister's hand and pulled her down to sit. "If you stop and think about it, we were safe, safer than we would have been if she had kept us with her."

Kellesha sighed. "Fine, I'll try to let it go. No promises, though. If she had kept us with her, maybe we would have been fighting for change instead of hiding. I'm so sick of hiding."

"Have you stayed in hiding because of me?" Kennara felt the guilt that normally simmered inside her build to a boil. Her eyes burned as they filled with tears, causing her to look away. She felt her sister's hand on her shoulder for a moment before it fell away.

"Kennara, look at me." Kellesha squatted down in front of her. "I said look at me."

She slowly raised her head, not wanting to see what was in her sister's eyes. She didn't want to see her sister look at her like she was a burden, like she was the one holding them back.

"I stayed in Wreswell to keep both of us safe. Like I promised our mother. Now that we don't have a home, I want to do something to change that. I don't want to hide, I want to change the world for the better. And maybe we can now—we know the rightful heir to the throne. Even more, we know that he's a good person. Maybe we can convince him to overthrow his uncle, take his rightful place in the kingdom, and give women their magic back."

CHAPTER EIGHTEEN

bria watched the twins walk off together. She wanted to go after them, listen in on their conversation. But doing so would only cause them to trust her even less than they did now. So instead of following the twins, she stayed at the table wondering what Kennara had learned that had her so upset.

The stairs creaked behind her. She turned to see Eljin and Cas making their way down.

"You know she isn't wrong," Cas said.

"Just because she's not wrong doesn't mean she's right." Eljin pushed his hair back.

Abria tried to look busy as she strained to hear what the two men were arguing about.

"You could change everything, though. You're always telling me how wrong the world is, and how much it bothers you to see people suffer. If you took your rightful place, you could make everything right. Not many people are in a position to make that sort of change." Cas stood in front of Eljin, using his bulky frame to force his friend to listen. It was a tactic that Abria was familiar with since she did the same thing if the situation called for it.

"There's more to it than that. My uncle is ruthless. It's not like I can just show up and everything will go back to the way it was."

Cas reached out to Eljin, offering a bit of comfort. "I know it won't be simple. But you know it's the right thing to do. You can't let fear make your decisions for you."

Eljin shrugged Cas's hand off his shoulder. "Who said anything about fear?" He pushed past his friend.

Abria's eyes locked with Eljin's. He might claim to not be afraid, but she could see one emotion shining through his eyes—fear, plain and simple. But what were they alluding to that no one here wanted to talk about, and was it related to whatever had Kennara running off earlier?

She shifted back in her chair, contemplating everything she'd just heard. None of it made any sense at all.

The cooing of a pigeon interrupted the thoughts whirling through her mind. A pigeon could only mean one thing: someone had sent Gallagher a message. She stood. Gallagher must have slipped out of the room while Eljin and Cas were arguing.

"I need some air. I think I'll go for a walk." Abria nodded to the group still sitting around the table.

Reilynne glanced up from her cup of tea, her eyes wide as if she was surprised. "Sorry, did you say something?"

"Just that I'm going for a walk." Abria nodded towards the two left at the table.

She opened the back door. The twins were sitting on the stoop, deep in conversation. Neither one of them looked up at her as she followed the sound of a cooing pigeon.

"I was just about to come and get you," Gallagher said,

swiping his hand through his hair. He sat next to a tower of pigeon cages, his features tight with worry.

Abria sat next to him. "I'm here now. What's the news that has you looking so concerned?"

"It's not good."

"Clearly."

"They're in Wreswell." Gallagher's leg shook. His nervous energy was palpable.

Abria didn't understand his reaction. They knew the king's men were in Wreswell. "We already know the king's men are there."

"Not just the king's men. Maeryn and Viggo are there."

Abria's head whipped around, her eyes wide. "Why are those two there? They're King Sheamus's council."

"They're the worst of his council. I'm not even sure King Sheamus is as evil as Viggo. And Maeryn—I'm not sure if she's actually evil, or if it's desperate self-preservation, but it is her magic that's used for the Quickenings."

"She's evil. The amount of pain she's causing women can't be ignored." Abria couldn't stop the shudder that ripped through her body at the memory of her magic being taken against her will. It might have happened a long time ago, but she still woke up some nights in a cold sweat, shaking from the phantom pain of her magic being torn from her body.

Gallagher wrapped his arm around her and pulled her close. She leaned into his comforting embrace, something she had done many times since they had met.

"The twins got out just in time," Gallagher said.

Abria sighed. "I'm so glad we met Quade all those years ago. He's been a godsend for watching over them."

Gallagher squeezed her shoulder. "They made it out before Viggo and Maeryn got there. Unfortunately, that's not all the news. They are only a few weeks behind us. And enough people saw the twins travelling that I'm sure they will turn up here. We should move on as soon as possible."

"No one is going to like that. I don't even know if we can convince Zenevieve to leave. And I believe Kennara and Kellesha think this place is going to be a safe haven for them." Abria shrugged off her friend's arm and stood. She took a few steps, then turned back towards Gallagher. "It's going to be hard to get them to leave, at least I think so. There's nothing safe or secure in their lives right now. They'll probably cling to anything that feels like a home."

"You need to tell them. We actually need to tell everyone." Gallagher rested his elbows on his knees, steepling his fingers in front of him. "You're the woman here that's not at risk of losing her power; the other four, though— I don't even want to think about what Viggo and Maeryn would do to them."

"I know, I know. At least we have a little time to prepare." She shook her head as if she didn't actually agree with the words coming out of her mouth. "I wish I didn't have to tell them, though. Not like it matters what I want. Might as well go tell them now and get it over with."

She turned and walked to where Kennara and Kellesha were still talking.

"Can you two come inside? I just got some news that's important to all of us here," Abria said.

Kennara stood, wiping her skirts off once she was standing. "Of course. Kellesha, are you coming?"

Kellesha sighed, but she got up and reluctantly followed.

"Thank you," Kennara said as she followed behind her sister.

Abria made her way through the house to the kitchen

table where Reilynne and Zenevieve were still sitting. As the twins took their seat, Gallagher entered with Eljin and Cas. She waited until the group was settled and then explained the situation they were in, trying to emphasize the perils of staying in place.

"We should stay and fight them," Kellesha said. "Think of how much it would hinder the king if those two were out of commission."

Abria's eyes widened at the fervor she heard. "I don't know if the majority of you are ready to take them on. Gallagher and I have tried many times, and failed every single time."

"Just because you failed doesn't mean we will." Kellesha tossed her braided hair, emphasizing her flippant statement.

Abria rolled her eyes. "While there's some truth to the statement, I'm not the one that Viggo and Maeryn are after, but you are. It changes everything about the fight."

"So what do you suggest?" Kennara asked.

Abria glanced over at her, thankful for the reasonable question. "I think we need to take some time here to train, especially you, Kennara . . ."

"She doesn't need . . .," Kellesha started.

"Yes, she does. She needs to know she can take care of herself, and not depend on someone else. Training is imperative to make that happen."

"Kellesha, this is how we make the difference you were just talking about. We plan and we prepare. And whether you like it or not, we listen to the people who have more knowledge than us." Kennara made eye contact with Abria. "I'm ready when you are."

"That's good because Viggo and Maeryn are only a few weeks behind us, so we don't have long," Gallagher said.

Kennara glanced over at her sister, then at Abria. "Well then, we better get started. Time isn't on our side."

CHAPTER NINETEEN

Kennara strummed her fingers on the table in front of her. She had been awake all night trying to figure out a way to ask Reilynne to heal her. It didn't feel right to just go up and ask, but was there really another way?

She stood, it was time. Maybe today would be the day everything would change.

"Can I come in?" A man's voice asked from outside her room.

She wasn't sure if she should let him. Eljin had made her angry the other day with his big reveal. To have the power to change a world that was falling apart and do nothing was something she could not understand.

The door creaked as it opened. She turned, expecting to see Eljin standing there, but the noise stopped, and the door was only open a couple of inches. In the crack, Kennara saw a pair of brown eyes looking back at her. He blinked, but did not move to come into the room.

"Get in here, say what you want to say." Kennara pushed the door completely open.

Eljin looked around the room before his eyes rested on his feet. His fingers tapped out a pattern on his leg. She was about to tell him to just say what he had to say when his eyes met hers. He ran his hand through his riotous brown curls, creating more disarray than normal.

"Come on, Eljin. Whatever you have to say can't be that bad. Just say it and get it over with." She sat on the bed, tapping her thumb in an impatient rhythm.

He shuffled his feet. "It's not as easy as all that."

"I need to go train." Kennara stood. "When you're ready to actually talk, come find me."

She walked past him, but his arm encircling her waist stopped her.

"Kenna— Please— Stay a moment and listen." Desperation shone in his eyes.

Her hands settled on his chest. The plan was to push him away, but how could she when he so clearly needed a friend? She thought back to all the times he had stood by her side, helping her both physically and emotionally. There was no way she could leave him alone and in turmoil.

"Fine." She thought about pulling him closer, but in her moment of hesitation, she felt his arm drop. Taking a step back, she said, "Let's at least sit down." She sat on her bed, ensuring there was room for him to sit as well, but he just stood there.

"I don't know how to say this without you truly thinking I'm a coward, and that's the last thing I want. But you have to know I'm deeply afraid of my uncle. He terrorized my family, held my brother and me captive until one day he decided we would be better off dead." He sighed. "I want nothing more than to fight. To take back the throne for my people. And if it wasn't for my uncle, I would have started already." He paused.

Kennara waited for him to continue. She knew what it was like to battle within, and Eljin didn't need her input—yet.

"When we were in Wreswell, I was ready to stay and fight. But Quade insisted it wasn't the time. And now—now it feels like I have more to lose." He dropped his head into his hands.

She reached over and gently stroked his back. The gesture mimicked how her mother had comforted her when she was a child, making decisions she didn't know how to make at the time. They sat in silence for a bit, comfortable enough around each other that neither one of the friends felt forced to speak.

Eljin sat up straight and turned towards her. "How do I take the throne back?"

"Is that what you want to do?" She fought the smile threatening to take over her face. It felt wrong to be happy with someone choosing to do the thing that scared them the most.

He held her gaze. "Kenna, how can I not? I was raised on the belief that these lands and people were my responsibility. And my people are suffering. I'm in a house that is nowhere near civilization because half the people here are hiding from the king. A king that would destroy them if they were caught. What sort of man would I be if I did nothing?"

"You know you don't have to face this alone. There's a group of people in this house ready to fight the king and his minions."

"That almost makes it worse. How can I ask any of them to fight with me? Ask them to risk their life on an unknown?" He fell back onto the bed.

Kennara turned towards him, but it wasn't enough to

really be able to make her point. So she kicked her leg over him and shifted her weight until she was straddling him. She felt the heat of his body and blushed as the realization of how this looked hit her. She wouldn't let that deter her, though. Leaning forward until they were eye-to-eye, she knew she had his attention.

"No one here other than me and my sister, and—I'm assuming—Cas, know who you are and we're *all* getting ready to go to battle for our magic. You may be a prince and I'm sure at one point that meant you mattered, but for most people, you are either dead already or a hope for salvation. Either way, no one here is going to wait for one of those things to be true before they act. You're not asking anyone to risk their life. We've all decided to do so already. At least if you're by our side, it legitimizes our cause."

Eljin continued to stare at her after she stopped speaking. Kennara wasn't sure if he had heard her words or not. He reached up and his fingers tangled in her hair and he slowly pulled her down until their lips met. Her body tingled everywhere they touched. She felt his tongue swipe across her lower lip. She sat up, her eyes darting around the room.

"Thank you, I needed to hear that, especially from you."

She leapt off him and ran out of the room as fast as she could.

Kennara went in search of Abria or Reilynne or even her sister, her mind was spinning with everything that had just happened. Their renegade group had a prince, and having the prince gave them a solid purpose: get Eljin on the throne.

Thinking about Eljin, though, made her think about the kiss—they had kissed, he had kissed her. Why had he kissed her? And she had run like escape was her only option, leaving him there, lying on her bed.

"Abria, I wanted to talk to you," Reilynne said around the corner.

Kennara stopped, curiosity getting the better of her.

"Can it wait? I'm supposed to be meeting Kennara for training and I'm running late," Abria said.

Kennara leaned against the wall to relieve some of the pressure off her leg as she listened to the conversation happening just out of sight.

"It's just— That is— I think I can restore your magic. When I healed your leg, I could feel it pulsing inside you, like it was trapped. I can't be sure, though. I've never tried it before. But—if you'll let me try . . ." Reilynne trailed off.

"No—my magic's gone. It's been gone for over five years. I can't deal with this right now." Abria's boots pounded the ground as she walked off.

Kennara pushed herself off the wall, took a deep breath, and rounded the corner. Reilynne still stood there, watching Abria storm off.

"Hi, Reilynne, are you okay?"

She shook her head. "I'm fine; just not the reaction I was expecting." Reilynne focused on Kennara. "How are you? Aren't you supposed to be training?"

"I am, but I was delayed." She took a deep breath. "Can I ask you something?"

"Of course."

She twisted her hands, afraid to ask and be rejected. "I've wanted to talk to a healer for a long time, but have never met one because—well, you know why—but I was hoping I could find someone to fix my leg. It has always given me problems. I often need to use a walking stick or even a chair with wheels to get around. And I don't want it to impede our rebellion. Can you help?"

Reilynne's eyes darted towards something behind her. Kennara turned to see Eljin there.

"You don't need to be fixed, Kenna, you're perfect exactly as is." He had clearly overheard at least part of the conversation.

"Don't listen to him. He always has his head up in the clouds." Kennara took Reilynne's hands in hers. "Can you please heal my leg?"

"I can try. But healing magic is unlike some of the other types of magic: I can only do what the body allows me to. Which is easy when it's healing a cut or a broken bone, but some things just aren't meant to change." Reilynne chewed her lower lip. "Do you want to do this now?"

Kennara could barely contain her excitement. "Can we?"

Reilynne hesitated, but eventually nodded. "Let me go get a few things. I'll meet you out back."

"Thank you! I'll let Abria know. If my leg can be fixed, it will only help with training. I'm sure she'll understand." Kennara turned, stumbling as her leg trembled beneath her. She grabbed on to the wall to regain her balance and continued to the area Abria had designated for training.

She heard Eljin following her, but she didn't want to hear his concerns or his doubts. This was something she'd wanted for as long as she could remember, and it was finally happening.

"Abria," she called out, waving to get the warrior woman's attention. "Over here."

Abria jogged over to her. "You're late."

"I know," Kennara said sheepishly. "But Reilynne said she can try to heal my leg. Let's train after that. It's going to make such a big difference."

"If it works," Eljin said under his breath."

Abria looked at the two of them. "Go, it can't hurt to try."

Eljin crossed his arms. "Except her mental state if it doesn't work."

"Try to believe it will work," Kennara pleaded.

"Fine, but I don't like it at all."

Eljin wrapped his arm around her waist as they walked towards the back of the house. The day was beautiful. The sun was shining, she could hear the waves crashing on the shore, and she could smell the salt water in the air. She sighed and leaned into Eljin's embrace. His physical support was nice, but it would have been better if he supported her decision to be healed. She didn't understand his hesitation at all.

Reilynne and Kellesha were there waiting.

"Are you sure you want to do this, Kennara? You know you don't have to." Kellesha clasped her shoulders.

"Of course I'm sure. We've talked about it for ages. The day is finally here." She shrugged her sister's hands off her.

Kellesha nodded. "Right. I just want to make sure you're doing it for you and not me. I love you no matter what."

She wrapped her arms around her sister, ever the warrior, never the one to put her words to her feelings.

"Let's do this," Kennara said as she stepped away from her sister and turned to the healer.

"Okay, I'm going to have you lie down here." She pointed to a large table. "I'm going to use this crystal to amplify my magic. Healing something that's been present for a long time uses a lot of magic and skill. While I'm the strongest healer I know, I want to ensure that I'll be enough."

Kennara lay down on the wooden table Reilynne had pointed to. "I'm ready whenever you are."

Reilynne walked over. "Close your eyes. This may feel strange at first. It could be painful, I'm not sure." Reilynne gestured towards Kellesha and Eljin. "If she thrashes, I'm going to need you to hold her down."

She closed her eyes as instructed. At first there was nothing to feel other than the table under her and the salty breeze caressing the little bit of bare skin she had. Then everything changed. Magic pulsed through her body. She could feel it moving through her from the top of her head to her toes. It was energizing. But she didn't feel anything change in her body.

"What, that can't be," Kennara thought she heard Reilynne mutter.

The feeling would stop and start over. Kennara wasn't sure how many times it happened or how long she lay on the table, but eventually it stopped.

She heard Reilynne panting next to her.

"Can I open my eyes?" Kennara asked.

"Yes, I'm done," Reilynne said between gasps of air.

She opened her eyes. Eljin helped her sit up. While she felt invigorated, that's all that felt different.

Reilynne held up her hand. "Don't jump down." She took a deep breath. "I couldn't change anything. Your body wouldn't let me because it's the way it is meant to be."

"What do you mean?" she asked, unable to comprehend what Reilynne was saying.

Reilynne sighed. "There's nothing for me to heal. Your

body is exactly the way it wants to be. There's nothing wrong with it."

"How can you say there's nothing wrong with it? There are days I can't walk. That's not normal." Kennara twisted her hair around her finger.

"I didn't say 'normal.' I said there's nothing wrong with your body. I said it's exactly as it wants to be, as it's supposed to be. Your body will not let me change it because it doesn't need to be healed."

Kennara jumped off the table, landing on her left leg only. She felt her eyes fill with tears. It was not okay for anyone here to see her cry, so she limped off without saying another word.

CHAPTER TWENTY

Sobs racked through her body as Kennara threw herself face down on her bed. The violent tremors of her tears shaking her to her core. All hopes for the future turned to dust at the hands of the healer. How could her body betray her like this? This couldn't be the way she was supposed to be? The healer's words echoed in her head, mocking her and her inability to walk without stumbling or falling, and that was on the days she was capable of walking. The tears came faster when she thought about the days she had to use a cane, or a chair to get around. How could she help with this rebellion if she couldn't stand and fight? If her body continued to conspire against her?

How dare her body think it was perfect the way that it was. The small room was suffocating, filled with her stifled sobs as she scrunched up her blankets in her fists and screamed into the pillows.

"Knock-knock," Kellesha stuck her head into the room.

"Go away," she yelled into her pillow.

Kellesha ignored her and walked into her room. "No, I'm not going to leave you alone right now."

She felt the bed dip as her sister sat down offering a silent strength Kennara was used to leaning on. Kellesha began rubbing her back as she lay there. Her sister said nothing. The silence was comforting. Maybe having someone with her as she cried her eyes out would actually make her feel better.

"You know I love you just the way you are," Kellesha said as she continued to rub Kennara's back.

Kennara shrugged. "I'm still a broken burden that's just going to hold you, and everyone else here, back."

"That's not even close to the truth. First, you're not broken. You're just you. Second, you've never been a burden, you're my sister and I love you. And third, stop taking so much on yourself. I make choices not based on you, just like you make choices not based on me."

Kennara pushed herself up on her elbows. "Are you trying to tell me I'm not the center of the universe?"

"There's my sister's normal sense of humor, and is that a bit of a smile?" Kellesha teased.

"Shut up. I want to sulk." She pulled the covers over her head.

Kellesha stood. "Today you can sulk. But tomorrow you train." The words hung in the air, a steely promise of resilience in the face of adversity.

She hadn't left her room for hours. All she wanted to do was stay in here and sulk. Her head ached from the amount of tears she had shed, leaving her eyes swollen, and her face red and splotchy. But someone was knocking on her door, the noise reverberating through her skull, causing her to wince with each thud.

"What?"

"We need to talk, Kenna."

It was Eljin. Did he want to talk about the kiss? She didn't know what to say about it.

"Now's not really the best time." She pulled the blankets up, ready to continue her pity party.

"Kenna, we need to tell the others who I am, and I don't want to do it without you." Eljin pushed open the door as ran his hand through his hair.

She threw the blankets off and sat. She really didn't want him to see her in such a state, but it seemed she didn't have a choice.

Eljin looked at her. "Are you okay?"

"No. Not yet, maybe not ever. But apparently there's no time for me to feel sorry for myself." She pushed herself out of bed and smoothed her skirts down. "Let's go."

"Everyone is gathered already in the common room."

Kennara squeezed his shoulder. "Are you ready?"

"No, but it's something that I have to do. I have a responsibility to the people." He shrugged and continued walking towards the common room.

She followed behind him, hoping he felt the support she was giving him. They turned the corner to find everyone looking at them. Abria and Reilynne's eyes immediately fell on her, assessing how she was doing. She just shrugged as each of them made eye contact with her. Right now, she was ignoring what happened earlier in the day. If she thought about not being healed, she would break down again. And now wasn't the time for that.

"What's going on?" Gallagher asked.

Eljin took a step forward and paused. He looked back at

her. Kennara nodded and took his hand in hers, lacing their fingers together. She squeezed it, as if to say, you've got this. His lips quirked up in a lopsided smile before he turned back to those gathered in the room.

"Some of you have known me awhile, others just met me the other day. But plans are already in the works to fight Viggo and Maeryn, so I'm here, standing in front of you, to tell you we can overthrow the king." He paused. "I am the prince that got away. I am Prince Bryok."

The collective gasp of shock that went through the room probably could be heard all the way in Wreswell. The group started muttering to each other, ignoring Eljin and Kennara standing in front of them.

Kellesha stood, put two fingers in her mouth, and let out an ear-shattering whistle. "We should use this time to come up with a plan together and figure out how to get Eljin his throne back."

"How do we know he's the right person for the throne?" Abria leaned in, her elbows resting on her knees.

Kennara stepped forward. "I'll vouch for him. He's helped me through so much since we met. And when he found out we had magic, he brought us here. He didn't turn us in to any of the king's men."

"Could he though? Or would they recognize him? If he's caught, he's dead, just like his brother," Gallagher pointed out.

Cas was in the back, leaning against a doorframe. "I've been protecting him since before King Sheamus. I can confirm he's nothing like his uncle. His mother and father raised him to be fair and just."

"Then why has it taken this long for him to step forward?" Reilynne asked.

Eljin ran his hand through his hair. "Honestly, because

I'm not ready to die. And if I went up against the king with just Cas and myself, both of us would be dead."

Abria and Gallagher nodded. They had the most experience fighting and were at least listening to what Eljin was saying. Kennara wasn't sure they were ready to believe him, or her, but they heard his reasons and thought they were logical.

Zenevieve stood. "I know him. Well, I knew him. My mother's the one who helped him escape. She gave him the name he's using and left him to fend for himself when that became the best option for his survival."

"But now he's turned up on your doorstep and the king's henchmen are following. What if this is all a plan to catch all of you who have magic?" Abria raised an eyebrow.

Kennara threw up her hands. "Fine, don't believe me. But you said we had a couple of weeks to train. Take that time, see if you can learn to trust him like I have. Don't forget how much he's trusting you with his identity. That should mean something."

She grabbed Eljin's hand and dragged him outside.

"I can't believe how stubborn they're all being." She plopped down on the ground.

Eljin sat next to her. "It makes sense. Everyone here has been on the road or in hiding for years."

"So have you. Everyone here has been living a secret life. Even Gallagher."

"Exactly. They might not be trying to keep their magic, but Gallagher is Abria's right-hand man, fighting the Quickenings."

"Quit being so understanding. It's annoying." Kennara leaned over, resting her head on his shoulder.

She closed her eyes, feeling the sun hit her face and the

breeze caress her skin. Her anger blocked her disappointment.

Abria came outside and stood in front of the couple, casting a shadow over them.

Kennara looked up. "What?"

"He trains with us. Give me a chance to determine if he's trustworthy."

Then Abria turned on her heel and strode back inside.

CHAPTER TWENTY-ONE

"Again!" Abria yelled at her trainees. How these two expected to take on anyone was beyond her. Kennara was pretty good with a bow and arrow, but those weapons only worked in certain circumstances. What she wasn't consistent at was hand-to-hand combat, and Abria thought that was a problem.

Then there was the prince. It was like he hadn't trained a day in his life. If forced, she'd admit he could throw a punch, but there was no strategy behind what he did. It was all flailing arms and legs with no target. Everyone, including Kennara, had taken him to the ground in mere seconds.

"Water," Eljin gasped.

Abria looked over at him; he was hunched over, gasping for breath. "Fine, get some water. But if we're going to get your throne back, you have got to build up some stamina. Get a drink and go run up that sand dune and back."

Eljin looked at the sand dune she was pointing to. She could see his jaw tighten as he ground his teeth together. But he didn't fight her. He took a drink, dumped the rest of the water on his head, and took off running. The fortitude was there, the skill not so much. Abria shook her head.

"Now, Kennara, I think we need to work on balancing and using the environment to your advantage."

"Whatever you say, Abria." Kennara shrugged, her shoulders falling back into their tired, slumped position as she limped back to the center of the training field.

This would not do, Abria thought. She needed Kennara to want to train, to be excited for it . . . anything but the woman in front of her who had already given up.

"Come here," Abria said.

Kennara looked up, her sea-green eyes rimmed in red. She had been crying, a lot.

"What is it, Abria?" She stood there, her shoulders hunched as if her body was trying to close in on itself.

Abria grabbed her shoulders. "Do you want to win this fight we're headed towards? Better yet, do you want a chance of surviving it?"

Kennara sighed. "Of course."

"It doesn't look like it. You look like you've already decided not to live."

"That's not true."

"Really? Look at you, your posture is atrocious, like you're ashamed of yourself. It looks like you've spent time crying or drinking, maybe both, they do go hand in hand. And by the look in your eyes, you've already decided that you can't do any of the things I'm asking you to do. At least not anything you haven't already mastered." Abria tossed her braid over her shoulder.

Kennara stared at her, mouth agape. "You wouldn't understand." She folded her arms across her chest.

Abria laughed. "You don't think I understand? You got some bad news, news that doesn't change your life, just closes a door on a path you wanted to take. You don't think that's ever happened to me? That I haven't had my magic ripped from my body against my will and I haven't used it or felt it since. I had to learn how to live without magic, something I had used every day to grow herbs and vegetables for food. No, I wouldn't understand having a door closed on me and my life being nothing like I thought it would be."

"But you could have your magic back if you let Reilynne try. Your body wants it back. Mine wants to be like this. I don't even know why you're bothering to train me. It's not like I'll ever be a warrior." Kennara turned away, but not before Abria saw the tears form in her eyes.

She reached out and squeezed Kennara's shoulder. Kennara shrugged her off. "I don't need your pity."

"You mistake my compassion for pity. I don't feel sorry for you. I've seen how strong you are. You just need to see it yourself. So maybe instead of pouting all day, you can decide to work with me and actually train."

Kennara just stared at her, her mouth moving but no sound coming out. Eventually, she turned and walked towards the center of the practice field. "Okay, what do you want me to do?"

Abria could see the change in Kennara: her shoulders were back and her expression screamed determination. This was what Abria wanted to see.

"I want you to reach both arms up, bend over and put your palms flat on the ground then jump back so your body is parallel to the ground. Go down onto your elbows, then back onto your hands, jump back in as far as you can, and stand up straight."

Kennara started the movement, standing on both legs. She reached up to start the exercise.

"Oh, and do it all on your left leg."

Kennara's head snapped towards her, but she didn't say a thing. Just started the movement over again. Every time she did it, she fell. Sometimes it was as she bent over, other times it was as she jumped back, one time she even made it as far as standing back up, but she never made it through the sequence.

At some point, Eljin made returned from his run. Every time Kennara fell, he rushed over to help her up. It was sweet, and it was kind. But it was counterproductive. Kennara needed to learn how to do this on her own, to fall, to fail, and to get up and start over without anyone helping her. She needed to know that she was capable of doing it on her own.

"Don't help her up." Abria grabbed Eljin by the arm as he went to help Kennara.

"But she's fallen again."

"True, but she needs to do this on her own. You're only going to hold her back if you're always there to lend her a hand."

"But..."

Abria held up her hand. "Again."

"No, I'm done." Kennara sat in the middle of the training space.

"Did I say you were done? No. Which means you're not done yet. Now get up and do it again."

Kennara picked herself up off the ground.

Abria nodded her approval. "Now do it again."

Kennara balanced on her left leg. Even from where Abria stood, she could see the leg tremble with fatigue. But that didn't matter, her trainee was focused on her assignment. Kennara reached up and slowly bent forward, her right leg extending to help her balance. Her palms hit the ground. She tucked her right leg behind her left and jumped back. Her wobble had Abria holding her breath. But Kennara persevered and steadied herself, went from her palms to her elbows with ease, then jumped back. She scooched her feet forward little by little until she could balance on her left leg and her palms. Abria could see her whole body shake as she stood there folded in half on one leg. But this was the farthest Kennara had made it. She started to roll her body up; her ankle shook, and her heel moved back and forth as her muscles refused to help her balance any longer.

"Bend your knee!" Abria shouted.

But it was too late. Kennara tumbled to the ground, again.

For a moment she just sat there. Abria fought the urge to run to help her up. After what felt like ages, Kennara pushed herself off the ground.

Standing, Kennara threw her head back and screamed. Every ounce of frustration and disappointment could be heard. Her outstretched hands were filled with flames. Wind whipped around her, at first only causing her hair to fly, but after a few seconds, Kennara rose off the ground as if she was a fire goddess levitating above the surface.

"Kellesha, put me down!" Kennara hollered over the sound of the wind.

"I'm not doing anything."

Out of nowhere, a wave engulfed Kennara, putting out the fire and knocking her to the ground. Abria searched the area for the source of the water, and saw Zenevieve in the doorway, hands extended.

"No fire," Zenevieve stated, turned, and left.

Abria looked back to the training area; Kennara was drenched and sputtering.

"What was that about?" Kennara asked.

Abria made her way to Kennara, offering her a hand up. "I don't know, but you were the one on fire, levitating in a cyclone. At least you were until Zenevieve literally doused your flames."

"It was amazing, Kenna. Can you do it again?" Eljin stared at Kennara as if she was a goddess.

CHAPTER TWENTY-TWO

Kennara stood there, water dripping from everything: her hair, her sleeves, the laces in her shoes. She barely heard Abria say something about her being on fire and Zenevieve dousing her with water.

There. Kennara's eyes fell on her sister.

There she was.

Why would her sister do something like that to her?

Kennara pushed past Eljin, who had the goofiest expression on his face, to storm towards her sister. At least, she tried to stomp her feet in a way that fully expressed her anger as she went to confront Kellesha. It didn't work because exhaustion screamed from every single muscle in her body as she made her way over.

"Why?" Kennara stood in front of her sister, arms crossed, teeth grinding. "Why would you do that?"

"I didn't do anything! You know I would be on the ground, exhausted, if I had used my magic to do whatever it is that just happened." Kellesha's eyes were wide, bewilderment written across her face.

Kennara glared at her. "As if there's anything that you can't do. You've probably been holding back your power because you didn't want to make me feel even worse. Faking how tired it makes you to use it."

"Kennara . . ."

Kennara held up her hand. "Don't. You can't even let me fail on my own. You're always doing something to stop me from being independent."

"I didn't do anything. I've been trying really hard to—"

"How can you say you didn't do anything? I saw you. I saw your hands move. You were using your hands to perform magic. Don't deny it."

Kellesha threw her arms up in the air. "I don't have to put up with this. I did nothing wrong, and that's the truth —whether or not you want to believe it."

Kennara watched as she stormed away. Just one more thing her sister could do that she couldn't.

KENNARA LAY IN HER BED STARING AT THE CEILING AS SHE contemplated what had happened earlier. The pure frustration she'd felt as she failed once again at the movement Abria had assigned her had coursed through her, needing an outlet. So, she screamed. She hadn't expected what happened after that, not flames bursting from her hands, not seeing her sister use magic to pick her up, not levitating, and not crashing to the ground in a wave of water.

The worst thing was her sister's denial, though. Kennara couldn't believe her sister insisted she hadn't used her magic. Why would she do that when it was so obvious that she had?

She groaned and covered her head, tired of all the emotions coursing through her. It was exhausting. She didn't want to deal with anyone else for the rest of the day. Especially since it felt like she couldn't trust anyone anymore. Her sister, the one person she should be able to trust no matter what, was lying to her. If Kellesha could so blatantly lie to her, why would she ever think anyone else was telling her the truth?

A knock on the door interrupted her personal pity party.

"Go away," Kennara yelled at the door.

"I would rather come in," Cas said from the other side.

Kennara rolled over, shoving her face into her pillow. "What about what I want?"

Cas walked into her room. "I didn't hear the last bit." The bed dipped where he sat.

"What do you want?"

"To talk." Cas looked at her, opened his mouth, then closed it a couple of times; a long sigh followed all of this.

"Just get on with it. You're cutting into my 'woe is me' time, and I would like to get back to it."

"Your sister is really upset. I've never seen her like this." The bed shifted as he stood. His heels struck the wood floor with every step. "She's in her room sobbing because you don't believe her."

"My sister never cries," Kennara stated, folding her arms across her chest.

Cas raised a questioning eyebrow. "She's in her room crying now, and this isn't the first time I've sat with her as she's cried. She's trying to respect your wishes and not protect you from everything, even if it hurts her to see you in pain."

Kennara wanted to laugh at his last statement. If he only knew how many times she'd had that conversation with her sister. Why would she think this time was when her sister would finally listen?

"She's been watching you train with Abria, barely a shell of yourself. Today, you finally got up there and tried. And then you failed. It gutted her. I watched as she stood there and did nothing," Cas said.

"Nothing?" She threw her hands up in the air. "I saw her gestures . . ."

"You saw her talking to me. She wasn't using magic. She's told me she hardly ever uses magic, and then, it's only when it's completely necessary. Even then, she's terrified her magic will sap all of her strength, that she's not strong enough to use it when needed, or using it will get the two of you caught." Cas stopped talking and sat. "Please don't tell her . . . I wasn't supposed to say anything to you about her fears."

Kennara stared at him, confused. "What do you mean, she's worried about not having enough strength? She's the strongest person I know and she just used it the other day when those bandits came upon us."

Cas stared at the wall. "I know we all saw wind and fire magic used that day, but she swears she hasn't used magic since the storm. She's afraid to, because of the exhaustion."

"That's ridiculous. Kellesha isn't afraid of anything." Kennara waved the thought away with her hand. "Clearly, her magic works. I've felt her use it when she's stressed and anxious and in battle. She's the only one with wind magic. It was used, so it had to be her."

"There's a lot she and I have talked about that would suggest otherwise. But you won't find out about any of it until you talk to her."

He walked to the door.

"Why would I want to talk to her, for her to just lie to me some more? She's lying about using her magic or lying about being too afraid to use it. Either way, she's not telling me the truth."

"If you talk to her, you could find out if she's lying and why." With those final words, he left.

Kennara stared at the door for a long time after that. She didn't really believe Cas when he said Kellesha didn't use her magic. Of course she did. She'd proved it earlier today with her little stunt.

She flopped back on her bed and stared at the ceiling. The thought of her sister crying, sobbing, didn't sit well with her. There was a part of her that wanted to go to Kellesha and work everything out. But the other part of her felt betrayed, again, by her sister. Kellesha had promised to stop her overly protective ways, stop doing all the things that made Kennara feel helpless. Picking her up after she fell today was the epitome of making her feel helpless. She wanted to succeed and fail based on her own capability, not because someone was helping her out or stopping her from taking action because she might fail. Her success was going to feel so much better if she worked through her struggles to get to that point. That's what she wanted for herself.

Another knock on the door interrupted her thoughts. She sighed. *Why couldn't everyone just leave her alone.*

"Come in."

Reilynne popped her head in. "Are you all right?"

"Not really, but that's normal for me." Kennara pushed herself up on her elbows. "Do you need me for something?"

"No, I just wanted to check on you. The training was hard today. Would you like me to help with the sore muscles you must have after this morning?" Reilynne pushed the door open a little farther. "Just because I can't heal your leg, doesn't mean I can't make it hurt less."

"No, it's not like any of this changes anything. I'm still a burden on the group because I can't count on my own body to support me."

Reilynne stared at her as if she was trying to decide whether to say more. "Kennara, you are so much more than you think you are. Once you stop defining yourself by what you think holds you back and start looking at what you can do, you'll be surprised by your own power." With those last words, Reilynne closed the door, her footsteps fading as she walked away.

CHAPTER TWENTY-THREE

Kennara pushed herself off the ground as she balanced on her left leg. She kept her bow out of the way as she swung her right leg around and grabbed an arrow with her left hand. She planted her right foot, notched the arrow, aimed, and released. A moment later, the satisfying thud of the arrow hitting its target reached her ears.

She whooped with excitement. Jumping up and down, she celebrated her success until she fell, only to be caught and whirled around by Eljin. He set her down, the wrinkles by his eyes and broad smile making her heart skip a beat. Their eyes met. For a moment, it felt like the world around them disappeared and only the two of them existed.

That was until she heard Abria praising her success.

Kennara carefully stepped back, making sure to stay upright the best she could. She didn't need to give Eljin another reason to touch her, at least not right now. Pivoting on her left leg, she turned to Abria.

"Can you believe it? That's five shots in a row that have hit the target."

"Actually, if I hadn't seen it with my own eyes, I would never have believed it. You've progressed faster than anyone I've ever trained." Abria looked at Eljin before continuing. "You're doing extremely well compensating for your right leg. I'm proud of you."

Kennara couldn't help but beam at the compliment. For the first time she felt competent at a physical activity, and it was more than competence right now, it was success. Sure, she'd learned how to use a bow and arrow back home, but now it felt like she didn't need to hide when a fight broke out. If it came to it, she could defend herself and others.

She walked back to the edge of the training field, only the slightest limp in her gait to indicate just how tired she was. The red hair of her sister snagged her attention momentarily, long enough for her right toe to catch because she wasn't concentrating on lifting her leg high enough to clear the ground. She groaned as she stumbled, glancing up to see her sister instinctively move towards her. Kennara steadied herself and turned away from Kellesha, still unable to talk to her after the other day. It was petty; she knew it was, but for once she didn't feel helpless, and she wasn't ready to feel that way again. So she avoided her sister, which was difficult to do in Zenevieve's beach cottage.

By the time she had reached the edge of the training area, Eljin had started his attempt at what she had just done. She held her breath as he practiced the evasive movement and grabbed an arrow. His movements were smooth and controlled. At least they appeared that way, but instead of the satisfying thunk of an arrow hitting its target, Eljin's arrow flew over it and landed at least ten feet past it. She bit her lip to stifle the giggle she felt coming. If it was her, she would be so annoyed, but Eljin just laughed and asked for a different weapon.

"Unfortunately, I'm no match for Kenna and her skills with a bow and arrow. I promise there's a weapon that does suit me. We just have to find it first."

Abria rolled her eyes at him. "You don't seem to be taking this seriously."

Eljin locked eyes with Abria. "Trust me, I'm taking this seriously—but there's no point in training with a weapon I'm never going to master. I'd rather spend my time doing something much more productive. Especially since we have no time to waste."

Kennara watched Eljin storm off, his mask of cheerfulness slipping more and more with each step he took. It was clear the stress was getting to him and his lack of warrior-like skills wasn't helping.

She shifted her weight to go after him. But Cas caught her eye and almost imperceptibly shook his head before he followed Eljin out of the room. She sighed, wanting to go help, but understood that she might not be the best person to do so. That left her on the edge of the training field watching everyone else prepare for the journey ahead. Gallagher and Kellesha sparred off in a corner. Reilynne was healing a rather nasty bruise Zenevieve got the other day sparring with Kellesha. Not one to waste time, Zenevieve manipulated water with her magic. She preferred fighting with her magic than hand-to-hand combat. To that end, she insisted on using her magic for everything, even when it wasn't necessary. Abria had made her way over to Kellesha and Gallagher; Kennara assumed it was to join them in their training.

Her training done for the day, Kennara turned to leave. Staying to watch everyone else wasn't all that interesting.

She made her way to the back door of the cottage. In her inattention, she almost ran into two men she didn't recognize walking through the courtyard. Lucky for her, she was able to duck down the hallway before they spotted her. She peeked her head out after they passed. One man's cloak caught the wind and underneath it she could see he was wearing the king's insignia.

This couldn't be good.

She made her way to Eljin's room, praying to the Five Sisters that he would be there. Her leg, tired from today's workout, wouldn't cooperate with her desperate need to hurry. She cursed under her breath until she was standing in front of his room. For a split second, she wondered if she should knock. She shook her head and opened the door. This was urgent. No time for any formalities.

As she stepped into the room, she looked up to see Eljin standing there, shirtless. She stopped, eyes wide. She felt her tongue dart out and lick her lips. Where did he get those muscles? They weren't like Cas's, big to the point of being intimidating. Instead of bulk, his muscles were sinewy and every one of his movements caused them to dance. His hair was damp. She watched as droplets of water fell from his curls and ran down his naked torso, caressing his moving muscles. She stared, she couldn't seem to help herself, imagining her fingers following the path of the water droplet. Eljin cleared his throat, snapping her thoughts back to her reason for being there.

"I'm so sorry." She turned her back towards him. "There are king's men here, now. They were headed to the training field. Everyone but the two of us and Cas are there right now." Kennara turned back and looked around the room, remembering Cas had followed Eljin not too long ago. "Where's Cas?"

"I told him to leave." His voice muffled as he pulled on his shirt.

Her head whipped around until she was staring at Eljin. "We have to find him. The others are going to need us. What if Viggo and Maeryn are here?" Her voice rose an octave by the time she posed her question.

"Maybe you should stay here. I don't want you to risk losing your magic."

His words of caution caused something to snap inside of her. "Like hell I'm staying here. I'm so sick of being protected." She grabbed his hand. "Let's go find Cas and save the others."

She heard Eljin mutter something about protecting her because she was special, not because she wasn't capable. But she ignored whatever he said. Instead, they ran through the halls as fast as her legs would take her. She wasn't sure where Cas was, but he normally spent his free moments in the kitchen, so that's where she dragged Eljin to. She careened around the corner, taking Eljin with her; if he hadn't reached around her waist to steady her, they probably would have ended up on the floor. Her eyes darted around the room—sure enough, there was Cas eating.

She tried to regulate her breathing by inhaling through her nose and exhaling through her mouth, which would allow her to communicate better. But concern for the others was overtaking her rational thought.

"King's men—training field—now," she said while gasping for breath.

Cas glanced over to Eljin, who shrugged.

"Come on, we can't leave them out there by themselves," she said, turning towards the doors. She took a deep breath and pushed open the doors.

The three of them cautiously made their way around

the building, taking measures to stay unseen and unheard. Cas took the lead, signaling when to move, when to stop, and when to stay hidden. Eljin was behind her, doing what he could to keep her safe, a gesture that was both sweet and infuriating, but he wasn't locking her away until the danger was over. So in her mind she relented and found his insistence on keeping her safe mostly endearing.

Cas gestured for them to halt as the clashing of metal on metal could be heard from around the corner. Kennara stopped for a moment, but she couldn't help if she stayed still. She needed to know what was happening; she needed to know that her sister was okay. Moving around Cas, she did what she could to hide behind a large tree, but she still couldn't see enough. It was impossible for her to tell if her sister was in danger. She crept forward, not listening to Cas and Eljin calling her back.

To the left, about twenty feet away, out in the open, were her bow and arrows. Too far away for her to be of any assistance to the battle at hand, at least not immediately. However, her cane wasn't far away at all. She must have left it out here yesterday after dinner. Which wasn't the smartest thing to do. She still had days where she could barely walk. At least today wasn't one of those days.

To win, they needed the element of surprise. She grabbed the cane and hobbled out to the training field, glancing at Cas and Eljin behind her. Cas gestured, letting her know that he and Eljin would take the perimeter if she insisted on going out there.

She rounded the corner, leaning heavily on her cane as she walked. Her eyes darted from one group to another, all engaged in combat with one or more of the king's men. She took a deep breath, willing herself to sound calm as she intentionally stumbled towards the battle that ensued. The clattering of her cane drew the attention of two opponents. They immediately stalked towards her, believing they had found a weak link.

Little did they know she was prepared and wanted them to think that exact thought.

When the first soldier was close enough for her to reach, she acted. As he bent over, she shoved her cane into his stomach and again between his legs. Kennara didn't wait to see if he was down for the count. Instead, she swung her cane around, hitting the second soldier in the back of the knees. He fell to the ground with a thud.

She rolled over to her bow and arrows, grabbed them and stood with most of her weight on her left leg. Her eyes darted from one group to the next. Cas was with Reilynne and Zenevieve: things seemed to be going their way. The other three were desperately holding off six men.

Kennara notched an arrow, lighting the tip with her magic as she did so. She drew her elbow back, keeping it level with her hand near her cheek, and let it fly. It hit the ground between Kellesha and the soldiers she was fighting, catching the grass on fire. One of the men grabbed her sister and dragged her through the fire. Kennara watched, a sense of helplessness coming over her. She couldn't shoot another arrow—in fact, her fire magic was worthless as well—because she couldn't risk hurting her sister. She wished she could put out the fire she had just started, the one licking at her sister's boots as the man dragged her.

Suddenly, water fell from the sky around Kellesha and her attacker. Wet, her sister slipped away from her captor. As soon as Kellesha was far enough away, she lit the grass on fire again with a gesture of her hand.

Kennara notched a lit arrow, letting it fly to cover up the use of her magic. She quickly repeated the movement until the soldiers had two choices; to risk walking through the fire or to run. She tossed her head back laughing, adrenaline coursing through her, as they turned and ran, one of them trying to put out a spark that had landed on his tunic. When the six men ran, those fighting Cas and the others also made their escape, leaving her with the two men she had downed, both recovered now and circling around her, plotting their attack.

She stood there for a moment, noting the amulet hanging from a leather strap around one of their necks. Why did the king send out groups of men with only one able to access magic? It didn't make any sense. She did know that she was going to take that amulet if she could. Just knowing it held a woman's magic meant Kennara wanted to steal it back from the thief. He was too far away for her to grab it, and she wasn't fast enough to get to him before he ran.

Kennara's shoulders drooped with the feeling that she still wasn't able to do enough. She wished the necklace would fly off his neck and into her hand or just explode—

That was it. Maybe a little heat would destroy the amulet. She focused on it, heating it up enough to cause the amulet to splinter, then explode. Blue mist escaped and dissipated into the air. Kennara hoped the magic made it back to its original bearer.

CHAPTER TWENTY-FOUR

Abria watched as the last of the king's soldiers ran off. They needed to leave. They were no longer safe at the cottage. It was only a matter of time before Viggo and Maeryn would be here.

As soon as she was sure the men had left and weren't coming back, she gestured for everyone to gather round her. She stood there, arms crossed, trying to figure out what to say. Even though they all knew they were going to have to leave soon, soon had become now, and she wasn't looking forward to breaking the news.

Abria rolled her shoulders back. "I'm pretty sure you all know what I'm going to say, even if you don't want it to be true. But we have to leave, today."

She looked around. Reilynne nodded her head in agreement. Cas and Gallagher stood between the group and any entrance to the training area, watching for more of the king's men. Kennara leaned against Eljin, who had his arm wrapped around her waist. It looked like he was taking the place of her cane. Abria didn't think Kennara even realized how much she leaned on the prince, both physically and emotionally. Kellesha stood off to the side, away from her sister. Her shoulders slouched, struggling to catch her breath as the post-fight exhaustion was setting in. Zenevieve, the one person Abria thought would fight her, looked . . . almost excited about being forced to leave.

"We should start packing, no reason to stick around and wait for something else to happen," Zenevieve said. She turned and took a few steps, but stopped when no one followed her. "Why is no one moving? It's time we get on with this mission we've all agreed to go on."

Abria didn't know what to think. Zenevieve's reaction to leaving was . . . surprising. "She's right. I just expected more of a fight." She raised an eyebrow. "Especially from you. This is really the only place you've lived."

Zenevieve shrugged. "It is, but now I have a chance to see the world. Might as well take advantage of it. Especially since I've been alone here for way too long. I may not have picked this as the reason to finally leave here, but I fulfilled my promise to my mother, and now there's nothing keeping me here." She turned and walked away. Clearly, she decided the conversation was over.

"I guess we should all go pack and meet back here," Abria directed the group.

There were some grumblings, but after the fight, everyone knew it was time to move on. If they wanted to succeed at stopping the king, they had to stay one step ahead of Viggo and Maeryn, who would strip the magic away from the women without asking, without thinking of what it did to the women who lost an essential part of themself. Abria felt like it was her job to ensure that didn't happen.

They had to succeed at stopping the king. Failure was not an option.

ABRIA LOOKED AT THE BAGS IN FRONT OF HER. MAYBE SHE WAS THE one who didn't want to leave yet. She was so used to being on the road that being in one place had never felt normal. But since she had shown up here, reunited with the twins, it felt like something had shifted inside her.

It wasn't about going from town to town trying to stop one Quickening at a time. Now she had a group of people that wanted to stop everything. They wanted to overthrow the king. They wanted—

A soft knock on the door interrupted her musings. Probably a good thing because her thoughts weren't really getting her anywhere, just making her more and more nervous about their journey and how they would successfully achieve their objective.

Someone knocked again, but louder this time.

"Come in," Abria said.

The door creaked open and Kennara stuck her head in.

"Are you sure? I know we're all in a rush. You know what, I can come back later or we can talk on the road. I shouldn't be interrupting you while you pack."

Kennara turned to leave, but Abria grabbed Kennara's wrist before she got too far.

"What is it?" Abria asked. She watched as Kennara fidgeted with the laces of her bodice.

"It's nothing. I should be gathering my things."

"Clearly it's something. We can take a moment to talk about whatever is bothering you." Abria sat on her bed, pushing her bags out of the way. "Sit. Talk."

Kennara flopped onto the bed. "Fine. I don't know. I'm worried about leaving. I know it's not safe here—I understand that, I really do. But it's not safe out there either . . ."

"I feel like I don't understand anything that's going on. Why are the king's men after us? More than that, I'm not ready. I don't know what I need to know, whether it's how to fight or about how to accomplish our mission, I just don't know." She sighed. "It's overwhelming that it's all happening now."

"I feel the same way, but maybe I can answer some of your questions."

"Why are they after me and my sister?" Kennara asked without a second of hesitation.

Abria stared up at the ceiling and cleared her throat. "I'm not sure. I know they're looking for you and your sister. Your mother told me to protect the two of you at all costs."

"But why? Because she didn't want us to suffer, or for some greater reason? I just don't understand why we would be targeted. Maybe I'm jumping to conclusions and this has nothing to do with me or Kellesha. Maybe the king's men are after Eljin. I mean, he is the prince and a serious threat to King Sheamus." Kennara was practically hugging herself. Her arms were so tightly wrapped around her knees as she sat with her feet on Abria's bed.

Abria placed her hand on Kennara's arm. "I wish I had an answer. Your mother sacrificed herself for you and Kellesha. What that means for us—I'm not really sure."

"She could have saved us just because we were her daughters. It doesn't have to mean anything." Kennara rested her head on her knees. "But someone just tried to grab my sister, and I want to know why. Did you notice they didn't even look twice at Eljin? He was just another person here, not the target. I would think they would be after him, not us."

CHAPTER TWENTY-FIVE

They left the beach cottage the day after the attack. Kennara was dreading the journey: it's where she always felt the weakest. Like right now, she was the only one riding—not that she wanted to be walking, but with the distance they needed to travel, she would never be able to keep up. So here she was, riding Whiskey, while Shadow was loaded down with their gear and food. Everyone walking had broken off into groups and were talking with each other. She rode above everyone, unable to take part in any of the conversations. Once again, she felt like she was on the outside looking in, a feeling she was all too familiar with and hated more than most things.

She watched as Kellesha talked with Abria and Cas, their arms gesticulating wildly as they walked. Gallagher was walking with Zenevieve and Eljin. She felt an unfamiliar twinge as she watched Eljin walk with Zenevieve, wondering if he was connecting with the daughter of the woman who saved him.

"How are you doing, Kennara?" Reilynne asked.

Shocked, Kennara looked down to see the healer

walking beside her. "I'm okay. But if I'm being honest, I'm feeling a little sorry for myself. I feel so distant from the group up here. And while I know it's a necessity, I don't like being apart, feeling on the outskirts. So I'm up here moping while everyone else trudges through the forest." She knew she sounded silly, and she should have kept it to herself, but she wasn't interested in hiding her feelings right now.

"I understand. I've felt that way many times in my life. And it's hard to feel, and harder to express." Reilynne continued to walk next to Kennara, hands clasped behind her back.

"True. I always feel like I'm whining when I try to say something about it. Normally I just stew in my feelings for way too long." Kennara let her body move with the horse, letting some of the tension in her body dissipate.

Reilynne glanced up at her, then went back to looking straight ahead.

Kennara watched as Reilynne did this over and over again. "Whatever it is, Reilynne, you can just say it."

Reilynne took a deep breath. "How much do you know about the Five Sisters?"

Once again, Reilynne surprised her. "I know the basics. Five Sisters, each with their own element of magic." Kennara paused. "I know that there is more, but I'm not exactly sure why they're important. Just that the thought of them calms me when I'm feeling overwhelmed—and I visited them on our journey to the beach for some reason."

"So you've never researched the Five Sisters?" Reilynne asked.

Kennara glanced over at Reilynne, curious as to where this conversation was going. "I have, but it's been a while. I was quite obsessed when I first started working at the library. But I haven't thought about them for years. It didn't help my research that a lot of the books on the Five Sisters were missing or lost."

Reilynne shook her head. "The current king's reach is wide. He doesn't like people knowing about or believing in the Five Sisters, so he's tried to erase their story. He's a fool to think all of us would just forget. The Sisters have too much of a pull on anyone with potent magic."

"What do you mean by too much of a pull?" Kennara wanted to stop Whiskey and sit and have this discussion, but being on the run didn't leave time for sitting around talking about the mythology of the land.

"You felt it when you went to look at them. If you have strong magic, it's like they call to you, trying to show you a path. You might not want to follow the path or you might not see the path they intend for you—but they pull you to follow the path they have set for you." Reilynne gazed off into the distance as she walked and talked.

"Are you trying to say that they have plans for me?" Kennara asked. It felt like everything around her became more distinct: the clopping of Whiskey's hooves on the dirt, the rocks shifting under Reilynne's feet, and the wind rustling the leaves of the trees all seemed so loud. But she couldn't even hear the others talking around her. It was like she could only listen to Reilynne and whatever point she was trying to get across.

"They have plans for us all. Maybe I should start with going through the lore and then you can decide if they have plans for you." Reilynne took a deep breath. "Tanwen, Vala, Morgann, Awel, and Ened are the Five Sisters. Each one of them had access to one type of magic. They were the only five people in the world that had any type of magic at all.

"Tanwen was able to control fire. She was a lot like you, with a strong set of core beliefs that went into every decision she made in life; and, of course, you two share the same element of magic. Deep down, she believed that everyone should have access to the magic in the world, not just her and her sisters. It was such a firm belief that she went around the world teaching anyone who wanted to learn how to find magic in themselves and the world around them. She had some success, but it wasn't until her sister Ened joined her that people really succeeded at finding their magic. Tanwen always believed because Ened's power was heart, like mine, she was the one who helped people find their magic."

"Like you can feel Abria's magic in her, even though it was stolen from her years ago?" Kennara asked.

Reilynne's head snapped towards her. "How did you— Never mind, it's not like it was a truly private conversation." Her gaze returned to the road before she continued. "But yes, healers, or those of us with heart magic, are more tuned in to the human body and we can sense where a person's magic is inside them. Not only can we sense that, but we can sense what type of magic and how powerful they could be."

Kennara waited for Reilynne to return to her story, interested in what happened with the Five Sisters. The only thing she could remember about them was how they walked out into the ocean and let their magic seep into the world, and how they became jutting stones changing as the ocean tried to wear them down, day after day, year after year, century after century. But they still stood there, each of them on their own, but together—their strength standing up to the waves. They were supposed to remind women of their strength, something so easy to forget with everything King Sheamus had done since taking the throne.

"Anyway, the other three sisters joined Tanwen and

Ened after their initial success, until Awel, air magic, fell in love with a human. Vala worried about her sister because her air magic disappeared every time the human was around. She went to Awel and told her, but Awel would have nothing of it. She only wanted what her heart craved and could not be convinced of anything else." Reilynne paused. "You can guess what happens from here."

The story absorbed all of Kennara's attention. It was more than she had ever been able to learn about the Five Sisters. "What I know doesn't quite match up with the story you're telling. I've always been told that the Five Sisters stand in the ocean to remind us of our inner strength. But information has always been so limited."

"That has become the watered-down version that people tell when selling oil paintings and other art. But the actual story is so much more. Despite the warning of her sister, Awel fell deeper and deeper in love until she chose to give her lover her magic power of the wind . . ."

"Why would she give up her magic?" Kennara interrupted.

Reilynne shifted her pack before answering. "From what I have read, he got jealous of her having more power than him. It didn't start out that way, but over time, his jealousy grew. But Awel wanted him to love her so she gave up herself a little at a time. First, it was giving up her sisters and giving him all her time. Then it was his desperate need to have a family to carry on his legacy. And finally, he wanted her magic. The only good that came out of the relationship was a daughter."

"What happened to the daughter?"

"No one really knows. It's like history forgot her. Some say the four sisters who had watched Awel become a shell of herself took the child away and hid her among the humans, but she's rarely, if ever, talked about. What is talked about is how the human left Awel, uninterested in her once her magic was gone. So her sisters took her to the ocean to heal. There they decided to stay, Morgann standing taller than the rest, since she could use magic to control water. They let the ocean wash away their magic and the earth soaked it up as they turned to rock. Rocks that can still be seen today," Reilynne finished.

"I can't believe that's how they ended." Kennara kept plodding along on the back of Whiskey, sad for the five magical women who gave everything up for their betrayed sister.

Reilynne clasped her hands together. "But they are still there, the story continues on. So it's not how they end; plus there's a little known tale that talks about Awel's heir and the strength of her magic. I've never seen the actual writings, though I hope to someday. It could answer so many of my questions."

Kennara and Reilynne continued down the trail in silence.

Day turned to night as everyone trudged on. Stars could be seen through the tree branches by the time Abria decided it was time to set up camp. Kennara dismounted and would have fallen to the ground if she wasn't holding on to Whiskey. She leaned up against her horse for a moment, trying to find the strength in her legs to support herself on her own.

"Are you okay, Kenna?" Eljin asked as she felt his hands on her lower back and quickly move around her waist.

She wanted to stand on her own, but it was comforting to have his support. So instead of pushing him away, she let him escort her to the center of camp and what looked like an abandoned firepit. "I'll get dinner together for everyone while they set up camp."

Eljin set up the pot stand and hung the pot between the two sticks on a sturdy pole. "You don't need to cook dinner. I can do it for you."

"I can sit and cook dinner. In fact, I would like to. It will make me feel useful." She stacked the wood so the fire would get enough air to continue to burn, then started the fire with a flick of her hand. She grabbed an onion, some carrots, potatoes, and a little bit of salted meat. The onions went into the pot first, filling the area with their savory aroma. She added the rest of the vegetables and salted meat to the pot, then filled it with water, creating a quick stew for her and the others.

The campsite buzzed with activity around Kennara while she stirred the stew and thought about the lore of the Five Sisters.

"Is the stew done? It smells delicious." Kellesha squatted next to her.

The spoon clattered against the pot as Kennara looked up at her sister, her thoughts about the Five Sisters interrupted. They hadn't really said anything to each other since she had started her training. Kellesha still insisted she had not used her magic, but there was no other rational explanation for what happened. This made it impossible for Kennara to believe her sister.

"Almost." Kennara picked up the spoon and stirred the stew, not exactly ignoring her sister, but not giving her full attention.

Kellesha sat down next to her. "I'm sure it will be good, especially after our long day."

"It's the least I can do after riding a horse all day long while everyone else walked. I figured everyone must be famished and camp still needed to be set up. The least I can do is cook something." Kennara stopped stirring. "Anyway, help yourself. It's done."

Kennara stood, wiped her hands off her skirts, and limped away to go talk to someone else, anyone else.

CHAPTER TWENTY-SIX

Sun filtered through a small opening in the fabric of her tent. Kennara covered her eyes to block out the offensive light. There was no way it was morning already. She rolled over, snuggling into her bedroll. Light burst in from the other side of the tent and Kellesha poked her head in.

"Time to get up and on the road, Kennara."

Kennara covered her head with the blanket. "Go away."

"Sorry, not an option." Kellesha grabbed the blanket and yanked it off her body.

Kennara curled into a ball, willing the cold to go away. "Why are you so mean? I just want to sleep a bit more." Her entire body shook as the cold set deeper into it.

"That may be, but I'm not being mean. I'm just trying to make sure no one is waiting for you because I know that will make you feel bad."

"Fine. I'll get up." Kennara's teeth clattered as she forced the words out. She hated that her sister was right about her. If she delayed their travels—or more accurately, their escape—she would feel terrible for days. Which was why she dragged herself out of her tent and outside of their campground to freshen up for the day. The morning dew had frozen onto the grass, causing it to crunch under her feet as she walked, and the sun sparkled off leaves dusted with ice. The cold and damp weather was not doing her any favors: she was already in pain, which was never promising at the start of a new day. She rubbed her leg before she walked back to camp, hoping no one noticed.

"There you are, Kenna." Eljin sidled up next to her. "I saved you some breakfast." He held out a ration of bacon, cheese, and bread.

She smiled. In response, Eljin's face lit up with his smile.

She took the meal he offered her and took a bite. It might have been simple food, but it tasted so good. It was all she could do not to moan in satisfaction.

"Thank you. It's so sweet of you to think of me." Kennara blushed, looking down as the words came out of her mouth sounding much more meaningful than she had meant them.

Eljin reached out and tilted her head up with a finger under her chin until their eyes locked. "I'm always thinking of you—" He dropped his hand and cleared his throat. "Or so it would seem."

Kennara didn't know whether or not to look at Eljin, so after a moment, she glanced away. She was touched by his admission, but uncomfortable with what his words meant for their friendship. Instead of pressing further, she looked straight ahead as they walked back to camp, side by side but not touching. It was strange not leaning on him, something she had become all too comfortable with.

"Thank you again," she said as they reached camp.

Eljin stopped and shifted his weight from one foot to

the other, looking like he wanted to say something to her but didn't know how to bring it up. She wanted to tell him to spit it out. Instead, she just stood with him in silence.

"Well then"—she brushed off her skirts—"I should really make sure all my things have been packed. I'm sure Abria wants us on the road soon."

"Yes, yes, of course." Eljin stood there, not moving.

She turned and walked away, leaving him there.

What was that all about? Shaking her head, she found her bedroll and sat. She finished packing the few things that were left out. She stood and the sharp pain that shot through her leg had her stumbling to the ground. Shrugging the pack onto her shoulders, she made her way to Whiskey. She had another day of riding ahead and she wasn't looking forward to it. Not that she would ever tell anyone. It wasn't right to complain about spending a day riding when everyone else was walking. So she kept her mouth shut and tied her pack down. Before she mounted, she offered Whiskey a carrot she had set aside the night before.

"Come on, girl, we have another day on the run. Are you ready to carry me through the woods?" she asked. Whiskey whinnied. Apparently, the horse was ready for another day even if she wasn't.

"Are you ready to head out?" Abria asked everyone around the campsite.

There was a murmur of assent heard from the group. Kennara sighed, but joined them, agreeing she was ready to go. Kennara grabbed the pummel and pulled right as she felt a pair of hands clasp around her waist and lift her onto the saddle. She looked down to see Eljin looking up at her.

"Thank you," she said. "But I could have done it myself."

Eljin looked down sheepishly. "I don't doubt that, but I wanted to help."

She chewed her lower lip, unsure of what to say. He had overstepped, which annoyed her, especially when it was someone other than Eljin. But sometimes when he did the things that annoyed her, her reaction was quite different.

"Kenna, are you okay?"

She shook her head ever so slightly. "I'm fine, and thank you for your assistance. It would be nice if you asked first, though." She smiled down at him, hoping that he would know she wasn't upset.

"I promise, I'll ask next time." He smiled back, causing her heart to skip a beat. She felt heat in her cheeks and knew she was blushing.

"We better get going before Abria comes over and tells us to hurry," she said as she looked away.

Eljin laughed. "True, I don't want to be the one holding up Abria's escape plans."

Kennara clicked her tongue, urging Whiskey to move to the rest of their band of renegades. Despite the long arduous days of walking they had already done and in the days ahead of them, everyone was in good spirits. Gallagher and Cas were in a deep conversation about the benefits of certain types of weapons. Some of their gesticulations caused her to wince. The dagger they were analyzing looked like it was close enough to draw blood at one point. She really wished they would put down the weapons they were discussing before conversing about them.

She shifted her focus to the next group. Abria and Kellesha were sitting together, almost touching, looking over what Kennara could only guess was a map. They were probably planning out the rest of their route all the way to the king's castle, which was built into the side of a mountain, making it almost impenetrable. For her, getting into the castle was a thought for another day. She was more concerned with getting there first. The journey itself seemed almost impossible.

On the other side of Abria and her sister, Zenevieve and Reilynne huddled around what was left of the fire trying to stay warm—and failing, by the looks of it. Kennara was tempted to set the fire ablaze to help them out, but she knew they would be warm soon enough despite the chill of the morning.

Abria looked up from the map, whatever decision that needed making having been made. She clapped her hands and everyone's head snapped towards her. She pointed towards their path. "Let's go."

As one, or so it seemed to Kennara, everyone picked up their small pack, the rest already loaded on Shadow. For some it was mostly weapons; others, Reilynne mostly, kept the tools of their trade close to them. As Kennara thought about it a little more, really all of them kept the tools of their trade close. Reilynne's were carried in a sack since she was a healer, while most of the others were more warrior-like, explaining why they needed access to their weapons.

On the other hand, Zenevieve carried very little. Kennara was still trying to figure her out. She didn't interact much with anyone, really. She had trained with Reilynne, learning to use her magic in different ways at her cottage, and she begrudgingly talked with others when approached, but isolated herself more often than not.

Kennara swayed with her horse's movement, the rhythmic pattern lulling her to sleep. Her head bobbed and her eyes snapped open. Crap, she needed to stay alert. There was no way she would risk falling off her horse. She thought about walking for a while, but her leg twinged in pain just at the thought of supporting her weight. If she was back in Wreswell, today was one of those days she would have been forced to use her chair.

"Why don't I ride behind you?" Eljin asked. "You can rest. I'll make sure you don't fall."

"I should just walk for a while. That would wake me up." Kennara shrugged. It wasn't what she wanted to do, but it made sense.

"Nonsense." Eljin shook his head. "I've seen you rubbing your leg all day. It's clearly bothering you. Walking would just slow everyone down."

"Well, when you put it that way, I guess your suggestion makes a lot of sense," Kennara conceded and held out a hand.

Eljin took her hand, placed one foot in the stirrup, and lifted himself onto the horse behind Kennara. As soon as he was behind her, she leaned back into his warmth. She felt his arms circle around her and a wool blanket drape over her legs. For the first time today, she was warm and comfortable.

"Kennara, wake up. Someone is following us," Eljin whispered into her ear. She could feel the urgency of his tone throughout his body. What had been a cozy place for her to nap was now hard, muscles taut, waiting for something to happen.

She sat up straight in an instant. The sleep that had taken over her gone. "Is it just one person? Can you tell?"

"I think there are more, but I can't be sure how many."

Kennara pressed her heels into Whiskey just enough to let the horse know they needed to move. The clip clop of her hooves belied her change in speed as they made their way to Abria and the others.

"Cas, Abria, I think someone is following us. I heard the snapping of branches and murmuring that didn't seem to come from you." Eljin's tongue seemed to trip over itself as he relayed the information to the warriors in their little group.

"You two go on ahead. We'll see who these people are and fight them off if necessary."

Kennara held up a hand. "I don't want to go off where it's safe. What was the point of all the training if I run and hide every time there's trouble?"

Abria rolled her eyes. "It's keeping the prince safe. Without him, we don't have the rightful heir to the throne. So you keep him safe. Help us out with the strategic use of your bow and arrow."

"Oh, that make sense." Kennara turned Whiskey towards a hill, figuring higher ground would be to their advantage.

"I'm not completely helpless, you know," Eljin muttered.

Abria laughed. "We know, but you are the key piece to taking the throne back, so you're stuck being protected, for now."

Kennara clicked her tongue and tapped her heels on Whiskey's side, directing her up the hill. Both she and Eljin dismounted, hoping the trees would hide their location. Kennara watched as Abria covered up their path by kicking some fallen leaves over Whiskey's hoof prints. She then conferred with Cas, Gallagher, and Kellesha before sending Reilynne off to a safe spot with Shadow. Kennara was fairly certain whatever direction Reilynne went, Zenevieve followed.

Those that remained on the trail went about like it was time for a snack. Kennara watched their movements, each one sharper than it needed to be. It wasn't long before a group of soldiers came into view. In the middle of the soldiers was a woman with long white hair, dark eyes, and blood-red lips. Kennara trembled at the sight of her. Was that Maeryn? She had never seen the woman who assisted the king in his mission to steal all the magic women possessed. But the woman standing down there looked powerful enough to be her.

"Her." The white-haired woman pointed to Kellesha. "She's the one the king wants."

Abria stepped forward. "Maeryn," she spat. "Do you really think I'm going to let you take a member of my family?"

"I don't think you're going to have a choice."

Abria gasped as if she couldn't breathe. She clawed at her throat, trying to remove something that wasn't there.

The soldiers stepped forward, swords drawn, ready to attack.

Cas and Gallagher moved in front of Abria and Kellesha, weapons at the ready.

Abria fell to her knees.

Without another thought, Kennara drew and lit an arrow, then sent it flying. Shooting faster than she had ever shot arrows before, she let loose four more arrows before the first one struck the ground. Each one landed near Maeryn, cutting her off from the soldiers with a wall of flame. The flames licked at her clothing, but she did not catch on fire. However, the flames distracted her enough that whatever she was doing to Abria suddenly stopped.

Maeryn looked around. Kennara ducked behind a tree, but it was too late. She had locked eyes with the evil woman and, for a moment, she was frozen in place. Now with her back to the tree and whatever was happening below, she panted, afraid to look around to see if Maeryn's gaze was still focused in her direction.

"Is she still looking this way?" she whispered.

"Who?" Eljin asked, his face filled with concern as she clung to the tree to prevent her hands from shaking.

"Maeryn, the woman with the white hair," Kennara said through clenched teeth.

Eljin's eyebrows shot up. "If she's here, you aren't safe. We have to move."

"Don't be daft, Eljin. There's no way I'm leaving anyone here, especially not my sister. Now find out if she's still looking this way."

She watched as Eljin snuck around the tree and hid in some tall grass. "No, she's focused on the battle in front of her."

Kennara thought about peeking her head out, but the feeling of dread that came over her was so overwhelming she stayed frozen where she was.

Eljin nudged her. "They need help."

His words were enough. She burst into action again. Looking at the scene below was troublesome. Their friends were not faring well. The combination of magic and combat was overpowering them. Especially since Maeryn did not care if her magic killed someone, which was not true for either Zenevieve or Kellesha.

Kennara did not want to kill anyone with her magic, but fire burned and had a mind of its own. If a person didn't heed its power, the damage it did to them was on them. With that thought, she released one arrow after another, each landing at the feet of a soldier. Despite Maeryn's orders, the soldiers ran from the flames falling from the sky. It gave her sister and their friends time to run—or stumble away: Abria and Cas were practically dragging Gallagher between them.

CHAPTER TWENTY-SEVEN

Abria was angry. There were no other words to describe how she felt.

Wait, yes there were. She also felt guilty. Maeryn had got the drop on her and Abria vowed never to let that happen again. She hated that they needed to run, because she wanted to stay and destroy that woman. But that wasn't the goal right now—the little band wanted to dethrone the king, as did she.

"Cas, will you put me down now?" Gallagher yelled, his words punctuated by the bouncing of Cas's steps.

She looked over to see her friend thrown over Cas's shoulder. His white shirt was soaked with blood near his shoulder and there was another gash on his leg. Guilt overwhelmed her. Here she was thinking about what she wanted while her friend was badly injured.

"Nope, we need to get to a safe spot before I can put you down," Cas said.

"I can walk. I'm not that injured."

Abria interrupted their argument. "The gash in your leg says otherwise."

They continued down the trail until they came upon Reilynne and Zenevieve hiding across the stream in a beautiful copse of trees while Kellesha was standing guard watching for her sister—or so Abria assumed that's who Kellesha was looking for. Abria hoped Kennara and Eljin were following behind them and staying out of trouble.

"Bring Gallagher over to me," Reilynne ordered. She laid down a wool blanket and gestured for Cas to lay the injured man on the blanket.

Cas and Abria carefully laid Gallagher down. Reilynne fell to her knees beside the injured man, her hands hovering over him. Abria watched as the healer first focused on the gash in his leg. Gallagher winced as the wound closed, but unlike Abria during her healing, he was able to stay still. Reilynne moved on to his shoulder and chest. It was such a relief to watch her friend heal so quickly.

She heard a snap of a branch and turned with her sword drawn. The neighing of a horse caused the tension in her shoulders to ease. She relaxed even more as Kennara and Eljin came into view. They didn't look any worse for wear.

"Oh no, what happened?" Kennara said as she dismounted. She stumbled as she stepped away from Whiskey, but righted herself.

"He's okay, or at least he will be when Reilynne is done." Abria reached out and grabbed Kennara's arm.

Kennara turned her head to look at Gallagher, who was clearly in pain as Reilynne did her work.

"I promise he'll be okay," she said. "We need to be ready to move when Reilynne is done. I think Gallagher and Reilynne will need to ride for a while today."

"I understand. I'll do what I can to make that happen." The look on Kennara's face didn't match what she was saying. It was even more obvious how unsure Kennara was as she unconsciously rubbed her right leg.

Abria wanted to take back her words and let Kennara continue to ride. But she knew that Reilynne and Gallagher would be exhausted after the healing session. She would love to stay here and let them rest, but it wasn't possible. They needed to keep moving for as long as they could today, and it wouldn't be long if her injured friend and the healer had to walk.

"I'm done," Reilynne said before collapsing to the ground.

She watched as Kennara scurried over to Reilynne and dropped to her knees. Kennara checked for the healer's pulse. Finding it, she moved her friend into a more comfortable position, resting Reilynne's head in her lap and stroking her hair.

Abria sighed, thankful that everyone was okay . . . for now.

Gallagher sat up and rolled his shoulders. "That's amazing. I can't believe I was sliced up and bleeding just a short while ago."

"Don't go running off like you're completely healed. You could undo everything that Reilynne did, which wore her out completely." Abria nodded towards the healer.

Gallagher looked back. "Is she okay? She should have left me injured if it was going to exhaust her to the point she lost consciousness."

"We couldn't have stopped her if we'd tried, which none of us did." Abria steepled her fingers in front of her and tapped them on her lip. "Hopefully she wakes up soon, though we need to continue moving before Maeryn comes back."

It was like she had made it happen: Reilynne's eyes

opened. "What happened? Why am I on the ground?" She pushed herself up on her forearms, looking around, confused.

"You fainted after healing Gallagher." Abria helped Reilynne off the ground. She looked back to see Eljin helping Kennara.

Reilynne's eyes widened. "I've never fainted after a healing session before." She pushed her black hair back. Worry creased her forehead and showed in her dark brown eyes.

"How are you feeling now?" Abria asked.

Reilynne flexed her fingers, rolled her shoulders, and tilted her head from side-to-side. "I feel fine, maybe even better than I did this morning. Did anything happen after I fainted?"

"No—well, Kennara sat with you while you were unconscious."

The healer raised her eyebrows.

"That's interesting," Reilynne murmured, more to herself than to anyone else.

"Kennara is giving up Whiskey for you and Gallagher to ride."

"That's unnecessary. I'm fine." Reilynne walked towards where Kennara and Eljin were talking.

She ran after Reilynne. "Like hell you're fine. You were unconscious moments ago."

"But Kennara can't walk long distances, her leg won't support a lot of walking, and we need to get far away from here." Concern was written all over Reilynne's face.

Abria stopped. "We aren't that far from the end of the woods and Bellecote. With any luck, we can find an inn with rooms for all of us and recuperate there. Hopefully, we can disappear among all the other people."

"Fine, I understand why you're making this decision, but I don't agree with it." Reilynne stormed off towards Kennara once again.

Abria went to talk with Gallagher. He was going to fight her too, but she couldn't have him undoing all of Reilynne's hard work.

"Gallagher, you're going to ride Whiskey with Reilynne. I want you to rest as much as you can today so we can keep going as soon as possible."

The look of shock on his face was almost comical. "I can walk just fine."

"No, you were cut up. If it wasn't for Reilynne, you wouldn't be walking at all. I will not let you mess up her work because you don't think you ever need to rest."

"I know I won't convince you otherwise, so I'll do it. Just know I'm fine and can walk."

Abria looked around at their little group. They all looked worn down. Now she was going to tell them they had to make it out of the woods and into town tonight. She sighed. Leading was natural for her, but it didn't mean she always enjoyed it.

"Okay, as much as I would like to stay here, we need to make it to Bellecote by tonight. I think everyone needs the opportunity to stay in an actual bed—a small reprieve before we continue on our way."

"A proper bed would be wonderful." Zenevieve held her hands over her heart, her eyes wistful. "Does that mean we might even have the ability to take a warm bath?"

"Maybe, if we hurry along. I don't want to stay in town too long. We can't risk being discovered."

"I'll walk all night if it means a warm bath is in my future. Let's get moving so I don't have to, though." Zenevieve grabbed her pack, ready to go.

Abria wasn't surprised at Zenevieve's eagerness. "If everyone is ready, we're going to go more north than before. I wasn't planning to stay in Bellecote, but now it's a good place to stay out of sight since we'll be around so many people."

She watched as everyone gathered their belongings. Kennara had her cane in hand, and as usual, Eljin was near her, waiting for her to need to lean on him. It amazed her at how he was able to be there for her without making her feel helpless. It was something Kellesha hadn't been able to do, and Abria felt helpless as she watched how much it strained their relationship.

Kellesha and Cas led the way with Shadow in tow, Zenevieve close behind them. Reilynne and Gallagher looked miserable on the back of Whiskey, even though they both knew it was the best thing for them and the group. Behind them, Kennara and Eljin took their spot. Abria could see that Kennara was going to struggle. She hoped they were closer to the town than she thought. If they weren't, they were going to have to figure out how to carry Kennara.

Abria pushed that thought from her mind and caught up with Kellesha and Cas. She led the way as the light changed, filtering through the branches of the colorful leaves of the oak tree. As the sun went down more, the light went from bright rays, to pink and orange streaks painting the sky, to dusk with just enough light to see the outskirts of Bellecote.

She encouraged the travellers on as the roads turned from dirt to cobblestone. Buildings of stone and mortar lined the streets, starting off somewhat sporadically and ending up as dense as the trees in the forest.

Abria stopped the group in front of the Dragon and Unicorn. It was an old stone building covered with plaster and wood beams. The thatched roof gave the overall appearance of a cozy place to stay, as did the smell of burning peat coming from the chimney. The village outside of the inn was eerily quiet.

She opened the door and the savory smell of meat pies overwhelmed her nose. Inside the inn was quite the opposite, filled with chatter, the clanking of tankards, and the clinking of flatware. It seemed like all the locals from the village were in the tavern. Every chair in the public area had someone sitting on it, each patron enjoying food and drink. It was so busy she hoped that there was still room for all of them to stay the night, maybe even the next night.

She waved down a server and asked for the innkeeper. It wasn't long before he showed up.

"Good evening. We were hoping you have room for the eight of us."

The innkeeper looked at the loud crowd before responding. "I actually have three rooms left. Would you like all of them?"

"That would be wonderful," Abria responded.

He handed the keys to Abria and directed her to the three rooms. The band of weary travellers followed her towards the stairs.

"Here you go." Abria handed a key to the three men in the entourage.

Eljin snatched the key out of her hand. "Let's drop our stuff off and head to the pub. I think we could all use a tankard of ale after the last few days."

Cas clapped Eljin on the back. "I think that's the best idea you've ever had."

Abria rolled her eyes as they made their way up the stairs, Gallagher following behind.

She turned towards Reilynne and Zenevieve. "Here's

your key. I'll be in the room with you two. I'm going to see if food can be sent up to the room. I'm not in the mood to deal with the intensity of the crowds tonight."

"If you can get food sent up, I would love something as well," Reilynne requested as she walked up the stairs.

Zenevieve looked at the public rooms. "I could use a tankard. I'll meet the boys down there. After my bath."

Last, Abria turned to the twins and tossed the last key. Kellesha caught it.

"I figured the two of you are used to sharing a room, so you wouldn't mind it now." Before either of the twins could say anything, she turned and walked into the crowd.

It was manipulative, but hopefully forcing the twins to share a room would force them to talk. Their fight had gone on for far too long. Abria needed them to get along if they were going to succeed in their goal.

CHAPTER TWENTY-EIGHT

Kennara watched Abria run off before she could protest. She looked back at her sister and saw hope in her blue eyes. Maybe she had drawn this out too long. It's not like her sister interfered because she wanted to cause harm. Kellesha always stepped in to help her as a way to protect her.

"Why don't you see if we can get dinner delivered to our room? The last bit of the day was rather hard on me." Kennara rubbed her leg with a slight grimace.

Kellesha smiled. "Of course, steak and ale pie and an apple tart?"

"If they have those things on the menu, they would be perfect. So much better than my terrible stew." Kennara laughed.

"Your stew is pretty bad—makes me wonder who put you in charge of cooking. I'll go get us dinner."

Kennara watched while her sister went into the pub to order food. She turned to walk up the stairs, using the handrail to leverage every step she took. Halfway up the stairs she] the pain sharp after the walking she had done today. She dragged herself up the rest of the stairs to the room she was sharing with her sister.

She leaned up against the door for a moment before unlocking it. She pushed the door open to find a roaring fire. The mantle had figurines of small animals. Her favorite was the fox. There were two small beds next to each other, both covered with handmade quilts. In the corner, close to the fireplace and a window, was a small dining table with two chairs. It was one of the coziest rooms she had ever been in. It was too bad they couldn't stay here for a while. She wanted to spend the day curled up under a soft blanket, reading a book, but that wasn't going to happen, at least not anytime soon. She sighed. Just the thought of reading made her miss the library in Wreswell.

The door crashed open, causing her to jump out of her skin, her dagger at the ready for whoever had come through the door. She dropped her arm as soon as she saw her sister peek around.

She glared at her sister. "Did you have to come through the door like that? You scared me half to death."

"My hands are just a little full. Get over here and help me." Kellesha precariously balanced food and drinks in her arms.

Kennara grabbed the drinks from her sister's hand and placed them on the table. Kellesha did the same with the food. Kennara might have drooled a little when she got a good whiff of the savory goodness that was on the table. She sat so the steak and ale pie was in front of her. The pastry was flaky. She should have waited for her sister before she took a bite, but it looked and smelled so good. As she cut into the pie, gravy spilled out along with bits of steak and mushrooms. On the side was a steaming pile of fluffy mashed potatoes covered in butter.

Her sister sat across from her and cut into a chicken and vegetable pie. It was filled with a cream sauce, carrots, peas, and other root vegetables Kennara wasn't familiar with. It looked good—not as good as the one that she was eating, but still good.

The two sat across from each other, silent. The only sounds in the room were the crackling of the fire and the clinking of the flatware. One of them was going to have to say something at some point.

Kennara looked up at her sister, who was devouring her dinner, and cleared her throat. "We should probably talk, or something. It's pretty obvious that Abria wants us to work things out."

Kellesha looked up from her food. "Do *you* want to work things out? If you don't, I don't really care what Abria wants us to do."

"I've missed you. I would love to put this fight behind us." She pushed her food around her plate. As much as she wanted to bridge the gap between them, she didn't know how to do it.

"How do we get past this, then? Especially when you don't believe a word I say." Kellesha placed her fork on her plate. "I don't know either. All I know is I didn't use any magic that day."

"But I was held off the ground by wind. If it wasn't you, then who was it?" Doubt wriggled its way into her head. Maybe her sister had nothing to do with it and she had been wrong all this time. Kennara couldn't think of a single reason her sister would continue on this path of denial unless what she said was actually true.

"I'm not sure what happened, just that it wasn't me. And I wish you would believe me." Kellesha pushed her plate away.

Kennara stared at her sister, hunched over, the pain of her distrust evident. "I believe you. I can't imagine you would lie to me like this for so long. But how do I explain it? If it wasn't you, then what happened?"

Kellesha tapped her fingers on the table. "I'm not sure. Doesn't Eljin have an amulet from his mom? Maybe he did something without realizing it. He might not even know he has magic in the amulet since he's so opposed to his uncle's actions."

Kennara raised an eyebrow. Her sister's suggestion was preposterous, wasn't it?

"Never mind, forget I said anything." Kellesha looked down, her nails suddenly becoming very interesting.

"You could be right. It would at least explain what happened that day." She reached across the table for the untouched plate of what she assumed was an apple tart. As she cut into it, the smell of cinnamon, apples and butter wafted towards her—one of her favorite smells. She pushed a slice over to her sister and dished one out for herself.

"Thank you," Kellesha said, but didn't even reach for her fork.

Kennara rolled her eyes. Her sister hardly ever ate anything sweet. "Come on, have a bite." She took a bite, and the crust melted in her mouth. The filling was sweet, but when she bit into an apple, the tartness balanced out the sugar.

"You'll enjoy it more." Kellesha pushed her plate towards Kennara.

She was going to protest, but why? The apple tart

would be wasted on her sister, and she would truly enjoy it. "Fine, I guess I'll suffer and eat the entire thing myself."

"I'm sorry to make you eat your favorite dessert all by yourself." Kellesha stood. "I'm exhausted. I'm sure you are too."

She sat down her fork. "It was a long day. I'm definitely ready for a week or a year of rest."

LAST NIGHT KENNARA FELT THE ANGER SHE HAD BEEN HOLDING ON to regarding her sister slip away as they finally talked to each other. She wouldn't say things were perfect between the two of them, but she no longer thought Kellesha was willfully lying to her. That didn't mean she understood what had happened that day, but it didn't feel like there was any time to figure it out. Tomorrow they were back on the road, and today they needed to stay unnoticed.

"What can I get for ya?" the serving girl asked.

Kennara looked up at her, giving up the inspection of her hands while her mind refused to focus on anything, instead bouncing from topic to topic. The young woman looked at her impatiently with her large brown eyes.

"A steak and ale pie with some mash, please." Kennara smiled at the server before returning to the study of her fingers.

She sat there, her thoughts racing until a woman's voice pierced through the fog she was in.

"I'm so thankful for King Sheamus and what he's doing with these Quickenings," the nasal voice said.

Kennara's eyes darted around the room, trying to determine who was talking. She wanted to see the person spouting such nonsense.

The voice continued, "I never liked the burden of having magic. I never knew what to do with it. It's so much better just letting men have it. They can deal with making all those decisions now."

Kennara narrowed in on a table with three women sitting around it. The one speaking was wearing a large floppy hat with an orange ostrich feather in it. As she spoke, the feather continually fell into her face, causing her to blow the feather out of her eyes. The other woman listened and nodded as the one with the orange feather continued to speak.

"Life is so much easier now that I don't have to worry about having powers."

Without a thought, Kennara stood, the legs of her chair scraping against the rough wood floor of the tavern. She was going to have a little chat with Lady Orange Feather.

The pressure of a hand on her shoulder forced her to pause. She reached up for it, about to use one of the moves Abria had taught her to incapacitate whoever had interfered.

"Woah, slow down. We don't need to draw any unnecessary attention to ourselves," Reilynne said, her tone tense.

Kennara turned towards the healer. "How can I stay silent? Those women are advocating for removing magical powers from women."

The nasal voice pierced the air. "Really, all the women fighting the Quickenings should just stop. It's not like we need the extra burden."

Kennara gestured towards the table. "Did you hear that?"

"I did, but you'll never change their mind. They've decided that what's happening makes sense. And if they don't want their magic, let them be rid of it." Reilynne sat at the table.

"But they're for taking it away from *all* women, not just those who choose to throw their magic away. Why should men get to choose to have magic or not, wear the amulet or not, and women, born with magic inside of them, are forced to throw it away?" She sat with a huff. "They want to toss away their essence. Fine, do it. But don't make others who want to keep their magic do the same. It's abhorrent."

The server approached the table as Kennara finished her rant. "Here you are, miss, one steak and ale pie." She turned towards Reilynne. "Can I get ya something, miss?"

"I'll have whatever she's having, thank you." Reilynne smiled at the young woman before turning back to Kennara.

"You're not wrong. And hopefully somebody someday will get through to her. But if you go over there now, all you're going to do is make a scene and draw attention to us. Which would go against what we are trying to accomplish here."

She sighed. The healer was right, but it didn't mean that she had to like it. Instead of getting up, she took a bite of the pie in front of her. The savory gravy and flaky crust were lost on her as she thought about what the woman had said. How many women were out there happy the king had taken away their choices? Were there others that would happily give their magic away if given the opportunity? Their mission felt so right, but could it be wrong? She looked over at Lady Orange Feather as she took her last bite of food, everyone else in the room forgotten.

She stood calmly, heading to the stairs, passing Lady

Orange Feather along the way. When she stood beside the woman still spouting her nonsense, blowing her feather out of her eyes every thirty seconds, Kennara stopped, leaned over, and whispered, "Just think, if you had air magic, you could keep that feather from falling in your face."

CHAPTER TWENTY-NINE

Kennara looked back at the Dragon and Unicorn. Two nights, Abria had let them sleep in actual beds for two nights. Their orders for today were to pack up and leave for more walking and more camping for days and days on end. She looked back at the room she'd shared with her sister and sighed at the thought of leaving its cozy comfort.

She mounted Whiskey; her leg muscles twinged as she settled in the saddle, causing her to rub it absentmindedly.

Eljin walked over to her. His easy gait caused a spike of jealousy that had her rolling her eyes at her own thoughts.

"Good morning, Kennara." His smile was infectious no matter how she was feeling about this morning in particular.

She felt her lips quirk up into a smile of their own. "It is morning. I will grant you that."

"How can you not say that it's a good one? In fact, I would go as far as to say it's a marvelous morning. Just look at the rays of light filtering through the trees over there." He took a deep breath. "And feel the cool air enter your lungs. It's invigorating."

"That's one way to look at things. And maybe in a few moments I'll see it that way. But right now I'm mourning the loss of a comfy bed, in a warm room, with all the quilted blankets I could ever want." She drew her cloak around her tighter, trying to replicate the warmth they were leaving behind.

Eljin glanced back at the inn. "It was a nice place to stay. But Reilynne and Gallagher are completely healed so there's not any reason to stay—unless you've changed your mind and we aren't going to overthrow the king."

It was then she noticed the shadows under his eyes, realizing his cheerful persona was just that: a persona. She imagined it was to hide his fear of King Sheamus.

She made a point of looking around at everything. The sleepy town wasn't awake, the sun's light had just filtered through the leaves of the trees, but it wasn't high enough in the sky to melt the frost on the grass or brighten up the rooms of many of the homes surrounding them.

"You're right, Eljin. It's a lovely morning. A perfect day to change the world. Or at least continue on our path to change the world." She clicked her tongue and Whiskey plodded forward. "Come on, girl, you heard Eljin. It's a beautiful day and we have fresh supplies. I know you'll miss the stables here, but hopefully, we'll find something better."

Whiskey's pace quickened ever so slightly. It was enough that she was out of town and on the forest road before the town came alive. Eljin loped along next to her. She would have liked to have said he plodded or trudged, but his movements were fluid, and he looked refreshed, yet also like he was on the lookout for something. What, she wasn't sure.

"I think we need to stop at the Rare Quill," Zenevieve said as she approached.

Kennara looked down at her with a raised eyebrow. "What sort of place is the Rare Quill and why do we need to stop?"

Zenevieve raised an eyebrow right back, clearly not used to being questioned, which made sense: she had been living a rather solitary life. "It's a bookshop that caters to those searching out antiquities. My mother mentioned it more than once. I think there's something important for us there."

"I've heard of this shop before. Many believe it's not just antiquities it carries, but prophesies. Are you looking to see if there's a prophesy that applies to us?" Eljin fell in beside Zenevieve, matching her shorter stride.

"I didn't say that, but I would like to look and see. It's not far out of our way, and might throw off who that are following us." She shrugged as if to downplay what she wanted.

Kennara chewed on her lower lip. "I don't see how it would hurt to stop. Go tell Abria. I'm sure she'll stop if she knows the reason."

She watched as Zenevieve hurried over to Abria, interrupting a conversation Kellesha was having with the woman. There was some gesticulating, lots of pointing. A map even came out of the pack. But in the end, Zenevieve got her way, which was made abundantly apparent when they stopped for an early afternoon respite.

Abria found a clearing for them to stop. Others must have used the spot because there were logs spread out like seats. Everyone grabbed some cheese and bread out of their pack and grabbed a log to sit on.

For a moment Kennara thought about eating while still astride Whiskey. If she was sure her leg wouldn't give out on her, she would have dismounted already. But that wasn't the case, at least not for her.

"Can I help you down?"

She looked down to see Eljin's brown eyes staring back up at her. As much as it annoyed her that she needed help, it was sweet that he asked before helping her.

"Help would be very much appreciated."

She swung her leg over the saddle. He reached up, his hands clasping her waist. Pushing off Whiskey, she slowly slid down the front of Eljin until her feet touched the ground. But he didn't let go. Instead, they stood there, gazing into each other's eyes, touching from chest to knee. She remembered their kiss back at Zenevieve's. It seemed ages ago, and somehow, like it was just yesterday. Her eyes dropped to his lips. She bit hers. It would be so easy to lean in and press her lips to his, remind her what that moment had felt like, let her know that she was remembering it correctly.

Someone clapped their hands, cutting through the haze she had been in. Eljin cleared his throat and took a step back.

"Gather round. Don't forget your lunch," Abria said with authority.

Kennara moved to the last wood stump available and sat with her snack of bread and cheese. Eljin stood behind her, almost touching, but not. It would have been so easy to lean back against him. She refrained, though, and listened for the announcement she assumed was coming.

"We're going to make a stop at the Rare Quill."

Gallagher's head popped up. "Are you sure that's a good idea? We've already been blindsided once by Viggo and Maeryn. I don't want it to happen again."

Kennara watched the exchange, surprised Gallagher was the one to question Abria's decision. She always thought of him as a lost puppy that followed along with everything Abria told him. Apparently, that was not the case.

Abria cocked an eyebrow. "Zenevieve believes there will be vital information there that could aid us in our mission. It's something her mother mentioned would help if the prince ever showed up. It would be foolish to ignore an opportunity to learn more, especially if it'll aid us in this impossible task. The more information we have, the better." Abria took a seat on the stump she was standing in front of.

"Who knows, it might take us far enough away from the main path that Viggo and Maeryn won't think to look for us there," Cas added.

Kellesha glanced up. "That was my thought."

Reilynne sat there, looking at her hands. It was almost like she wasn't listening to the conversation at all. But Kennara saw her nod when Cas spoke up, and again when Kellesha did. It was clear she wanted to stop but didn't want to be part of the conversation, and Kennara wanted to know why.

It took two days to get to the Rare Quill. Kennara wished she was better at geography because this seemed farther off their path than she thought would have been acceptable. They rode on wide dirt roads lined with evergreen trees, narrow paths that seemed more like wildlife trails than actual routes for travellers, and one time Abria even cleared a trail for them. It was clear the plan was to stay as far away from as many main roads as possible.

Through all of this, Kennara rode Whiskey, watching everyone in their band of renegades from her perch.

Gallagher spent his time sulking. He clearly didn't see the purpose of going to the bookshop and didn't want to take the time to go. Every time Abria tried to speak to him, he gave her one-word answers before turning away. The only person he seemed willing to converse with during this leg of the trip was Reilynne.

His insistence on only speaking to Reilynne made it impossible for Kennara to pull her to the side. She wanted to know why the healer had agreed to go to the bookshop. What did she know or expect to find out there?

Meanwhile, it seemed Kellesha was over her anger at Abria's abandonment. The two of them spent most of the day together, walking side by side, sharing whatever secrets they had.

Since Eljin was normally at her side, this left the unlikely pairing of Zenevieve and Cas. Although, the more she thought about it, the more the two of them spending time together made sense to her. They both craved adventure more than anyone else in the group. Cas was so happy every morning getting on the road and every night setting up camp. And Zenevieve, well, she still was ecstatic about leaving the beach cottage.

"Lead the way, Zenevieve." Abria gestured to the door. "You have an idea of what you're looking for. Let us know how we can help."

Zenevieve opened the door to the shop. A small bell tinkled above her head, alerting the shopkeeper to their presence. Reilynne followed close behind. Kennara dismounted, holding on to the saddle until it felt like her leg would support her weight. She grabbed her cane out of her pack as pain pulsed up her leg.

She felt Eljin's hand on the small of her back and smiled as she turned towards him.

"It's been a while since we've been surrounded by books. I miss the library." Her tone was wistful.

Eljin pulled her closer, supporting her in such a way that she didn't need to lean on the cane. "But now we are on a grand adventure. This is so much more exciting."

"True, but I think I'll spend my time here perusing the books and enjoying the smell of them."

"Enjoy your strange hobby. I never did understand why you insisted on sniffing the books." Eljin laughed.

She laughed with him. "I don't know either—there's just something about the smell. Now that I'm on a real adventure, it's not that they smell of adventure at all, but it is something special."

"They smell of dust and paper," he said, looking at her as if he was waiting for a reaction.

She glared at him, unable to ignore the bait. "And ideas and stories of lives lived and lost. Tall tales, and great feats of real people. There's way more to it than dust and paper."

"Anyone ever tell you that you're a romantic?"

She stuck her tongue out at him. "No, just cause you don't get it doesn't make it any less real."

"Whatever you say, Kenna."

He held the door open for her as she walked into the Rare Quill. It was almost like coming home. It wasn't as large as the library at the university, but it might have had almost as many books. There were mismatched shelves everywhere, some filled with books, others with scrolls, one even had stone tablets. She couldn't imagine that there were stories in this world that weren't being kept here in this bookshop that was somehow bright and inviting despite all the shelves of books.

"How can I help you, miss?" An elderly woman with white hair pulled back in a top knot appeared from behind one of the many sets of shelves. She looked soft in her bright blue dress and a pale pink shawl. Her rosy and plump cheeks and easy, friendly smile matched the rest of her.

Kennara smiled. "Our friends are here looking for something in particular. I'm here to enjoy being around books again after a long journey away from them."

The shopkeeper tapped her nose. "You know, I think I have something for you." She scurried to the end of the row where they were standing. Stopping, she perused the shelves until she found what she was looking for. "Yes, this one." The woman grabbed a small leatherbound book—it almost looked like a journal—and handed it to Kennara.

It was in fact a journal; inside was a loopy script that wasn't easy to read.

"I can't take this from you." Kennara handed her back the book.

The old woman shushed her, refusing to take the journal back. "You have to take it, it belongs with you."

CHAPTER THIRTY

Thankfully, no one found them at the Rare Quill, something Abria had been worried about ever since they had agreed to stop there. Zenevieve had found what she was looking for, but she'd only shared it with Reilynne. Every time they stopped for the night, the two of them would huddle near the fire, poring over the scroll they had purchased at the bookshop.

Meanwhile, Kennara would use her magic to light her tent and spent her time deciphering some journal the shopkeeper had insisted she take with her. Abria didn't understand how anyone could be that fascinated with a journal, but Kennara was, and she refused to let anyone or anything distract her from it whenever they were stopped.

"You know, she's always been like this. Put a book in her hand and you're not allowed to speak to her until she's finished." Kellesha watched her sister huddled off to the side, poring over the pages of the journal. "I was happy she found work in the library. I don't know if she would have been content anywhere else."

"You're a good sister," Abria said.

Kellesha laughed. "Would you mind telling her that? We worked through something at the tavern, but it still feels like I'm one step away from messing up again. I've been protecting her for so long, I don't know how to turn it off."

"You know it's not about not protecting her; it's about letting her know you believe she can protect herself." Abria squeezed Kellesha's shoulder. "She loves you and just needs to know you love her."

"Sometimes that seems easier said than done." Kellesha nudged a rock with her toe.

Abria wrapped her arms around Kellesha, who rested her head on Abria's shoulder. They stood there for a few moments before each stepped away. Kellesha was becoming more than the girl she abandoned all those years ago. She was a friend, and it killed Abria to see her in pain.

"Why don't you go spar with Cas? A good workout might help with some of your worry." Abria watched as Kellesha nodded before turning away.

Should she go talk to Kennara, try to get her to talk to her sister more? Or should she leave it alone? For now, Abria would let it be, and try to work out her own issues with Gallagher. She just needed to figure out what he was doing tonight. It seemed impossible for a person to hide in a clearing this small, but he was rather good at it.

Glancing around, she saw Eljin with Zenevieve and Reilynne—interesting. He had been invited to know more about whatever it was they were going over. She was headed over there when she heard the thud of an ax. Gallagher must be chopping wood. It was one of his favorite ways to work out his frustrations.

She followed the rhythmic thudding of the ax until Gallagher stood before her. He wiped the sweat from his brow and picked up the ax. She waited for him to split the wood before saying anything to him.

"Seems like we have enough firewood to last us a while," she joked.

He looked up at her, placing another log on the stump he was using. "At this rate, we're going to need it. All these detours." He sighed, leaned his ax against the log, and sat.

She sat on the ground beside him. "I don't really understand why you're so upset. We always end up going astray for information."

"Not so soon after being attacked. How do we know they aren't hot on our trail?" He glared at her.

She shrugged. "We don't, but Zenevieve insisted we needed to stop. Reilynne agreed, even if she stayed silent for the most part. Have you seen the two of them poring over that scroll? It must have something interesting and hopefully useful in it."

"But what?" Gallagher spat. "They aren't sharing what they/re finding. It's like we're made up of small factions instead of one cohesive group. And only the chosen few can intermingle."

"I'm sure they'll tell us what's what when they've figured it out. Or you can go ask. I don't think they're being secretive on purpose. You know Zenevieve is used to being alone. And Reilynne doesn't have her apprentice with her. So it's different for them."

Gallagher picked up his ax.

Kellesha burst into the clearing. "Do not swing that ax." She held her hand up as if she could physically stop him. Maybe she could. Abria didn't remember what it was like to have magic, much less use it.

Kellesha flicked her wrist, and the ax flew out of Gallagher's hand and into hers on a large gust of wind. She had managed to control the wind for the few feet she needed to get a hold of the ax.

"What's going on?" Abria asked.

"Shhhhh." Kellesha held a finger to her lip. She walked behind Abria and Gallagher. "We have company nearby. I think it's them, or someone here on their orders."

Abria's eyes darted around. "I need to get to the others."

"No, you don't—they're safe. Cas is keeping an on eye on whoever is near us while the others move away from them." Kellesha put a hand on Abria's forearm. "I made sure they were as safe as possible. At least for now."

Abria couldn't just stay there and wait. "If that's the case, I'm going to help Cas." She didn't wait for Kellesha to say okay, or for her to stop her. She just left and made her way back to the campsite.

The hill was to the west of the campsite, and that was the direction Kellesha had gestured to when talking about her sister and the others. So she went east. It wasn't long before she crossed paths with Cas.

"What's going on here?" she asked.

Cas pointed towards a small gully. "They're down there. I don't see Viggo or Maeryn, but the uniforms definitely indicate the king's men."

"Crap, how did they find us so quickly?" Abria watched as the men set up camp. There was no way they could stay here tonight. They needed to pack up camp as quickly as possible and move on. They might even need a new plan. This was too close of a call, especially so soon after being attacked. "Cas, you keep watch. I'm going to tell the others we have to move."

Cas stared at her. He sighed and shifted his focus to the gully.

"Just say whatever it is you're thinking."

Cas turned towards her. "They're in a vulnerable position. We could attack."

"If it was just us, I would attack. But there are too many women with magic here. I don't want to risk any of them getting caught."

"Shouldn't you let them decide whether or not they want to take the risk?" Cas asked.

Abria shrugged. "Probably, but I can't risk them, not yet. We need to be at our best if we are going to defeat the king."

"I'll defer to you." Cas looked back at the campsite below. "I think we're passing up on an opportunity to even the playing field, though."

"I hear you. I just can't risk it, not yet." Abria made her way back to the others, Cas's words repeating in her head. He was right, but she couldn't shake the sense of dread that came over her any time she thought of a sneak attack.

When she got to the clearing where Gallagher had been chopping wood, everyone but Cas was present. Kellesha must have gathered everyone here since it was farther away from the campsite of the king's men, and Abria now had six sets of eyes staring at her.

She cleared her throat. "I don't know what you've been told, but there's a campsite in the gully. It's all king's men."

Someone gasped. Kennara took a small step back. Eljin reached out and put his arm around her, drawing her to his side.

"Are we going to attack?" Gallagher asked, looking fierce with his ax in his hand.

Abria rolled her shoulders back. "No, we're going to pack up quietly and get as far away as possible. Then we'll come up with a new plan."

"But we have them at a disadvantage." Kellesha gestured towards the enemy's camp.

"That's true, but something tells me it's a bad idea to attack. We need to get away and regroup."

Reilynne nodded in agreement. "It's too easy. It could be a trap. Better to sneak away this time. Rushing into a fight is never a good idea, especially with so much at stake."

Abria sighed in relief. At least someone agreed with her. "Reilynne's right. We don't have enough information. Not yet. Now move, quietly."

Thankfully, everyone did just that. Gallagher looked like he wanted to argue, but he stayed quiet. Abria doubted he would have kept his mouth shut if Reilynne hadn't spoken up.

They broke the campsite down in near silence. Everyone moved deliberately, trying not to disturb the sounds of the night. Eljin did more work than anyone else: breaking down Kennara's tent, his tent, and packing up Cas's gear. Everything was almost packed when Zenevieve dropped a cooking pan on a rock, sending birds up into the air and flying away. Abria heard Cas curse, the thud of his footsteps as he ran to the campsite.

"Let's go," he hissed. "They heard that and plan to investigate."

Eljin mounted Whiskey, then offered his hand to Kennara to help her up. Once she mounted, the horse moved with precision, leading the way. The others followed, making as little noise as possible. They were careful to stick to small trails, trying not to disturb the plant life. Once they crossed a main road, they ran, hoping they were far enough ahead to not get caught.

CHAPTER THIRTY-ONE

The sky was streaked with pink clouds as the sun made its way above the horizon, a pleasant sight to see after an arduous night on the run. Kennara tried to keep her eyes open to see the sunrise. She was desperately trying to stay awake as they continued on a narrow path that cut through a meadow. It was unfair of her to sleep while the others walked, even if it was technically possible for her to sleep while sitting on the back of a horse and supported by someone else.

Kennara's head jerked back of its own volition as she tried to stay awake, hitting the surprisingly solid chest of Eljin. His arms tightened around her and his breath tickled her ear.

"It's okay, I won't let you fall," he whispered. "You can sleep. I've got you."

The tension in her body left as she exhaled. She still didn't want to fall asleep, but the cocoon of his arms was warm and safe, and that, coupled with the rhythmic gait of the horse, she was going to lose the battle, so she let herself drift off.

Only to be awakened by Abria calling for the group to halt. It was like she could feel the collective sigh of relief at the thought of stopping, even if it was just for a few hours. She felt Eljin shift behind her as he stopped Whiskey and dismounted. Their eyes met as he looked at her from the ground. He raised a questioning eyebrow, then held his hand out for her. Kennara nodded her assent and dismounted with the help of the prince. This time it felt like she was sliding down his body because he wanted her to, and she wasn't about to complain. When her feet hit the ground, she turned around, his arms still around her waist. She leaned back ever so slightly, just enough to take some of the pressure off her leg.

Kennara watched the others figure out what it was they needed to do to be able to rest as soon as possible. It seemed to take twice as long to do the most mundane of tasks. And it wasn't just her. Everyone moved like they were asleep on their feet, as they did just enough to have a comfortable place to lie down for a brief nap.

She lay down on her bedroll, the same as the rest of the group. Despite her exhaustion, she couldn't sleep. Her mind played their escape over and over again. After what felt like an eternity, she gave up on her quest for sleep. Instead, she snuck away to a small clearing next to where the others slept that was close enough no one would be concerned for her when she wasn't in her bed, but far enough away she would not disturb anyone.

Standing in the clearing, she began the movements Reilynne had taught her during their journey. Her intention was to use this time to calm her nerves and work on her balance. So, she started on both legs and inhaled. Raising her arms out in front of her and balancing on her left leg, she lifted her right leg so her foot was even with her knee.

She let her hands float over her head, bringing them out to her sides in one sharp movement. She tucked her right foot behind her left and slowly turned to the right, letting her arms sweep through the air as she moved. Her goal was to do these movements in one fluid motion. And she was almost there.

She lunged out with her right leg and collapsed to the ground. The day and night of riding wasn't the rest her body needed for her leg to feel strong. She pushed herself off the ground and started again, her movements mirroring what she had just attempted. Except, when it came time to lift her left leg, she kept her toes on the ground to help her balance and to compensate for her lack of strength. This round of the movements was stilted as her leg trembled even with the assistance of the left. She lunged, wobbled, but stayed standing.

Kennara heard a clap from behind her. She turned to see her sister leaning up against a tree.

"Your movements are so fluid now. I'm impressed."

Kennara looked at her sister, trying to decipher if she was placating her. "I fell and wobbled. How can that be fluid?"

"It's a movement you wouldn't have even attempted before this adventure. And now look what you're capable of. I'm proud of you." Kellesha pushed off the tree and walked towards her.

Kennara's eyes burned with tears she refused to let fall. She looked away before her sister noticed her watery gaze. "Thank you."

"Can I join you?" Kellesha asked. "You're doing the patterns Reilynne taught everyone, right?"

Her head jerked back to her sister in surprise. Kellesha wanted to join her? She almost said no. Watching her sister best her at another physical activity wasn't going to help.

Instead, she heard herself say, "Of course, anytime."

The two sisters stood next to each other and went through the movements Kennara had been practicing on her own. For the first time in a long time, Kennara felt like they were in sync. Her sister only paused when she fell, waiting for her to stand. Kellesha never offered advice or told her not to do a move because it was challenging. In fact, it surprised Kennara when her sister didn't even offer her hand to help her up. Someone else might have been bothered by that, but for her, it meant Kellesha had been listening and was adjusting.

Kennara flung herself at her sister, wrapping her arms around her in a crushing hug. She felt Kellesha move her arms to hug her back, which was how they were found moments later, when everyone else stumbled into the small clearing.

"It's about time the two of you made up."

Kennara smiled. "We're getting along—for now." She winked at her sister.

"That's a relief. It will make it easier for me to lay out the plan." Abria turned and walked towards their gear. She clearly expected everyone to follow.

She made eye contact with Eljin and raised an eyebrow. He shrugged and shook his head. Apparently, Abria hadn't shared her plan. Rolling her eyes, she followed everyone back to their gear and food.

Reilynne was busy putting together cold beef and cheese sandwiches for everyone. Gallagher took his place next to Abria like he did whenever she needed moral support. It surprised Kennara to see her sister on the other side of Abria, hand on her shoulder as if she already knew what was going to be said and that it wasn't going to be liked by many.

"Grab some food. Keeping up your energy is going to be important." Abria watched as Reilynne handed out sandwiches.

Kennara watched Abria, the dread that had kept her awake creeping back in and growing to something akin to panic. "Just tell us what you've planned, so we can discuss it." She wasn't sure how well she hid the quiver in her voice.

"I second Kennara." Zenevieve crossed her arms. "Waiting to speak is creating unnecessary tension."

Kennara sat on the ground with her food, Eljin beside her, their knees touching as if he was offering her physical contact to keep her calm. She skimmed over the group, stopping on her sister. Their gazes met and Kellesha nodded, her face filled with concern. Kennara knew her sister was telling her to agree with what Abria had planned. But the lengthy build up and her sister's silence was foreboding, as was the dread that had taken residence in the pit of her stomach. She didn't know what was going to be said, but she felt like she should fight whatever the plan was.

Cas cleared his throat. His hands rested on his hips. "Okay. Enough waiting. What are you proposing?"

Abria looked over at Kennara. "We need to split up."

"No." There was no way she was leaving Kellesha's side.

Abria sighed. "Specifically, you and Kellesha need to split."

"I can't see one reason we need to be separated." Kennara looked to the others to back her up.

No one said a word.

She nudged Eljin. He shrugged.

"We are better together. Especially when we're

speaking to each other." She stared at each person, pleading for someone, anyone, to agree with her.

Reilynne cleared her throat. "She's right, Kennara, splitting up makes sense. Especially since . . ." She trailed off. "That is, both of you are targets of the king. If we split up, we might put a strain on his resources."

"He could be after Eljin. That makes more sense. Are we going to split up into three groups and weaken our resources?"

"He's not after me. You heard them last time. They want your sister," Eljin said.

"Then I need to stay with her. Make sure she's not taken," Kennara protested.

Cas came over and sat beside her. He wrapped his arm around her shoulders. "It's not just your sister that we need to keep safe. You need to stay safe too. And the best way to make sure both of you are safe is to split the two of you up." He squeezed her shoulder. "I know it seems wrong right now. But trust me, it's the best way."

"Would you be so sanguine if you were being split from Eljin?" She spat the question out as the feeling of betrayal weaved its way in with her dread. Why was everyone against her right now?

Gallagher stepped forward. "Actually, that's exactly what's going to happen. Too many people recognize Eljin and Cas together. We need to change the look of the groups."

Kennara almost laughed in Cas's face. She wanted to ask him how it felt being told you couldn't protect someone you cared about. But she kept her mouth shut as she felt tension run through the man who had tried to comfort her and the one who had attempted to make her see reason. She waited for them to argue. But there was silence—

silence so tense it felt like a living, breathing thing, and still no one spoke.

"Here's what I propose: Kennara, Eljin, Reilynne, and Gallagher take the northern route to the castle. It's shorter, but with fewer settled areas. The rest of us will take a more southern route." She drew a map in the dirt in front of her. "We can meet here. At the Grog Barrel."

"Your route is so much farther," Reilynne said, looking at where they would have to backtrack.

"It's a bit longer, but it allows us to gather information and supplies before we head to the castle," Abria explained. "At least this way you can continue to work with Kennara."

"There's a safety concern. If one route is so much longer than the other, one group is going to be sitting around for too long, risking being caught just by not continuing to move," Gallagher added.

"The difference isn't that great when you consider how far south we went during our escape last night, then, calculating the difference in our speeds, everything should work, especially since my group could really use the horses," Abria said as quick as she could.

Kennara's head snapped towards Abria. "I'm to give up my horse as well as my sister? How do you expect me to make the journey without Whiskey?

"The four of you will work together to figure it out. There's a river you have to cross. The ferry is too far away, so it would be difficult to get a horse across, anyway." Abria avoided eye contact while she explained the situation.

Kellesha squatted down in front of her. "Kennara, it's a well-thought-out plan. It should keep both of us safe, and I know you can take care of yourself."

Betrayal joined with all the other emotions she was feeling. "Is that why you were so nice earlier? You knew this was coming, and you were trying to make me feel better about myself?"

Her sister recoiled. "You can't actually believe that." She stood and took a step back, pain crossing her face.

Kennara' twisted her hands together. "No, I don't. Not really. But I don't like this. Everything was decided without talking to all of us. But you knew at least some of it, if not all of it."

"It's not like you think it is." Kellesha glanced back at Abria. "It's not underhanded. And we should have talked to everyone together, but things just sorta happened."

Kennara saw something she couldn't explain pass between her sister and Abria. She wanted to ask her sister about it, find out more. That wasn't going to happen, because they were splitting up, and she was the only one opposed to it.

She stood. "Well, I guess we should get going then, since everyone else is in agreement with this plan. We don't want to waste time and end up getting caught." She limped over to Abria. "You better take care of my sister. I will never forgive you if something happens to her."

Kennara hugged her sister, but didn't have any words. She just clung to her for as long as she could.

CHAPTER THIRTY-TWO

The trail Abria had set for them through the woods was not as easy as Kennara had expected. Even with the use of her cane, she could barely put weight on her leg without fear of falling. It would have concerned her more, if she'd been looking at miles more of forest. That's what should be in front of them, according to map. They should still be days away from the river, but here they were, standing on the edge of the water. Rays of light filtered through trees that appeared to grow out of the rippling river for as far as the eye could see.

It didn't look real to Kennara. How were the trees growing from water so deep they'd need a boat or raft to cross it? It was like the river and the forest were at war with each other. Neither one was willing to give an inch, so, for now, they occupied the same space. It was a stunning sight, even if it brought their travels to a complete halt.

Kennara looked at her companions. They all looked as lost as she was. If the banks of the river were in their normal location, it would have been easy to find a boat to cross. But, here? How were they going to find the necessary transportation?

"We need to find a place to set up camp for tonight and figure out how to cross the river," Kennara said as she looked out at the expanse of water and trees. "Maybe things will look brighter in the morning."

They walked along the new riverbank until they found a clearing wide enough for their tents. Since Kennara didn't have Whiskey, they had decided to only bring two tents. Eljin and Gallagher would share one, while she and Reilynne would take the other one.

Kennara built a fire and lit it with a flick of her wrist. The dinners she made weren't good, but she was proficient at setting up the cook pot and boiling vegetables with a little bit of dried meat for a stew of sorts. She spooned four bowls of stew and broke off some bread. After a day struggling while everyone else carried extra—carried what she should have been carrying—cooking a meal was the least she could do. She moved away from the fire and sat with her bowl of food.

Eljin sat down beside her. "Looks good."

"There's no need to lie. It looks terrible. But at least it's good for you. I'm looking forward to never having to cook again when this is all over," Kennara said as she pushed the vegetables around in her bowl.

Gallagher grabbed one of the bowls she had filled up. He shoveled the food into his mouth. "I think you're getting better, Kennara. Either that, or I'm starving. I'd almost say this tasted good."

She laughed. "At least you're honest. There's nothing quite like hearing your food *almost* tastes good."

Reilynne took her bowl and sat. Kennara waited for her

to join in, but the healer stared out at the river, now shrouded in darkness, in complete silence.

"Is everything okay, Reilynne?" Gallagher asked.

"Yes—well, not really. How are we going to take the northern route as planned if we can't cross the river? I don't see a straightforward solution, just something that will take us days to put together." Reilynne's shoulders sagged. "We don't have days to sit around here building a raft."

Kennara leaned forward, clasping her hands in front of her. "It seems we need to come up with a plan. Anyone have any thoughts?"

"I was trying to figure out how to build a raft, but Reilynne's right. We don't have that much time to spend here." Eljin leaned back on his elbows, kicking his feet out in front of him. His languid pose was a stark contrast to the tension in his eyes.

"I know we're on a bit of a timeline, but it's not like there's a deadline to overthrow the king. What's the big deal if we take a day or two to build a raft? At least we can guarantee that it gets done," Kennara asked. "We can try to make up time later, maybe even buy a horse and cart or something, make it easier for us all to travel."

Eljin's weight shifted beside her. She glanced over to see him raise an eyebrow. She turned to see who he was communicating with. Reilynne shook her head, her movement almost imperceptible.

Their brief exchange irritated her. She crossed her arms. "What's going on? Is there something you two are hiding from me?"

"I don't know what their private conversation was just then, either. If it will help us, I think we should all know about it." Gallagher set his bowl down.

"It's nothing that will help." Reilynne rolled her shoulders back. "The scroll made for some interesting reading, that's all. Nothing to share. And if you really want to know, you can read the scroll yourself."

Kennara wanted to believe her, but there was something Reilynne was holding back, with Eljin's help. If she hadn't been so exhausted, she would fish out the scroll to see what they were hiding. But she was tired, and whatever was in the scroll would not help them come up with a plan. At least it didn't seem like it. Eljin wouldn't keep it a secret if it was that important since they needed the information to put him on the throne.

"Well, if you won't share, maybe this information from my travels will help." Gallagher pulled out a map. "This looks like woods, but about a half-day walk along the river there's a fishing village. It's between a river and a lake. We should be able to find a boat or raft there. It's still a bit of a trek, but it will go quicker than chopping down trees and making a raft."

"How do we know the village isn't flooded?" Reilynne asked.

"We don't, but it hasn't been in the past," Gallagher responded with a shrug.

THE FISHING VILLAGE WAS EVEN CLOSER THAN GALLAGHER explained over dinner. So despite the thick layer of fog making it impossible to see more than a foot in front of them, Kennara and her merry little band stumbled into town mid-morning.

"Eljin and I will go find us some boats. These are pretty

small fisherman boats meant for one to two, so we'll need two boats."

Kennara watched the two men head into town. She wasn't sure what to do while they went off to find transportation.

"Should we stock up on supplies for the rest of the trip? I'm sure our food stock is getting low," Reilynne asked.

Kennara nodded. She took a step forward using her cane, and winced. Yesterday's hike had done her in. But they didn't have room to carry her chair, so walking was a necessity.

Reilynne noticed the grimace. "Is your leg okay?"

"Not really, but we have to keep moving."

"I may not be able to do what you wanted, but I can still help you." Reilynne helped her over to a bench.

Their movements were slow. Kennara had pushed herself yesterday, and her leg was telling her it was time to take a break. Too bad that wasn't an option. Instead, she let Reilynne push her down on to a stone bench. The healer looked around as if she was making sure no one was watching them. The town seemed empty even though it was late enough that it should have been bustling. Kennara attributed it to the gloomy morning. She would have stayed in bed and let the weather pass before doing anything. That was, if she had a proper bed and not just a bedroll on the cold ground.

"This may hurt."

Kennara felt Reilynne's hands brush over her leg, followed by a tingling sensation that turned hot. It didn't feel good, but the tight, gripping pain she had been tolerating all morning dissipated.

"It feels like I've rested for days. Still weak, but I'm not fighting through agonizing pain as well. Thank you."

Reilynne nodded and turned towards the center of town. Kennara followed, assuming they were heading to a market.

THEY HAD JUST FINISHED PURCHASING SUPPLIES IN THE MARKET when Eljin and Gallagher returned, both of them smiling from ear-to-ear. Their jovial nature as they walked up to where she and Reilynne waited not only showed their success in finding a boat, but also made her feel like they could succeed in their mission—something that had felt far away just this morning.

"Two small fishing boats have been obtained." Eljin clapped his hands together, clearly excited by their success.

Gallagher threw his arm around Eljin's shoulders. "It was like it was meant to be. This fisherman was retiring and had been trying to sell his boats for a while now. But he's been struggling."

Eljin picked up where Gallagher had left off. "He normally went off by himself, but sometimes his daughters joined him. So he had two boats for sale. Each one holds two people."

"Let's go, the boats are at the dock." Gallagher grabbed a bag of supplies; Eljin grabbed the other.

The two men led the way to the dock. Kennara assumed it was a temporary dock since the river wasn't always flooded. She would find out soon enough, it seemed, as they made their way through the town streets. One was lined with wood-and-stucco buildings with straw roofs and brightly colored doors. It was as if the townsfolk were trying to bring in color to an otherwise dreary locale. It was almost afternoon, and it was quite grey.

"There they are. Aren't they beautiful?" Gallagher's arm swept out towards two small rowboats floating in the water attached to a tree.

They were one step away from dilapidated. One boat had been painted blue at one point, at least that's what the bits of blue that could be seen here and there indicated. The other one was either never painted or was so worn it was impossible to tell what the original color was. If the two boats weren't already afloat, she would've asked if they were water safe.

"I guess we should split up and get on with it," Kennara said, not moving any closer to the eyesore the guys were calling water transport.

Reilynne looked at the rowboats and raised an eyebrow. "It's time to go. Hopefully, we stay afloat." She walked towards the boats. "Kennara, you and Eljin take that one." She pointed to the one with the peeling blue paint. "We'll take the other one." She gestured to the remaining boat. "How long are we going to be on the water?"

"The fisherman said the river is somewhere between ten and twelve miles wide. Which means we're going to spend a night or two on the boat unless we find an island somewhere along the way."

Kennara watched as the boats danced around in the water. What was it going to be like to sleep in a rowboat? At the moment, it didn't seem like a fun time. Especially as she realized there was no way to get into the boat without getting wet.

She thought about her options and sat on the ground to remove her boots. She wasn't sure how long it was going to take to paddle across the river, but she knew she didn't want to have wet shoes or clothes the entire time.

She tied her boots together and set them on the ground. She then reached for the hem of her dress and pulled it over her head. Standing there in her chemise, which barely brushed the top of her knees, she folded her dress and tucked it under her arm, grabbed her boots and tossed them around her neck.

Taking a deep breath, she stepped into the water. It was cold outside, but it had nothing on the chill of the water. Shivers coursed through her as she took another step forward. Someone else splashed into the water. She looked over to see Eljin hurrying to hold the boat so she could get in. Thankfully, the water was only up to her knees and she was able to climb over the side of the boat without it capsizing. Once in the rowboat she slipped her dress over her head, clenching her teeth to prevent them from chattering as the cold seeped in further.

Splashing continued around her, and she turned to see Eljin grab their packs and some food for the long journey. He leapt into the boat, causing it to violently rock. Kennara grabbed on to the edges, her eyes wide, as her heart plummeted into her stomach, terrified she was going to end up in the water.

"When you get into the boat, try to do it with a little more finesse than Eljin. I would prefer to feel as secure as possible in the boat, not like I'm going to fall into the water before we've even started this part of the trip." Reilynne's tone was clipped.

"Of course. I would never do anything to scare you," Gallagher said.

Eljin touched Kennara's knee. She looked at his hand and then up at him.

"I'm sorry. I didn't mean to rock the boat so much. I really didn't mean to scare you." He looked down at where his hand was on her knee. "You're shaking. Come over here. Let's get some blankets on you and warm you up."

She sat there, unable to stop her body from shaking. It surprised her that the short amount of time she'd spent in the water was affecting her so much. Although it might have something to do with stripping down to her chemise in the crisp weather of late autumn. Not that they could tell it was fall here, surrounded by evergreens.

Eljin pulled the wool blanket from her bedroll around her and tucked her into his side. He then grabbed the oars and paddled into the river. She snuggled closer to him and the warmth of his body. It didn't take long before she stopped shivering. When she did, she took in the sight surrounding her. Here they were floating on water blanketed in fog, surrounded by trees that seemed to grow out of the water. It was both breathtaking and unreal. Like they had paddled into another world. She had caught glimpses of the world from the shore, but skimming across the water with trees everywhere was even more poignant.

Her shivering subsided, so she reluctantly shifted away from Eljin. "I can help paddle."

She felt him stiffen, heard him exhale and his body relax. "Of course, why don't you take this paddle and we can work together, maybe even cover a greater distance?"

She took the paddle from him and sat so they were hip-to-hip. It was easy to work in unison, sitting next to each other. They paddled together in silence for a long time, allowing Gallagher and Reilynne to lead the way across the expanse of the tree-filled river. Kennara watched as the paddle sliced through the water, pushed it away, lifted, dripping, and hovered before slicing into the water again.

The repetitive moment was almost as mesmerizing as the scenery.

The trees thickened around them, slowing them down. The change in speed allowed Kennara a moment to rest. In fact, it seemed like a good time for all of them to rest and float through this patch until the river opened up once again. They needed to make sure they followed a path wide enough for the boat until they reached the river proper.

She put her hand on Eljin's. "Let's rest for a little while."

"You're right, a break will be nice." Eljin stopped and pulled the paddles in. She watched as he signaled their companions. They also stopped paddling.

He rummaged through one pack and pulled out some bread and cheese.

He handed her the food.

"Thank you," she said.

It was hard to see what was happening on the other boat. The fog was thicker than before and the sun had set, leaving streaks of pink and orange in the sky. It wasn't long before moonlight was the only thing illuminating the river.

Kennara sighed. She wanted to tell someone about the journal she had been reading and her theories about it. Actually, she wanted to tell her sister, but that was impossible, and she didn't want to wait until they were reunited to discuss it.

She took the last bite of her dinner and scootched closer to Eljin. He put his arm around her.

"Do you remember the journal the shopkeeper gave me?" She felt him nod. "I'm sure you've seen me reading it. I believe it's the journal of Awel and her human lover's daughter. The human lover is better known as King Balor. He used the magic Awel gifted him to become the first King of Maurasus. He took a queen, not Awel, and they had a son and a daughter. Maurasus has changed hands since then, so you aren't related to any of them. But I think Kellesha and I are the direct descendants of Awel's daughter. Which means we're related to the Five Sisters and King Balor."

Eljin moved them off the bench in the small boat and leaned back. She rested her head on his chest. She felt rather than heard the rumble of his response. He didn't stop her or say she must be mistaken, so she continued on.

"Dalaney—that was her name—lived a quiet life in hiding. She had magic, which was a surprise since her mother had given it up. In fact, according to this journal, she had the magic of more than one element." She looked up at the stars. "Do you think that's even possible, to possess the power of more than one element?"

Eljin pulled her closer to him. "I think it's more than possible. I think it's highly likely it exists, but I also think it's rare.

"What makes you think you're related to Dalaney?"

"There are sketches in the journal. They're of her twin daughters, and they could be Kellesha and me. It's uncanny how much they look like us." Her eyes closed. She felt sleep creeping in, overcoming her. "There's more. The king's other daughter— Maeryn looks just like her. I think we could be related. Not recently related, but through King Balor. It's all in her sketches."

"Did your mother ever say anything to you about it?" he asked.

She answered as she slowly drifted off to sleep. "No, but maybe that's why your uncle is after Kellesha: our relationship to the Five Sisters."

Eljin whispered into her hair something about searching for the wrong sister. She wanted to respond, but sleep took hold, leaving her question unasked.

CHAPTER THIRTY-THREE

The four of them made it to Dradon. Abria knew it was out of their way, but she wanted to check with the local pigeoneer to see if there was any news from others fighting the Quickenings. She also wanted to find out why the king was after Kellesha.

She looked over at the woman walking next to her. Kellesha's dark red hair was barely visible under the hood of her blue cloak. They had argued this morning when she had tried to convince Kellesha to wear something other than her leathers into town, something that might hide who she was, like a dress. The compromise was covering up with the voluminous cloak because a dress would be too much of a hindrance if something were to happen.

"Do we get to stay in a tavern tonight?" Zenevieve asked. "I'm tired of smelling like horse."

Cas laughed, one arm around her waist, the other holding Shadow's reins as the two of them rode together. "Horse smells good on you. And it beats walking."

"I long for a bed that's not dirt." Kellesha sighed. "And pillows. I never thought I would miss pillows so much, but

I'll never complain about a bed with too many pillows ever again."

Abria stopped, only to have Kellesha run into her. She slipped her arm around the twin's waist to prevent her from falling. At least, that's what she told herself. If only it explained why she didn't let go right away. She dropped her arm and took a step back.

"I'm sorry, I didn't mean— That is— I'm sorry." Kellesha looked at her feet as she apologized.

Abria squeezed her shoulder. "No harm done. But you don't need to crash into me to get me to hold you. All you have to do is ask." She looked away, shocked that those words left her mouth. She didn't wait for Kellesha to respond. Abria didn't even look at her to see what her response was. She just turned towards the public house she had stopped in front of. If they were going to spend the night, it would have to be at the Pilgrim's Respite. Not a very clever name since they were in Dradon, where everyone walked to on their pilgrimage.

The tavern stood next to the ancient ruins of a temple said to be the location where Awel gave her magic to King Balor and where they lived before he left her and moved the kingdom's seat to Aleria. It was not an area where Abria liked to spend time. However, plenty of the king's men came here, connecting with King Balor's history—which was why Abria brought them here. She wanted to find out why they were after Kellesha. During the last battle she shouted out that they were her family. She didn't realize until that moment just how important her former charges were to her now.

She glanced over at Kellesha.

"We can stay here tonight. Zenevieve and Kellesha, you need to stay out of the common rooms. I expect there to be king's men here. I'm hoping there's not a scryer in town."

No one moved towards the door. Abria didn't blame them. The building was not what she would describe as inviting. But it was the only place to stay in Dradon, so it would have to do. She looked back at the others. Each of them wore an expression of extreme doubt.

"Come on, it's not that bad." She shrugged. "At the very least, it has beds and hot water."

Zenevieve pushed her way to the door. "What? She said hot water. That's my love language. At least it is right now."

Cas shrugged and followed Zenevieve. "The lady has spoken. I'm going to make sure she doesn't get into any trouble in there." He followed behind the water woman with something akin to interest in his eyes.

Abria held the door for Kellesha to go through, then hurried to catch up to her. Getting more information was crucial, but she was also concerned about what could happen in this place—a place she would describe as hostile territory.

The inside of the public house matched the outside, dreary and drab, but at least for now, it was empty. Abria knew the dining room would fill up later, but the lack of patrons now gave her the opportunity to ensure Kellesha's and Zenevieve's safety. Focused on that current mission, she procured a couple of rooms for the four of them.

"Cas, as the only man in our group, you get a room by yourself tonight. Zenevieve, Kellesha, you're sharing with me." She tossed them the keys. "I've already ordered hot water for our room, Zenevieve. The bath should be ready soon."

Zenevieve rubbed her hands together, glee written all over her face. "I'm ready. The pure bliss of soaking in hot water, especially hot water scented with something, anything, that smells better than horse." She then took the stairs two at a time to get to the room.

Abria gestured to get Zenevieve's attention, but she was too late. "Someone tell her not to leave the room after her bath. We can't risk her or you, Kellesha, getting caught."

"I get it. I'll make sure she stays in the room. Just send up some food for us. If we're going to be stuck in a room, incapable of helping, we can at least indulge in a hot meal." Kellesha moved towards the stairs.

It was like waves of exhaustion radiated off her.

Abria knew she was tired. She also knew Kellesha was a woman of action. The fact she needed to stay hidden tonight would not sit well with her. Abria could relate. She would have a hard time if someone told her to lock herself away while someone else was doing something to further the mission.

"I know you don't want to be stuck in a room, but this would be a good time to rest. You've barely slept since we split from your sister."

Kellesha stopped on the stairs. She didn't turn around. Her lack of movement was the only sign that she was listening.

"I know you're worried about her, but she'll stay safe. The people she's with won't let anything happen to her." Abria watched Kellesha stand on the stairs. She saw her friend's shoulders sag before she continued up the stairs. Abria hated seeing Kellesha upset. She wanted to fix it, take away everything making her upset. She knew it wasn't possible, but it didn't stop her from wishing she could make it happen.

Kellesha moved out of sight. Abria sighed and contemplated going after her. Instead, she turned to the dining room. Might as well see if she could get the information she came for.

She made her way through the maze of empty wooden tables and chairs that had seen better days, noting how every piece she touched rocked due to either uneven legs or uneven floor. She found a suitable table and chair hidden in a corner, and sat. The chair seemed to mutter in protest as she settled in for the evening.

She tapped her fingers on the table as she waited. Sitting still was not a skill she claimed to possess. In fact, she wanted to jump out of her seat in the corner and find someone with information, convince them to talk. She might have done just that, but Cas folding himself to sit on one of the rickety chairs distracted her from her impatience.

He leaned forward, covering her hand with his. "Are you going to tell anyone what we are doing here?"

She looked at his hand and up at him. He squirmed and removed his hand from atop hers.

"I'm surprised you don't already know, or at least have some inkling as to why." She tapped her fingers on the table.

He leaned back in the chair and crossed his arms. "I have a theory. But I would rather hear from you why we backtracked. What do you hope to gain by coming here?"

"Information. Maeryn wanted to take Kellesha, and only her. I want to know why. And this is the only place I could think of that would have loose-lipped king's men." The speed of her tapping fingers increased of its own volition.

Cas nodded and leaned forward. "It's a solid plan. Why aren't you letting anyone else know about it?"

Abria's eyes widened. She had always explained just enough of the plan as she thought the others needed to feel comfortable following her. This group was the first time she had discussed what to do instead of just telling them.

"I'm not in the habit of sharing."

"This might be a good time to start," Cas said before leaning back in the chair.

The door to the public house opened, and a group in the silver-and-black uniform of the king filed into the dining room. They sat on the opposite side of the room, too far for her to hear anything that they had to say. Abria worried she had picked the wrong side of the room to lurk, but it was mere moments before another group filtered in, and then another. The dining room had gone from desolate to packed in mere moments. It happened so fast that it was almost unbelievable.

A small group of soldiers settled near Abria and Cas. She concentrated on distinguishing their voices from all the others in the room. One of the men's voices was deeper than the rest, standing out from the buzzing in the room.

"It's like we've been sent on a wild goose chase," he said as he rubbed his temples. "How are we supposed to find a redheaded woman—one redheaded woman, in a nation filled with redheads? The king is making us look for the proverbial needle in a haystack."

"It's not that bad, George." The guard to his left clapped him on the shoulders. "Didn't you hear? Maeryn and her troops found them, but they got away. I just want to know what's so special about this woman. Why are we after her in the first place?"

"Tomas, it's because of her magic. Magic is the only thing the king cares about nowadays, and she's apparently brimming with it," George responded.

A third man entered the conversation. "It's more than that, comrades. So much more. Maeryn and the king found a prophecy. And this woman is supposedly the only person strong enough to take away his power and, with it, his throne." The man leaned in and whispered, "Some even believe she's the direct descendant of Awel and King Balor."

The others laughed as if some fantastic joke was told.

Abria and Cas stood in silence. They made their way through the raucous crowd. There was much to go over before they left in the morning.

CHAPTER THIRTY-FOUR

Kennara shot up to a sitting position, causing the boat she'd forgot she was sleeping in to rock. She grabbed the side, fear of capsizing coursing through her as water came within inches of sloshing over the sides. Eljin's arm snaked around her waist and pulled her to him, and he wrapped his other arm around her until the rocking stopped. It wasn't until the boat settled that she could breathe again, her fear of ending up in the water dissipating as the two of them sat there together.

"I'm sorry. I forgot where I was." Her voice quivered as she thought about how close she had come to ending up in water she could knew was icy cold.

"Understandable. It's not every day you wake up in a small fisherman's boat." The pitch of his voice vibrated next to her ear.

She could see his exhale float by her. It was so cold. It took every ounce of her self-control not to burrow into Eljin's arms. Instead, she sat there as still as she could, worried if she moved, so would he. And she rather liked where they both were at the moment, even if she knew that the moment must end.

She wasn't sure how long the two of them sat in silence. But now light penetrated the darkness. A blanket of fog surrounded them that not only hindered their vision, but muffled the sounds of nature. She could only hear the lapping of water hitting the side of the boat and Eljin's rhythmic breathing.

"Kennara! Eljin!" Reilynne's voice pierced the quiet.

Kennara squinted, trying to see anyone or anything through the fog.

"Reilynne," she hollered back.

Eljin's arms tightened around her. "You could have waited before responding."

"But then they would worry, and that wouldn't be fair." She sounded breathless.

"True, but if you hadn't said anything, we could have stayed like this longer." His voice sent shivers of longing down her spine.

Where did that come from? She knew she took comfort being around him, but she hadn't realized it had moved past comfort into something more. Or maybe she had, but she hadn't wanted to acknowledge it. With everything changing around her, she was worried that admitting she was feeling something more than friendship for Eljin would somehow destroy the relationship they had. But would it destroy it if he was having the same feelings as her?

It was like he could read her thoughts. He pulled her closer, and the warmth of his body seeped through her clothes, warming her skin. He nuzzled her neck, placing his lips right below her ear for the briefest of seconds. Her head fell to the other side of its own volition, exposing more of her neck.

"Where are the two of you?" Reilynne's voice cut through the fog.

Eljin moaned, sounding frustrated. "We're between trees. There's no land around, though."

"You've described the entire river around us. How's that supposed to help her find us?" Kennara whispered.

She felt him shrug. "I'm not sure, but what else can I do? It's not like my description was inaccurate."

"We should try to paddle to them. At least then, we will be working towards something." Kennara snuggled into his warmth.

"Fine, but I would rather just stay here for a while." He moved away and grabbed the paddles.

"I agree, but we're on a mission." She shifted to sit across from him. The shock of cold against her back made her long to be back in his arms. But he needed to paddle while she talked to the couple in the other boat.

"Reilynne, keep talking. We'll paddle over to you."

The paddle splashed into the water as Eljin prepared to find their friends.

"Okay, Kennara, not sure what to talk about now that I'm put on the spot? But I guess you guys just need to hear where we are so you can make your way towards us." Reilynne's words tumbled over each other with the awkwardness of talking into the foggy void.

The boat moved backwards as Eljin paddled out of the nook of trees where they had slept. As the boat moved across the water, the trees grew farther apart. The river slapped the boat as they tried to move closer to Reilynne's voice. At least she thought they were moving towards the healer.

"She's sounding farther away now. What happened?" Kennara asked.

Eljin stopped paddling. "You're right, she does sound farther away."

She heard a muffled curse from where Eljin sat. She stared at him for longer than necessary; she wasn't sure she had ever heard him curse before. They sat and listened for a bit before he started paddling again. He started going in the direction of where they had slept, then paused. He altered course.

"I'm pretty sure this is the direction we should be going." He continued to paddle, the boat cutting through the water, hopefully in the correct direction this time.

They paddled towards Reilynne's voice for what felt like forever. Until, once again, they were surrounded by trees. The boat was too wide to fit through the openings. They needed to turn around again.

Kennara held out her hands. "I can paddle while you help direct me."

Eljin shrugged, handing her the paddles without a word. She moved to sit in between his legs so she was facing the correct direction. He whispered where to go in her ear as she moved the boat across the water, away from trees, and towards their friends. In her head she repeated, *Find Reilynne*, over and over again until it felt like a mantra. All the while she was paddling, it felt like the boat was pulling them towards something. The pull was always in the same direction as where Eljin said to go, or at least a very similar one. She let the boat lead the way. It wasn't long before they were gliding into place next to Reilynne and Gallagher's boat.

"I'm so happy to actually see you. I was so worried we had lost you during the night. This is such a relief." Reilynne's eyes were filled with water. It was clear she had been crying and was doing her best to hold back her tears right now.

Gallagher took her hand in his. Kennara''s eyes darted over to Eljin. They shared a secret smile at this little development.

"We should tie the boats together so we don't have another morning like this," Gallagher said, his thumb rubbing circles on the back of Reilynne's hand.

Eljin sighed. "That's a good idea," he said loud enough for everyone to hear. "But I would rather wake up with just you," he whispered just for Kennara to hear.

It sent a shiver through her. Maybe her concerns of ruining what they had were for naught. He seemed to have feelings similar to hers. She smiled to herself. They would have to talk once this was all over.

It took two more days to cross the overflowing river. Kennara was tired of sitting, exhausted from worrying about falling into the water, and sick of the lack of privacy. Things had been shared that should not have been shared, especially considering the feelings she had for Eljin. Just thinking about it made her cheeks feel warm. But now her feet were on solid ground and she couldn't remember ever being so happy to walk, especially since right now walking meant relying heavily on her cane.

"I was wondering if you wanted to work on using your magic while we travelled?" Reilynne asked, walking beside her.

The question surprised Kennara. "I've never really

thought about it. I thought I was pretty good at using my magic."

She focused on putting one foot in front of the other, scanning the ground for rocks or anything else that could cause her to trip.

Reilynne chewed on her lip. "You're great at using your magic, but I think it could use refining, especially for battles."

It felt like Reilynne was holding something back, but Kennara didn't know how to discuss what the healer was hiding.

"Okay, if you think I need it, I guess it can't hurt."

Reilynne sighed, the relief she felt palpable. Kennara listened to the instructions the healer gave her. She practiced searching for the element of fire inside her—something she wouldn't normally even think of before using her magic, but Reilynne was insisting on identifying the element she wanted to use. So that's what she did, repeatedly. She told herself she wanted fire, flicked her wrist, and fire appeared in her hands.

"Good. It appears you're right and you do have superb control over accessing your fire magic." Reilynne held her hand up, then dropped it to her side. It was like she had something more to say but didn't know how to say it.

Kennara felt like she needed to say something. "It's always nice to practice. For years, we didn't access our magic for fear of the danger it would bring." She bent over and rubbed her leg. It not only hurt, but she could feel it swelling. Training with Abria made her more comfortable with physical activity, but walking all day was very different from the exercises she had been doing at the beach cottage.

"This looks like a good place to stay for the night. What do you guys think?" Eljin stopped in front of a line of trees.

Kennara looked up at him. "What are you talking about? There's no room to camp."

"Look past the trees."

Beyond the line of trees there was a small clearing; it looked like enough room to set up their two tents. There was a felled tree where she could sit, and a circle of rocks already in place for a fire.

Pain shot through her leg, and she glared at it. Just because she thought about sitting down didn't mean her leg needed to remind her it was there. She took a step forward. If she hadn't had her cane, she would have fallen to the ground. It was probably time for her to stop, but she didn't want to hold her friends back.

Gallagher looked at her as she leaned on her cane. She thought she saw him sigh. "I concur. Let's stop for the night. We need to make sure everyone stays in fighting condition while we travel."

Kennara hated they were deciding to stop for her, but she wasn't willing to push herself any further, so she didn't fight them. She wasn't in the condition to, anyway. Instead, she sat next to the firepit. She got a fire going and set up to cook dinner. More of her stew. It still wasn't very good, but it was nutritious.

Eljin sat beside her, draping his arm over her shoulders. Her eyes darted around, looking for Gallagher and Reilynne.

"They're off collecting wood or some other excuse to go off and be together."

"So, we're alone." Once again, she sounded breathless.

"Yes."

She shifted until she faced him. His arm fell from around her shoulder to her hip. Their gazes connected. His eyes fell to her mouth. She reached up, tangled her fingers in his hair, and pulled his head down to hers until their lips met. He tensed and pulled back. She didn't let him escape. She leaned farther into the kiss, opening her mouth ever so slightly. The tension in his body melted away. He swept her into his arms and pulled her on to his lap.

Their kiss deepened. His tongue swept across her lips and into her mouth. Her tongue tangled with his as her fingers weaved farther into his hair. She felt the heat from his hands on her back and she couldn't help but shiver, wanting more.

When he backed away this time, she let him go, a slight smile on her lips. He kissed her forehead before his arms dropped to his sides, ending their embrace.

He cleared his throat. "Dinner smells good." He ran his hand through his already mussed hair.

"Sure, it does, and you wouldn't want me to burn it. That would detract from the wonderful food I make." She laughed.

"I'm sorry, I don't . . ." He trailed off, fidgeting.

"What happened to the flirty, confident man on the fishing boat?" She twirled the tie on her dress around her finger. "I figured we might want to talk about what's going on between us."

Eljin's eyes were wide. Maybe this wasn't such a good idea. His surprise made her want to take back everything she'd just said. But she didn't want to go into this battle with his uncle and never say anything. The danger was too real; she needed him to know how she felt.

"If you don't want to say anything, you don't have to, but I have to say something. I don't know if we're going to survive this mission we've set out to do." Kennara went from twisting her bodice rope to twisting her hands together.

He put his hand over hers but said nothing. Why was he staying quiet? Isn't the man supposed to express his feelings first?

She sighed. "I think I'm falling for you."

He gathered her into his arms again, holding her tight against his body. He kissed her cheek, then her lips. Then he said against them, "I don't think I'm falling for you."

It was her turn to pull away.

He stopped her, tilting her chin until their eyes met.

"I know I'm in love with you."

CHAPTER THIRTY-FIVE

The night came and went in a blink of an eye. Kennara was still exhausted from the day before, but she also felt like she was floating on air. She smiled thinking about last night as she packed up her bedroll.

"What has you so happy?" Reilynne asked.

Kennara's eyes shot up. "What— That is— It's nothing."

"Sure, you're always this happy packing in the morning." Reilynne raised an eyebrow. "Of course it's something. In fact, I'd be willing to bet it has something to do with how cozy you and Eljin were last night."

"No cozier than you and Gallagher."

It was Reilynne's turn to splutter. "We aren't cozy."

"Sure you aren't."

"Fine, if you don't want to talk yet, I won't force you."

Kennara smiled. "You're only saying that because you don't want to talk about Gallagher." She laughed.

Reilynne grabbed her pack, struggling to get it on to her

back. Not surprisingly, Gallagher was there to help her in mere seconds.

Kennara laughed even louder as she walked over to Eljin. At least she was nice enough to leave them alone to have their moment.

"Did you see Gallagher and Reilynne together? Something's definitely developing between the two of them," Kennara said, quiet enough that only Eljin could hear her.

Eljin wrapped his arms around her waist. "Are you seeing love everywhere because that's what you're feeling?"

She wiggled out of his embrace. "No." She pointed. "Look at them."

Gallagher had taken the pack Reilynne was trying to carry and was repacking so he took more of the weight. He helped Reilynne put on the pack, squeezing her shoulders when he finished. Then he turned her around and kissed her straight on the mouth. From across the clearing, Kennara could see Reilynne blush and smile.

"See. I'm not seeing stuff just because I've got feelings. They are having feelings, just like we are, and it's adorable." Kennara crossed her arms over her chest.

"I stand corrected. Love is in the air. At least something positive is coming from what we've decided to do." Eljin bent down to pick up his pack.

Kennara leaned on her cane. She didn't have a pack to carry. Without Whiskey she couldn't carry much. She shook her head and rolled her shoulders back, trying to push away the feeling of being a burden. Reilynne told her that her body thought it was perfect the way it was, and she was determined to feel the same way, even if thinking that way wasn't natural for her.

They started on their way in silence, the thought of how much fun an adventure would be wearing off with each step. Somewhere between leaving Wreswell and now, the day-to-day had become drudgery. She was ready to do something that made a difference.

Gallagher slowed so he was walking beside her, his pace measured to match hers. "If I'm correct, I think we're ahead of schedule. I was wondering if you would like to stay at an inn for a night or two while I try to contact Abria."

A proper bed with pillows and blankets? There might even be a fireplace in the room. She didn't like the idea of someone making concessions for her, but she also couldn't see turning down being comfortable and warm for a night.

"Honestly, that sounds wonderful. Especially if you think we have the time."

"We do. The flooded river was actually a boon. We covered more ground than we would walking." Gallagher glanced at her cane, then back at her face. "I hope you don't mind me saying this, but you've been doing really well. I don't understand why Abria took both horses."

Kennara smiled. "It worked out. What would we have done with Whiskey to get her across the river? I would have been beside myself if we had to sell her. As much as I wish I wasn't walking every day, it was the right decision."

"I guess I would've done something different, but we're here and you're doing fine," Gallagher said.

Kennara was ready for the conversation to be over. "How far is the inn?"

"I think it's another mile, more or less. Can you push yourself through?" Gallagher asked.

"Of course I can, but I'm definitely looking forward to some pillows. Have I ever told you how much I love pillows?" Kennara said, her tone wistful.

Gallagher threw back his head, laughing. "Kellesha

mentioned it. She told me how your bed was covered in them and how she never understood why you need so many. But after camping for so many nights, she missed your cozy bed."

"She said that? I'm surprised she missed anything about our cottage. She was always wanting to leave." Kennara let her hair shield her face, hiding the tears welling in her eyes as she looked down at her feet. She hoped Kellesha was safe, wherever she was.

"She talked about you all the time. I'm surprised she agreed to splitting up. She was always worried about you, but was so impressed with what you had set your mind to doing." Gallagher continued to pace his steps with hers. "She often wished she was as brave as you."

She was silent, contemplating what her sister had told Gallagher. It seemed out of character for Kellesha, but maybe she didn't know her sister as well as she thought. Maybe she had stopped seeing her twin a long time ago because she was so frustrated with Kellesha's promise to keep her safe. She sighed and shook her head. These were thoughts for another day. She couldn't do anything about it now.

"What has you so deep in thought?" Eljin asked.

It surprised Kennara to see him beside her. When had Gallagher left her side? How had she not noticed?

"It's nothing. Just thinking. Do you know where we're staying tonight?" she changed the subject, not ready to talk.

"I think he said the Faerie Glen Inn. Gallagher told me if we stayed on the path, it wasn't far down the road. Reilynne and Gallagher have made their way to the inn ahead of us. They're going to have rooms set up for us when we get there. Maybe even dinner."

"Dinner." She sighed. The thought of a meal that she

didn't cook had her salivating. If she could, she would speed up to get there quicker, but that wasn't going to happen.

Eljin took her free hand and laced his fingers through hers. They walked like this in companionable silence until they stood in the rain—well, mist—in front of the inn.

The Faerie Glen was an appropriate name for the small inn. It was built between two trees; actually, it would be more accurate to say it was built into two trees. There were ten stairs up to the blue front door that led into the wood-and-plaster building. The roof was made of leaves the size of a person. Condensation from the mist collected on the oversized leaves, beads of water gathered and ran from the green rooftop and dripped onto the ground.

"After you." Eljin gestured up the steps and bowed.

She stepped in front of him, climbing each stair with her left foot first. It was a slow and cumbersome way to climb, but it was all she could manage. She opened the door and walked into the coziest room she had ever seen in her life. If she could have run and thrown herself into one of the oversized armchairs, she would have. They looked like the perfect spot to sit by the fire and read a book. Staring at them wistfully, she couldn't help but long to spend the evening doing just that.

The fire was roaring. A gold-furred dog lay on the rug in front of the fireplace, napping. Kennara wanted to squeal. This place was perfection. She wanted to live here, to never leave. She tripped over a floor rug, but was too happy to care she was falling.

Eljin scooped her up into his arms before she fell and carried her over to the armchair she had been dreaming about.

"Maybe you should sit here while I find Gallagher and Reilynne." He plopped her down into the chair.

She smiled up at him. "Only if you bring me a book to read while you search."

He grabbed a book of lore and dumped it into her lap with a lopsided smile. He winked before he went off to find their friends.

She opened the book, found a story about the Five Sisters, and read. She was ready to get lost in the story.

The low rumble of a dog growling interrupted the words on the page. She reached over to pet the grumbling pup.

"Good book?" a woman asked.

Kennara looked away from the book to answer the woman. When she saw who stood there, her hands shook. They continued to tremor as she took in the white-haired woman they were running from. Her eyes darted around the room, searching for Eljin or Gallagher, but there was no one around to help her. Her palms were sweating, as were a few other places that she didn't want to think about. She didn't know what to do. Her magic wasn't the type she could use inside the inn without destroying it, and it wouldn't even guarantee her escape. Then there were the others. She didn't even know where they were to warn them.

"It is. I particularly like the story of the Five Sisters," Kennara answered, the quaking in her voice barely noticeable.

Maeryn rolled her eyes. "You would like them."

"I'm not the only one. It's a shame the king left her after she gave him her magic." Kennara sat there speaking about one thing, her mind racing as she tried to figure out an escape.

"She was a fool, giving up her magic." Maeryn spat. "Of course he left her. Anyone willing to give up their essence to another person doesn't deserve love."

"It's better to steal it from women?" Kennara asked.

"It's either help him steal it or have him take it from me." Her enemy stared at her as if she was willing her to understand. "Sometimes you don't have much of a choice. It's a kill-or-be-killed situation."

Kennara raised an eyebrow. "I don't know. Seems like you have other options. I know my options haven't been as limited as yours."

"Ah, but you didn't grow up in the castle, under the thumb of the person who now controls how you use your magic. You've been hiding." The woman stood.

Kennara tensed, waiting for Maeryn to make a move against her.

"Relax. I'm not going to do anything to you, this time. In fact, I'll leave you alone until you leave this inn." She brushed her white hair out of her face.

Kennara's jaw dropped. "Why?"

"King Sheamus is as evil as you think he is, and I don't really like him much. He doesn't know I'm here. Which means you get a pass because I don't need to report to him. It won't be like this the next time." She walked away, then stopped. "I won't do anything that risks my magic. It's the reason I help him. If my magic was safe, I might decide he's not worth helping anymore."

CHAPTER THIRTY-SIX

They slipped away from the tavern in the darkest hours of the morning. Abria wanted to avoid as many people as she possibly could, and the only way to do that was to leave while everyone else slept.

Zenevieve rode over to Abria on the back of Whiskey. "I thought we were going to get a good-night's sleep. Leaving while it's still dark out is not a good-night's sleep."

"I'm trying to keep us safe. At least you don't have to walk." She looked at the horse pointedly.

Zenevieve rolled her eyes but didn't say anything else. It was useless to argue. Abria would always decide to be uncomfortable if it meant keeping everyone safe.

Kellesha threw her arm over Abria's shoulder. "I'm glad to be moving again. The inn was dank and uncomfortable. I didn't even want to lie down on the bed, it didn't seem clean."

"You know I can hear you," Zenevieve called back.

Kellesha laughed. "I know, and you have to admit that the place was way worse than a bedroll on the ground."

"True, it was pretty awful. At least the bathwater was

clean and hot. Even if the soap was a sin against humanity. My skin may never be the same."

Cas set his pace to theirs, leading Shadow. "I hope it didn't destroy your lovely skin. That would be a shame."

Their relaxed banter continued as they made their way out of town. It was the most relaxed they had been as a group for a long time, maybe ever.

"Did you hear that?" Cas's tone had shifted from jovial to on-edge.

Zenevieve reined in Whiskey. "What? I didn't hear anything." Her brow creased as she tried to hear whatever Cas heard.

Abria held her breath; if someone was out there, they were in danger. A twig snapped. In a fluid movement, she turned her back towards Kellesha and Cas and drew her sword. She knew they had moved into position with their backs to her. The clopping of hooves on the ground let her know Zenevieve was moving somewhere safer, hopefully out of sight.

Silver and black crashed through the trees, men attacking them at every angle. Abria cursed. They had left in the middle of the night to avoid this. How had the king's men found them?

"There she is."

Fear coursed through Abria's body. She knew that voice. It was one of two that haunted her nightmares. It took all the willpower she had not to give up her position and search for the man who ruined her life. To search out his blond hair and his face with the scar she had given him, cutting through his eyebrow and down his cheek.

"Viggo's here," she spat, her hatred of him apparent to anyone who could hear her.

Cas's shoulder nudged hers as if he was turning to look at her. "Are you sure?"

"Yes, I would recognize that voice anywhere." She wanted to search him out and go after him, end him. But he was after Kellesha. There was no way she was going to let that man get his hands on her.

Swords clanged as the king's men descended on them. Abria knew they could all hold their own, but she didn't like the idea of Kellesha being seen, much less getting caught. Her concern created a new fervor. She used her sword with deadly accuracy, taking out one soldier after another.

There was a break in the onslaught. Abria took that moment to stalk after Viggo. She heard a horse run-off, the sound becoming faint as time lapsed.

"Where did he go?" Abria shouted as her eyes darted around.

Kellesha put her arm over her shoulder. "He fled."

"Which way did he go?" She ran the fight through her head.

"It doesn't matter, we can't go after him," Cas said.

Abria turned and looked in the direction they had come from. "He must have gone off this way. I would have seen him if he had gone the other way." She shrugged Kellesha's arm off her and stalked down to the road, determined to go after Viggo.

Cas's arms wrapped around her waist. He picked her up and threw her over his shoulder. She kicked and punched, swinging her arms this way and that, but Cas was as solid as a rock. And he wasn't letting her go.

"If you were thinking straight, you would tell the rest of us we don't have time to go after him," he said through his teeth, grunting as she squirmed in his arms.

When his words made it through her haze of fear and

anger, she stopped moving. He dropped her. She hit the ground with an *ooof*.

"Was that really necessary?" She stood, brushing herself off.

Cas raised an eyebrow. "If you saw the look in your eye and the grimace on your face, you would know it was necessary."

AFTER HOURS OF WALKING, THE SUN WAS FINALLY COMING UP. Rays of sunlight broke through the canopy of trees. Abria thought about the miles they had walked in silence. She was exhausted from the lack of sleep and the battle that still had her seething. She wanted to destroy Viggo, and the fact she knew he was still out there on a mission to make women miserable for their entire lives only fueled the fire inside her to destroy him.

"Are you ever going to stop sulking?" Kellesha asked as she sidled up next to her.

Abria swung her arm at an offensive branch that was in her way. "I'm not sure. I don't think leaving Viggo around to torture others was the right decision."

She could feel Kellesha's eyes on her.

"But to go after him would be to abandon the rest of us, or put us all in danger. Is that what you want to do? Or does that go against your actual plan?"

Abria could feel the heat of Kellesha's body. She was so close to her, but she was determined to ignore it and stay irritated. "Plans change. We had a chance to make a real change and we ran. It was the wrong decision."

Kellesha squeezed her shoulder, she shivered at the contact. "You know it was the right decision. You just aren't seeing things clearly right now."

"Maybe I am, maybe I'm not." She huffed as she folded her arms across her chest.

Kellesha stopped. "We're trying to overthrow the king. We have bigger fish to fry, as the saying goes."

Zenevieve rode over. "Did someone say fish? Man, that sounds so good right now. If we survive this, I'm going to have a nice fish dinner."

Abria rolled her eyes. "Leave it to someone with water magic to want fish. Now a nice juicy steak, that would be divine, anything but vegetable stew."

"Especially stew made by my sister."

Somehow, the talk of food broke through Abria's anger. She realized she was wrong, and her friends were right. Now wasn't the time to go after Viggo. If she had, it would leave the others abandoned, left to deal with the king on their own. And Viggo would still be around after all this. Then she would take care of him.

The thought of him getting what was coming to him after so long caused her to smile.

"Is that a smile I see? I knew your ire would go away. If I had known the talk of food would do it, I would have brought it up earlier." Kellesha laughed.

Abria laughed. "Well, now you know."

CHAPTER THIRTY-SEVEN

Kennara sat in the chair, unsure what to do. Maeryn said they were safe as long as they stayed here. But how could she trust someone whose purpose was diametrically opposed to hers? And yet, for some reason, she did.

She felt safer here than she would if they decided not to stay, which was why she was still curled up in the chair, a book in her lap, fast asleep, when Eljin came to find her. She felt someone's arms slip under her knees and around her back. For a moment she thought about opening her eyes, but when she took a deep breath in, she smelled pine, and rain, and something that could only be described as Eljin. She kept her eyes shut and burrowed into his chest, wishing she could stay like this forever. There was something she needed to tell him and their friends, though. It was important. And she couldn't go to sleep if she didn't let them know what she learned.

Her eyes popped open. "Put me down; I need to tell you, Gallagher, and Reilynne something important. Are they in the dining room?"

Eljin stopped in the middle of the hall. For a moment, his arms tightened around her, but he did as she said. Removing his arm from behind her knees, he let her legs slide down his body, then pulled her in so they were standing toe to toe.

She couldn't help herself, nor did she want to. Her arms snaked their way around his neck, fingers weaved their way into his hair, and she pulled his lips to hers. The kiss was brief. She didn't allow it to distract her, at least not completely. She sighed as she broke contact and turned to make her way to the dining room.

She could hear the rhythm of Eljin following her. It made her smile; she loved he was doing what she wanted, and she hadn't said much of anything. He lengthened his stride so he could step in front of her and open the dining room door.

She almost squealed when she walked into the room. If the overstuffed chairs by the fireplace were cozy, the dining room was like being wrapped in a blanket while it rained. The dark wood tables covered with mismatched place settings in an array of colors and patterns were so bright and happy she couldn't help but smile. The entire room vibrated with joy.

"Over there." She pointed to their friends who were having an intimate dinner. It was a shame she had to spoil their tête-à-tête.

They weaved through the handful of tables in the room, her eyes looking at every person, ensuring that it wasn't Maeryn. There was no sign of her. It was almost as if she had dreamed the entire encounter.

When they arrived at the table Reilynne and Gallagher were at, Eljin pulled out a chair for her before he took a seat.

"What's so important it roused you from a deep sleep?" Eljin asked.

Kennara leaned forward, placing her hands on the table. "Maeryn is here."

Gallagher's chair scraped against the floor.

"We don't need to leave. She told me we're safe as long as we stay here. King Sheamus doesn't know she's here, so she's not going to report us to him." She leaned back in her chair.

"We need to leave immediately. If she knows we're here, she can set a trap for us. It's too dangerous to stay." Gallagher's leg shook with nervous energy.

Reilynne leaned on the table. "I think we rest here like we planned. She knows where we are, she can attack us here, or she can wait until we leave. Either way, we need to be on guard. What difference does it make if we're here or on the road?"

"She's right, Gallagher, and I can really use a break from all the walking—at least a day." She winced as the request left her mouth.

Eljin looked at her, brow raised. "I was on your side, Gallagher, ready to leave, but maybe we should stick with the original plan. Like Reilynne said, does it matter if we're on edge here or on the road? At least here we have good food and soft beds."

"Do we have rooms for tonight?" Kennara asked.

Eljin's face broke out into a wide grin. "Actually, we have rooms for two nights. Gallagher wanted us to have a full day of rest since we paddled across the river faster than we could walk."

Her head whipped towards Gallagher. "Two nights. We have to stay. I promise I'll be able to move so much faster if I have an entire day to rest my leg."

The things she would do for a day of rest. A day of food that she didn't have to cook. That was something she could look forward to.

"Fine, it's clear I'm outvoted. We'll stay and rest. But stay alert. Maeryn is probably lying, or setting a trap." Gallagher sighed in resignation. "But no matter what we do, we're going to be in danger. Might as well try to get the rest we need before actually confronting the king."

Kennara couldn't help herself. She hugged him. A day without trudging through the forest was something she wouldn't have even dreamed wishing for. Maybe a night, but not an entire day.

AFTER EATING THE TASTIEST MEAL SHE HAD EVER HAD, KENNARA made her way back to her room. She stopped by the front desk just long enough to ask if they could bring hot water up to her room. When the innkeeper said the bath had just been prepared, she wanted to kiss the woman. Even though she assumed Eljin was the one who had ordered the bath, the innkeeper had made it happen.

"Miss, before you go, I've also arranged to have your dress cleaned. There's a dressing gown in the room for you. Just leave what you need cleaned outside your door, and we'll get it back to you as soon as we can."

Kennara smiled. "Careful, I may not be able to stop myself from hugging you if you keep offering to clean my things."

"I take it you've been on the road for a while?" The innkeeper asked.

"We've been travelling for so long, and when we last stayed in a tavern, I didn't appreciate it as much as I should have."

The innkeeper laughed. "Tonight, you'll have to make up for it. Now go, enjoy your bath. Don't forget to set out your clothes."

Kennara would have taken the stairs two at a time if her leg had wanted to cooperate. Instead, she hurried only in her mind, careful not to fall as she made her way to her room.

When she arrived, the maid was closing the door behind her. For a brief moment, something niggled at the back of her brain, but the excitement of soaking in hot water was more important than whatever it was she was supposed to remember.

"Thank you," she said to the maid with a wide smile.

The maid curtsied and scurried off. She shrugged and opened the door. By the fire, there was a copper tub big enough for two to soak in. The task of bringing up the hot water must have been an arduous one. She didn't envy the maid one bit.

Steam rose off the top of the water, and the air filled with the faint aroma of cinnamon and citrus. She sat on the edge of the bed and unlaced her boots. Her desire to hurry was actually slowing her down as she accidentally knotted her laces. She stopped and took a deep breath and carefully prepared for the bath. Taking care not to tie her shoes together, she kicked the boots off and stood. She pulled her dress off and let it drop to the floor at her feet. Naked, she walked to the tub and climbed in, careful not to knock it over or splash water all over the floor. As she sank down into the tub, a blissful moan escaped. The hot water seeped into her muscles, helping them relax for the first time in what felt like forever.

She ducked down under the water, allowing her hair to soak. Pushing it off her face, she came up for air, the steam and fragrance from the bath filling her lungs. She patted around for soap to wash her hair. Not finding it, she used her forearm to wipe away the water dripping from her eyes.

"Here, let me." Eljin's voice interrupted her private soak.

She sat straight up, then sank back down into the water, realizing how exposed she was. Her hand searched for the towel to cover up. Finding it, she pulled it into the water and covered up her front.

She glared at him. "What are you doing in my room?"

"You mean my room? Not that I'm complaining about you being here."

She used her arms to pull herself up until she sat straight with her back against the tub. The wet towel clung to her front, the modesty it provided undermined by how it had become a second skin, leaving next to nothing to the imagination.

Surreptitiously, her gaze made its way around the room, taking in the single bed, Eljin's pack, his coat hanging on the coat rack by the door. More importantly, she noticed the very obvious absence of a dressing gown. With a groan, she sank down underneath the water, the flaming heat in her cheeks a sure indication of just how embarrassed she felt.

Eventually, she peeked above the water, her hair a blanket of red covering her face. She opened her eyes. He was still in the room, facing away from her, but still there.

"If you wouldn't mind going to my room and getting my dressing gown, I'll be out of here as soon as I can," she said, her voice not much louder than a whisper.

He continued to look away from her. "I'll be right back, but there's no need for you to cut your bath short." He walked to the door. "I'm sorry I said anything. I should have just left. But, if you want help washing your hair, I'm willing to play lady's maid for the evening."

CHAPTER THIRTY-EIGHT

Kennara stayed where she was, the relaxed bliss she felt earlier was gone. How did she not notice this wasn't her room? More importantly, how was she ever going to look Eljin in the eyes ever again?

She heard the door open and shut behind her.

"I have your dressing gown." His back was towards her. "What would you like me to do?"

"If you bring it over here, I'll get out of your way." The words left her mouth one on top of the other. "I'll go downstairs and ask them to bring fresh water for you."

Eljin thrust his arm out, the dressing gown in his hand. "You don't have to go— I mean— That is . . ." He trailed off and dropped the gown into a puddle at his feet. He lifted his shirt over his head and dropped it on the floor.

"What are you . . ." She stopped. Whatever she was going to say disappeared as her eyes raked over his chest, barely noticing the amulet he always wore. Her gaze continued down his abdomen, his toned muscles dancing in the candlelit room.

He kicked off his shoes, and then his pants. She stared.

She couldn't help herself. He was so much more muscular than she thought, especially his legs. The definition of muscles in his thighs made her tingle as she watched the candlelight's shadows flicker across his body. Heat pooled between her legs. The thought that she should look away flitted through her mind. Instead, she watched him move towards her.

Who knew Eljin had been hiding that body under his clothes? She certainly hadn't.

"Move forward," he said, his voice strained.

Without thinking, she did exactly what he said. He climbed in behind her, his legs on either side of her. She sat there, back stiff, not sure what to do now, not really comprehending what was happening.

That's not true. She had an idea what was happening. She very much wanted this to go where it was going, but this was Eljin, her friend, and she didn't know how to go there with him.

His fingers weaved their way through her hair and massaged her scalp. The tension that had settled on her shoulders when he originally walked in melted away as his fingers worked through her hair and pressed little circles into her scalp. She sighed as her head fell . He rinsed the soap from her hair, any concerns she had washed away with the soap. He brushes eher hair off her neck, caressing where it had once been with his lips. She leaned back onto him, tilting her head to the side so he had more access to her neck.

He nibbled his way from the base of her neck to her ear, sending shivers down her spine. But she wasn't cold, all she felt was heat. The hot water, his warm body, and the intense fire of desire coursing through her body caused her toes to curl. He softly bit her ear, then nuzzled below it, his breath dancing over her skin, flaming the fire he had started with his lips.

She tilted her head back until her lips found his. She felt his arm behind her neck, and his other hand lightly touched her stomach. Self-conscious thoughts skittered through her brain but when his tongue swept over her lower lip and into her mouth those thoughts disappeared, along with every other thought. It felt like she was only sensations at this point. She shifted to gain better access to his mouth. Water sloshed over the side of the tub. They both stared at the offending spot, breathing heavily.

"Maybe we should take this somewhere with less water and more room," Eljin said against her ear. His breath sent tingles to her toes and everywhere in between.

"I think that's a good idea. I wouldn't want to damage anything." She scrambled out of the tub, no longer thinking about her nakedness, causing even more water to land on the floor.

His eyes raked over her body, much like hers had earlier when he had disrobed. Her hands clenched by her sides as she fought the urge to cover herself. She didn't mind him looking, especially since it was obvious he liked what he saw, but she couldn't remember the last time someone had looked at her naked. And when they did, their eyes definitely had not flashed with desire like Eljin's did.

He leapt out of the tub, and water poured off his body as he stalked towards her. She giggled as he swept her up into his arms and tossed her onto the bed, where she was engulfed by pillows and blankets. He jumped onto the bed and slid next to her. He paused, his eyes questioning. She took his face into her hands and brought his lips down to her, kissing him as if her life depended on it, and maybe it did. Maybe she needed this to feel like she was truly living her life before risking everything. Maybe he did too.

He pulled his head back, his lips so close she could almost feel them when he spoke. "Are you okay?"

She crushed her lips against his, pulling him atop her. Her tongue laying siege to his mouth as one hand tangled in his hair and the other caressed his back. She didn't want to talk, she only wanted to feel. When he moved away and slid down her body, she whimpered at his absence, at the lack of kissing. But then his hands caressed her right leg, starting at her hip and moving their way down to her toes. The light touch was followed by a firm pressure, his hands and fingers working their way up her leg. She lay back into the pillows and let him massage her sore, tired leg to his heart's content.

"That feels divine," she all but moaned into the pillows surrounding her.

"I'm glad you like it. I wish I could do this every night. Especially after a long day of walking or riding."

She smiled. "I'm not going to stop you."

"Oh, really?"

His lips traced where his hands had just been. The sensation changed as the heat she felt in the bath returned. His mouth got closer and closer to her center. She wondered if he would continue on or stop before he got there. It was impossible not to squirm as he inched his way closer to where all the heat in her body had taken up residence.

His arm draped over her hips, holding her in place. He used his other arm to move her legs over his shoulders as he made himself comfortable in between her legs. And then his mouth was there, right where she wanted it, but never would have imagined it. His tongue parted her and swiped up, sending fiery flames down her legs to her toes. His next caress sent the flames up her body, causing her to throw back her head. She wanted to do something, anything, as the sensations intensified, but his arm held her in place as he feasted off her desire.

When she was sure she was going to expire, her fingers found his hair and weaved their way through. She thought she was going to pull him up to kiss her; instead she held him there as he brought her closer to the brink with his tongue. Then his finger slipped inside her. She felt her body tighten. His tongue slowly swiped up one last time and it was like the dam burst. She rode the waves of pleasure and heat flowing through her. As he slid up her until they were face-to- face, he captured her mouth with his, rolling her on top of him.

She felt his hard length press into her core.

"Is this okay?" he asked.

She whimpered in response. When he didn't move, she nodded, desperate for more. Impatient, she didn't wait for him any longer; instead she grabbed his length and held him before she impaled herself and slid down. The initial tinge of pleasure was nothing compared to what she felt once she moved, gasping at the fiery feelings skittering through her. It felt so good she couldn't stop, couldn't think, she just wanted more.

As if he had read her mind, his hands were on her body, lightly caressing at first, but as the tension increased and the flames grew, she felt his fingers rake down her back and grab her ass. She heard a noise. It couldn't have come from her, could it? All thoughts stopped as they burst into flame, her hair wrapped around their pressed together bodies. Their lips met for a soft kiss as everything she felt subsided.

She collapsed on the bed as the room came into focus around her.

"That was . . ." She didn't really know what to say.

"Yeah, it was." Eljin smiled. "I wasn't expecting an actual burst of flames around me. I know I'm good, but I didn't know I was that good." He laughed. "How did you do that and not burn anything?"

"Hmm?" She lay there, not really listening to a word he was saying. Instead, she relished in the afterglow of what they had just done. But the words pierced through her happy haze eventually. "What do you mean, flames around you? Are you hurt? Did anything burn down?"

He grabbed her and tucked her into his side, stroking her back as they lay there. "I'm fine. I don't think anything burned."

She pulled away and leapt out of bed, taking the quilt with her. She scoured the room, looking for any sign of something burning. As she turned, her feet tangled in the blanket she had wrapped around her. She was headed for the ground with no way to stop her fall.

Eljin jumped out of the bed, but he wasn't fast enough. She tumbled to the ground, knocking a wooden side table in the process. "Kenna, are you okay?"

"I'm fine." She hit the floor with both her hands. "I've never accidentally created a fire around me, and I'm worried that I can't control my own magic. Now, as we go to fight the king, the time when I need the most control over my magic. I don't want to be the reason any of us die." Her voice caught on the last word, as tears streamed down her face.

Eljin sat on the floor next to her and gathered her into his arms. "You didn't hurt anyone tonight. In fact, you didn't even singe a blanket. And you will not be the reason any of us get hurt, ever."

"But . . ." She sniffed as she played with the blue amulet that hung around his neck.

"No buts." He pressed his finger to her lips. "You're the strongest one of us all. If anyone's going to save us, it's going to be you."

His words did nothing to set her mind at ease. Instead, her tears turned to sobs, the kind that shook her entire body. Thankfully, he held her and let her cry until there were no more tears left. Exhausted, she sighed against his chest and closed her eyes. He gathered her into his arms and carried her to the bed. There he sat her down, covered her, and climbed in next to her.

CHAPTER THIRTY-NINE

Abria would have thanked anyone that was listening to her when they set up camp that night. They had hiked until the sun rose, throughout the entire day, and well after sunset, shifting directions, even backtracking at one point. Anything to throw off the king's men or anyone else who followed them. Her relief at making it to a clearing and finding the area empty was almost visceral.

"Please tell me we're stopping here." Zenevieve moaned as she rode up beside Abria.

Abria smiled at her. "We are. I think we've lost anyone who might have been following us."

"If anyone was following us, they stopped long ago, probably after our second time backtracking." Kellesha bent over, stretching her back and hamstrings.

Abria stared for too long, but eventually forced herself to look away. "I'm trying to keep us safe."

Kellesha moved on to stretch her arms out, nudging Abria with her hip as she did so. "We know and appreciate it. My feet don't appreciate it, but I do. I feel safe here with you."

Abria blushed and turned away. "I'm not sure how safe anyone's going to feel about dinner. I know you don't want me cooking it at all. If you thought Kennara's stew was barely edible, anything I make is going to be a thousand times worse."

"Is it finally my turn to cook? Prepare yourself for a camp feast like no other." Cas rubbed his hands together. "I've wanted to take over for a while, but I thought Kennara might stab me if I did."

"She needed to feel useful. That's the only reason she took on the task of cooking, plus she's great at lighting the fire. If she'd been able to help set up camp, she would have done that," Kellesha defended.

Cas sighed. "I know. It's why I never offered before. Remember, I've spent a lot of time with her. I'm familiar with her quirks."

Kellesha rolled her shoulders back. "I know you get it. I can't help but defend her, though. It's habit."

"Maybe by the time this is all over, she won't need to do things like cook to know she's useful," Abria added.

Kellesha rested her head on Abria's shoulder. "Here's to hoping."

She froze for a moment, but then she let herself wrap her arm around Kellesha's waist. When Kellesha didn't move away, she sighed in relief. "You know, she was doing a lot better when we split."

Kellesha leaned into her. "I hope she's still doing okay. I really hope nothing has happened to her—them."

Abria didn't know what to say. She had gone to a pigeoneer while they were in Dradon. There hadn't been any messages for her from Gallagher. She'd sent one to him after her eavesdropping session, but they hadn't stayed long enough to get a response, if a response was coming.

"I'm sure they're fine," she said.

Kellesha stepped away and raised a questioning brow. "What makes you think that? Gallagher is the only one in the group trained to fight. Kennara and Eljin were training, but it was cut short when we were attacked. Yes, Kennara was excelling. But now she's walking long distances every day. How strong is she going to be if they're attacked? And their backup is Reilynne, a healer. It's not like she's good in a fight. Afterward, yes, but during, doubtful." Kellesha paced. "I should have fought to stay with them."

Abria grabbed her hand. "The king thinks you're the one he wants. The farther away you are from your sister right now, the better."

"Really? When did you learn that?"

"In Dradon. He thinks you're mentioned in some prophecy," Abria explained.

Kellesha stared at her. "You know I'm not the one that's in the prophecy, right?"

Abria thought about how she should answer the question. She shrugged, deciding the truth was always the best. "I do."

Kellesha tilted her head back and looked at the stars. "Then you must know it's Kennara. She's the one the king wants, the one in the prophecy."

"We don't know that. We just know the king thinks it's one of you." She leaned back to look at the stars as well.

"We know. It's why my mother made me promise to protect her, no matter what. She's the one who needs protecting because she's important. It has to be."

Kellesha's voice caught.

"We will protect her whether she's the one the king wants or not. She's taken care of."

"Are you two going to come and eat?" Cas called out.

They made their way to the campfire. Abria's stomach grumbled at the smell of beef. It had been too long without eating.

Zenevieve sat on a log, already eating a bowl of stew. Cas was next to her, his leg almost touching the woman.

"What were you two gabbing about over there?" Cas asked.

Abria handed Kellesha a bowl. She made eye contact with the redhead and raised a questioning eyebrow. Kellesha nodded almost imperceptibly, giving her permission to share.

Abria sat on a fallen log. The aroma of the stew wafted towards her. Her stomach grumbled and her mouth salivated. She longed to eat, but a conversation needed to happen first.

Abria told the group what she learned in Dradon.

Zenevieve nodded. "I figured as much. I picked up a scroll with the prophecy at the Rare Quill. At least I hope it's the prophecy. But it's not about Kellesha."

"Why do you say that?" Abria questioned.

Zenevieve shifted in her seat. "We all know you think she's pretty special."

Abria felt her cheeks grow warm at the water woman's statement. Was she really that obvious?

"But her magic is not diverse at all. She has decent strength in air magic. But it's not consistent, and it's only air magic. The woman mentioned in the prophecy can control all five elements," Zenevieve continued. She looked over at Kellesha. "I'm sorry. I'm not trying to be mean or anything."

Kellesha waved her hand.

Zenevieve nodded. "After watching Kennara and her use of magic, I'm certain it's her. But the king has no idea he's targeting the wrong sister. The one his spies have said is the stronger of the two."

Kellesha threw her head back, laughing. "Little do they know, my sister's stronger than all of us put together. She doesn't realize it. No one does except me."

Cas put up his hand and swallowed his mouthful of food. "Eljin too. He's known for a while."

Abria nodded. "He's known and fallen for her because of it."

They all had a good laugh on Eljin's behalf.

"It would seem like we need to get to Kennara as soon as we can. Looks like there's more long days ahead of us. We need to get to the Grog Barrel."

They sat around eating their dinner by the firepit, joking and laughing. The camaraderie she felt earlier deepened as they relaxed together.

Abria sat there watching the fire as Cas and Zenevieve went to their tents. The flames were hypnotizing. She felt rather than saw Kellesha sit next to her.

"Was Zenevieve right? Do you think I'm special?"

Abria shifted, continuing to stare at the flames. "What she said is accurate." She pressed her hands into her knees, willing the nerves to subside. This was not a conversation she was planning on having, at least not yet, or ever.

"I—umm—think you're pretty special too." Kellesha stumbled over the words.

Abria couldn't believe her ears. She slowly turned her head towards the woman she was falling for. She reached up, putting her hand on Kellesha's cheek.

"I've been dying to do this."

Abria leaned in until their lips met. Kellesha deepened the kiss, and she savored the feeling of soft lips on hers before she pulled away.

"When this is done, we'll talk about this thing between us." Abria was breathless.

"Yes, but we need to stay focused until this is all over."

CHAPTER FORTY

Kennara followed Gallagher out the back door of the Faerie Glen. Reilynne was behind her, and Eljin took up the rear. They were sneaking out in the middle of the night. She turned back, her eyes wistful as she said her goodbye to the little inn perched between two trees. She was going to miss it. The place had its own sort of magic, one she'd tried to create in her cottage back in Wreswell and had never quite got it right. A sigh escaped as she thought about home.

It wasn't long before the welcoming light of the Faerie Glen was long gone. They wanted to avoid Maeryn and anyone she had with her for as long as they possibly could, which was why they were slipping away in the middle of the night—a plan Gallagher landed on after allowing them to stay and rest for the day. He hoped to travel at night, away from prying eyes until they arrived at the Grog Barrel. She understood his thought process but didn't relish walking through the darkness night after night. Even if it was the smart thing to do. Needless to say, they were all on edge, worried there was someone waiting for them around every dark bend.

She wanted to light a torch or something, even just her finger, to help light their way, but Gallagher feared the light would attract attention. Instead, the mantra, *The ground is solid beneath my feet. I will successfully maneuver over any obstacle. My feet are steady*, ran through her head repeatedly. And for once in her life, it felt like the earth was cooperating. Definitely not something she was used to.

After an interminable length of time, the darkness lifted. Oranges, pinks, and reds painted the sky beyond the trees. She took a deep breath of the misty morning air. She wasn't a fan of waking up early in the mornings, but she loved the smell of them. There was something about a sunrise and morning dew that spoke to her of hope and made her feel like anything was possible. The feeling caused her lips to twitch upward. If they weren't hurrying to a destination, she might have even thrown back her head and twirled. Because this morning, watching the sunrise made her feel light, like they could succeed. She wanted to capture the feeling and bottle it up, hold on to it and use it to bolster her when she felt like all hope was lost. She knew she would feel like that at some point. The question was when and where.

Eljin sidled up beside her, draping his arm over her shoulders. "What has you smiling this morning?"

"The sunrise, isn't it stunning? Doesn't it make you feel like anything is possible?" She smiled up at him, wrapping her arm around his waist.

He smiled back. "And here I thought you were going to say it was me."

"I mean it's not *not* you."

Gallagher groaned. "You two are nauseating."

Kennara laughed. "You're just jealous. We know you want to be flirting with Reilynne right now. I don't mind. I don't think she'd mind either."

He threw up his hands and stomped off.

"Someone didn't have as much fun at the inn as we did." Eljin nudged her as they walked.

"Clearly. Should we help them out?"

Eljin raised an eyebrow. "You want to play matchmaker? I think it's better if they figure it out on their own. Maybe he wants to wait until this"—he gestured to the forest—"is all over."

Kennara shrugged, not really understanding the concept. "Why put off being happy? I'm so worried we won't survive. I feel like I need to live a lifetime while we walk through another forest."

"I don't understand it either, but it's their choice, not ours. We have to let them live their life as they choose."

She folded her arms across her chest. "Fine, I'll admit you have a point. It's just not one that I like very much at all. I would rather them find each other before we try to take the throne."

They walked together in silence for a long time. Kennara couldn't stop thinking about trying to take the throne back and what that would entail. She felt like death was on her mind constantly and she couldn't shake it.

Kennara watched from the tail end of their group as Gallagher stopped, Reilynne continued walking right into him. He caught her in his arms and held her there, pressed up against him. It looked like they were going to kiss. But then they both backed away from each other. Kennara wanted them to have something other than the mission to keep them going, like admitting they cared for one another, but they seemed determined to fight it.

"If we head towards the mountain a little farther, I think there's a cave. We can rest there during the day and travel again at night. We should be safe there, especially if someone stands guard. We can take shifts." Gallagher said.

"Sure thing, captain." Kennara gave a lazy salute, a huge smile on her face.

Gallagher glanced over at her. She thought he was going to reprimand her; instead, he burst out laughing. She was sure he'd laughed before, but whatever it was about her actions had him doubled over.

"Abria . . ." He tried to take a deep breath, but couldn't. "She's always in charge." He took a breath with more success. "I didn't realize I was being so bossy."

"Just a smidge. But we love you for it," Kennara said. "Let's go find this cave. I don't know if I've ever been in a cave. I know I've never napped in one. Or stood guard outside of one. I'm ready for some new experiences." She gestured for him to take the lead.

Gallagher laughed again, not so hard this time, and led the way to their safe haven for the day. They turned and started up the narrowest ridge she had ever seen. There was no way she was going to be able to make it up.

"Ladies first." Gallagher gestured to the path, if he wanted to call it that. She did not.

"Let's go together," Eljin said, holding his hand out to her.

"No." She stood firm.

Eljin took her hand. "It won't be too bad."

She didn't know why, but she took his hand and they climbed the narrow path. They faced the rock front and scootched their way along the narrow ridge inch by painstaking inch. Her back foot slipped. She felt his arm tense and his hand clasp down on hers. Her foot had only slipped a little before he pulled her back to the ledge. She was careful the rest of the way, inching along behind him until they made it to the cave. Once Eljin stepped aside, she threw herself through the opening, landing on her hands and knees, so very thankful to be safely off the ledge.

She stood, brushing her skirts down. The humid cave was behind the trickling of what was probably a roaring waterfall but today was just a steady flow of droplets. As much as she hated to admit it, this was a great place for them to hide for the day. She seriously doubted that Maeryn or anyone else would find them here.

Reilynne stepped through the droplets. "This is very secluded."

"Almost romantic, if we weren't running from an evil king bent on destroying the world as we know it," Kennara added.

Reilynne looked back as Gallagher stepped into the cave. "It could be quite romantic if someone wanted to take advantage of it." Her eyes were wistful.

"Eljin and I can stand guard first if you two want to rest." Kennara smiled.

"That would be lovely. I could definitely use some food and then a nap."

Kennara patted her on the shoulder. "That's exactly what you should do. I think there's some bread in my pack." She grabbed her pack and searched inside until she found the bread. She tossed some to Reilynne and took the rest over to where Eljin was laying out the bedrolls.

"We're standing guard while the two of them rest first. I volunteered us," Kennara said.

"You did? What if I don't want to stand guard first?" He smiled and nudged her.

"I just assumed you wanted to spend every second you could with me. If I'm wrong, I'm sure you could nap somewhere." She shrugged like she didn't care all that much.

"Let's keep this place safe while those two figure things out like you want them to."

CHAPTER FORTY-ONE

They stayed safe in the cave during the day. Kennara napped the last little bit before it was time to pack up and walk through the night. They made it down the ledge right before the sunset and were now headed to the trail towards the Grog Barrel. Gallagher expressed his hope they would make it to the tavern by morning. She thought there was a good chance that they would, barring something disrupting their travel.

The trail they took skirted the edge of the mountain. On the other side of the mountain was the king's castle. She had never been there, but the library in Wreswell had a painting of it in the entrance. She remembered thinking it was a foreboding place, built into the side of a mountain, ensuring it could only be accessed from one direction.

When she had looked at the painting, she never had a desire to see it in person. Now, that's exactly what she was going to do, and it felt like it was going to happen sooner than she was ready.

A chill raced down her spine as she contemplated the impending battle ahead of them.

"Are you cold? Do you want your cloak?" Eljin asked. He noticed everything about her.

As they made their way closer to the castle, she worried more and more about being a distraction when they challenged the king—once again worried someone she loved would come to harm because of her.

She forced a smile. "My cloak would be nice."

He took off his pack, opening it to search for her cloak. "Here it is." He pulled out the heavy fabric.

She stood in one spot, watching him. Tears welled in her eyes as she thought about everything that could go wrong. He stepped in front of her, whirling the cloak around her and fastening it at her neck. She tried to look away, but he captured her chin, tilting her head until their eyes met. A single tear fell and slid down her cheek.

"What's this about?" He wiped the water away with his thumb.

She shrugged. "Fear. I can't stop thinking about death. Yours, Kellesha's, all because I pushed this, or even worse, because I'm not enough to help finish it."

"One day, the voice in your head telling you that you're not enough will no longer exist. I long for the day you can see you like the rest of us do." He dropped a kiss on the tip of her nose. Then he swung his pack on to his back and continued walking, leaving her standing there, mouth agape.

She hurried to catch up, her mantra about not tripping repeating itself in her head even after she was by Eljin's side. She opened her mouth to speak, but the cawing of a bird stopped her.

"I don't think we're alone," she said, reaching out to Eljin.

Out of the corner of her eye, she swore she saw a flash

of white. But if she did, it was gone before she could pinpoint its location.

A stick snapped.

The sound of small rocks tumbling from their home could be heard to her left.

Her palms were damp. She wiped them on her dress as her eyes darted around. But she couldn't see anything in the dark.

Eljin shrugged it off. "It's probably just some nocturnal animals."

"I don't think so, and even if that's all it was, wolves kill humans." The pit of her stomach was in turmoil. Something was not right.

Something howled in the distance.

Why were Gallagher and Reilynne so far ahead of them? They should be closer. If an attack was imminent, their distance from each other made them vulnerable.

"We need to catch up to them. They're too far away." She felt the blood rush out of her face.

Eljin looked at her, and whatever he saw, he knew she was scared. More than scared, terrified. "Okay, we will. Can you run?"

She nodded. Somehow, she would make herself run like she'd never run before. She pictured the ground level in front of her, and her leg braced to give it extra strength. A breeze ruffled her hair and pulled her dress around.

"On the count of three, one . . . two . . ."

He never got to three.

She was running and, for once, it felt like nature was trying to help her rather than make everything more difficult.

Standing before Reilynne, she said, "They're here. It's disrupting the magic. I don't know, everything feels off."

Reilynne nodded, then grabbed Gallagher. He stopped. "This is it. They've located us."

"Are you sure?"

Reilynne nodded. "Kennara is, so I am."

No sooner were the words spoken, than men burst out from behind the trees. On a hill, there was a scryer searching for anyone with magic. The scryer's eyes passed right over her and focused on Reilynne.

What? Why didn't she notice her? She thought back to leaving Wreswell and looked down at the fabric engulfing her. It was the cloak. It hid her from those seeking magic. No wonder the woman wanted her to have it.

Gallagher's sword was drawn. Eljin had dropped his pack and had a dagger in each of his hands. She didn't like the idea of anyone getting close enough for him to actually use his weapons. She took her bow and lit an arrow on fire. Aiming at the scryer, she released it, praying it reached its target. The scryer's screams let her know her arrow had flown true.

She spun around to help Reilynne, who struggled in her fight with one of the attackers, but Kennara couldn't risk shooting him so close to the healer.

Kennara almost screamed, she felt so helpless. Rolling her shoulders back, she moved forward, determined to do something, anything to stop the fighting.

She grabbed her cane in both hands, ready to use it like a staff, when someone grabbed the hood of her cloak and yanked her back.

"I warned you," Maeryn said.

Kennara glared at the woman. "You did, and we've done what we could to avoid you. Now let me go." She grabbed her cloak and yanked it out of Maeryn's hand.

"I can't."

"You won't."

Flames erupted between them. Maeryn released her as the fire crawled over her body. Kennara ducked behind a boulder, out of sight of her enemy, as the woman tried to put out the flames. If only Maeryn knew the flames were an illusion that would not burn her, much like the ones from the other night—a fun new trick Kennara learned she could do.

Unable to move from her spot, Kennara shot multiple arrows into the melee surrounding Reilynne, hoping she didn't hit any of her friends. Those flames burned, and the silver-and-black uniforms of the king's guard were highly flammable. It didn't take long for them to disperse.

Kennara heard Maeryn curse. The white-haired woman flicked her hand and disappeared.

Their enemies having fled, Kennara stumbled to where Reilynne lay on the ground not moving. She fell on her knees at the healer's side.

"I did everything I could, but they just kept coming. I couldn't . . . I couldn't," Gallagher's voice broke, "I couldn't protect her."

Her hands were covered in Reilynne's blood. She searched for the source to find the healer had been run through with wounds the size of a sword's blade on her stomach and again on her back. Blood dripped from both wounds, soaking the dirt below.

Kennara sobbed, gasping for air. She should have stopped this from happening.

Reilynne took in a shaky breath. "I'm losing too much blood. You need to do something." Reilynne grabbed her hand, the grasp weak.

"Tell me what to do," Kennara said, wiping away the tears she couldn't stop with her free hand.

"Pressure, there needs to be pressure on the wounds," Reilynne said, her voice weak and trembling. Her face was pale and clammy under her natural tan, and her dark eyes, glassy and unfocused.

Kennara tore the bottom of her dress and shoved it into the wound on the healer's back. She did her best to ignore Reilynne's pain-laced screams. Gallagher stepped forward, his arm extended; he dropped it. Another strip of Kennara's skirt was pressed into the wound on Reilynne's stomach. She could feel Eljin pacing behind her. Gallagher dropped to the ground and cradled the healer's head in his lap. Kennara watched her grab his hand, grimacing in pain as she did so.

"It's not enough. You have to heal me," Reilynne said so softly Kennara barely heard her. A cough followed the statement, blood mixed in with spittle.

"What? I can't heal you. I don't have heart magic." Kennara sat back, unable to understand, tears streaming down her face. Reilynne must be delirious from the loss of blood.

The movement behind her stopped. Eljin put his hand on her shoulder.

"You can heal her, Kenna." Eljin took a deep breath. "You have to heal her. If you don't, she's going to die."

CHAPTER FORTY-TWO

The days and nights blurred together after a while. Abria had them hiking through the forest on little more than deer tracks or treacherous trails most of the way. It gave them little time to talk during the day because they were concerned more about where they put their feet. The last thing Abria, or any of the others, wanted was an injury. She sighed with relief every night they made it to camp safely after an uneventful day. But as relieved as she was each evening, she was also concerned. Viggo knew the direction they were going, and despite all the detours and cutbacks, she couldn't figure out why they hadn't been attacked again. She was thankful for the lack of attacks, but every night, the knot in the pit of her stomach grew tighter.

Something was wrong.

The others didn't feel it. Perhaps that wasn't true; maybe they did, but they ignored it. Cas and Zenevieve joked around the campfire every night. Abria would be surprised if they weren't sneaking off to each other's tents in the middle of the night. They seemed like an unlikely pair, but their need for adventure had bonded them in an interesting way.

Still, they never discussed what she felt in the air every day: this overwhelming sense of dread, like something was coming that she wouldn't be able to stop.

She didn't know what was wrong. She couldn't even put into words the overwhelming sense of foreboding she felt all the time. Something was going to happen, and she didn't know how to prepare for it.

She tried, though. Each night she worked with Zenevieve, trying to develop her combat skills. Zenevieve hated it, especially after a long day trudging through the forest. But Abria didn't know what was coming. Maybe training her would make all the difference.

After the additional training and dinner, Abria lay by the fire and stared up into the stars. Most nights Kellesha would lay next to her, looking at the stars. Sometimes, Abria expressed her concerns. Other times they just lay there holding hands, looking at the sky. It wasn't much, but it eased the tension she felt enough that she could make it through another day.

It wasn't long before they arrived in Ballenburg. She breathed a sigh of relief. Things felt safer in town. The king might perform the Quickenings in towns and villages, but she didn't think he would send his men to attack them here.

Abria relaxed. She loved villages like this one, where stone buildings lined the narrow streets, and every door was painted a bright color and above each was a sign with unique names that made her think of bedtime stories and better days. Carriages rolled down the main street where all the local businesses had their storefronts. If they were successful in this mission, this was the type of village she wanted to call home.

She directed them down an alley, her attempt to stay away from as many prying eyes as they could. Unfortunately, her plan failed. Men dressed in silver-and-black appeared out of thin air, or so it seemed.

"Where did they come from?" Abria drew her sword, cursing under her breath. The stone buildings closed in around her. Or maybe it was the fact the king's men were swarming them from every direction, trapping them in a narrow alleyway.

She swore under her breath. One more day was all they needed. They would be at the Grog Barrel in one day, meeting with the others. Maybe not safe, but together once again. Instead, they were in this village, surrounded by their enemy.

She felt Kellesha, covered in her cloak, at her back, and Cas to the side of her. They screamed their attack, blades swinging, cutting a path towards an opening in the alley.

"Help!" Zenevieve screamed from the opposite end of the alley.

An evil laugh echoed Zenevieve's screams. It was a laugh Abria heard in her nightmares. Viggo was here, and he had her friend. The words that left her mouth weren't fit for any company, much less decent company. She would not let that man take Zenevieve or anyone else for that matter.

She yelled, charging the men who stood in her way. Cas was beside her, plowing through the king's men just like her, ensuring that Zenevieve was not taken by anyone who supported King Sheamus. The clash of swords clanged in the alley. It was so loud it felt like the air vibrated with sound.

When she was close enough, she reached out and pulled Zenevieve behind her.

Abria looked back to see where Kellesha was. The king's men occupied the space between them. She watched as Kellesha kicked one man in the chest, fracturing an amulet. A blue mist escaped. Unfortunately, the move caused the hood of the cloak to fall off, exposing her deep red braids.

"It's her. The one the king is after," yelled one of the king's men.

Viggo laughed. "Remember, the king wants her alive."

Kellesha screamed as the hoard of attackers surrounded her. Abria watched as Kellesha climbed onto a shop's roof. She ran along the roof line trying to avoid their attackers. At first she succeeded, but the men followed her to the roof, trapping her there.

Abria frantically looked for a way to help her escape, but came up empty. Water flew through the air from somewhere, drenching some soldiers. But it did not distract them from their goal. Kellesha tried to use the water as a distraction; instead she slipped and fell on the other side of the building.

Abria turned towards the space where Zenevieve had been. There was another alley for her to take, the one the guards had been pulling the water woman towards. She stalked to that end of the alley. Turning the corner, she prayed Kellesha was there, hood back in place.

Her prayers were not answered.

Off to her left, there were muffled screams.

A blue cloak lay puddled on the ground, left behind.

She ran to the cloak, picked it off the ground, and let it slide through her fingers as she searched for the twin. Two men dragged a woman clad in leather leggings and a burlap sack over her head.

She knew that was Kellesha, and she had no intention of letting them take her.

She ran after them; her head swinging from one direction to another as she came to each corner. But the village roads had too many twists and turns, making it impossible for her to keep them within eyesight as she tried to follow them.

Was that a pair of boots? She came to the market in the center of town. The tents blocked every hope of her being able to see where Kellesha had been dragged off to. She stood there staring at those cursed white tents, her failure overtaking her.

Cas ran up behind her, out of breath. "Where is she?"

"Gone."

"What do you mean, gone?" he asked.

"What does it look like? They took her. I lost them in the market. I'm pretty sure the whole thing was a trap. And I wasn't prepared for it."

Zenevieve stood next to Abria. "What are we going to do to get her back?"

"Whatever it takes."

CHAPTER FORTY-THREE

Tears streamed down Kennara's face. She didn't know how to do what Reilynne and Eljin were telling her she could do. Why did they think she could heal? That's not the magical power she had.

Gallagher grabbed her shoulder. "You have to try, Kennara; if you don't, she dies."

"Will everyone stop saying that!" Kennara could barely breathe. "I don't have healing powers. I don't know what you want me to do."

Reilynne's lips moved. Kennara bent down to hear what she was trying to say.

"Like we practiced with fire, but think of heart instead. Think of me being healed. The magic will do the rest."

"What if I can't do it? What if I fail you?" Kennara wailed. Her biggest fears were all around her. She was being asked to access something she didn't even believe she had.

Eljin rubbed her shoulders. He whispered in her ear. "Believe. The rest of us already do. Now you need to as well."

She sighed. This was ridiculous, but there was only one

way to see if this was going to work, and it was to attempt what she was being told to do.

She held her hands over Reilynne's wounds and thought about accessing her heart magic.

Was it her imagination, or were her hands glowing pink?

"You're doing it. Don't stop," Gallagher whispered, hope tingeing his words.

"Hold her down. Healing often hurts," Kennara said while she thought about what she wanted to happen. She chanted in her head, *heal her wounds,* until those words were all she heard.

Reilynne gasped as the pink glow of her hands soaked into the wounds. Kennara ignored the healer's whimpers of pain. She let the world around her disappear as she focused on her task. There was nothing else, only healing Reilynne.

Suddenly the magic was gone, and she fell to the ground.

"You did it. The wounds are gone." Eljin's voice was filled with awe.

She lay on the ground, exhausted. Magic always took a toll, but this new level of tired was something else.

"Will somebody please explain how I did that? I have fire magic. That's it."

Reilynne sat up and grabbed Kennara's hand. "Thank you."

"Thank-yous don't answer my questions. How did I do that?"

"Do you remember when I attempted to heal your leg?" Reilynne asked.

Kennara sat up on her elbows. "Of course I do, how could I forget it?"

Reilynne cleared her throat. "Well, other than not being

able to heal your leg, I felt something shocking. I felt your magic. All of it."

She was sure doubt was written all over her face, despite what she had just done. "What do you mean, all of it?"

"You're the only person I've ever met that possesses all five types of magic. When I was attempting to heal you, it was all there at the very center of your being. I don't know how you hold it all inside you. There's so much power there." Reilynne shivered.

"Do you feel okay? Do you need a blanket? My cloak?" Kennara focused on what she understood and could control, not the words her friend was saying.

Reilynne glanced up at Gallagher. "A blanket would be nice. We need to move on soon. I don't want anyone coming back for us." She turned to Kennara. "You believe me, don't you?"

Gallagher came back with a blanket and wrapped it around Reilynne. He gently caressed her cheek. The healer leaned into the small gesture before he stood.

Kennara watched, feeling like she was intruding on a private moment even though it happened during her conversation with Reilynne.

"I don't know what to think. I know I just did something I never would have believed I could do. But wouldn't these powers have shown up before now? I'm sure I've wanted to access the other elements before this moment."

Reilynne smiled. "Are you sure you haven't?"

Kennara's mind raced as little realizations hit her. They had been hiking through rough terrain for days and she hadn't tripped once. She had been repeating something— she couldn't remember what right now—in her head as she walked, hoping she would be steady on her feet. And when they searched for the other boat on the river, in her head, she kept saying *find them*. She remembered the boat pulling in their direction, the same direction Eljin had told her to go, but it had felt like the boat knew the way. Even the ocean incident back at Zenevieve's cottage, she had pictured what she wanted to happen. But the water woman had been there with her magic, so that couldn't have been her. Or could it have?

"Did I cause the wind to pick me up off the ground? And I blamed Kellesha for it for days on end. Like she was trying to trick me. Was I actually the one that did it?"

"I think so. Kellesha had nothing to do with it, and you're the only other one with that magic," Reilynne said softly.

A sob escaped. "I almost let that ruin our relationship. The grudge I held lasted forever. I don't know if I ever really believed that it wasn't her." Kennara cried. "I have to apologize before . . . before we go to the castle."

Kennara stood. She looked around at what needed to be gathered. It wasn't much. She looked at the men. "We need to split up Reilynne's pack. She can't carry it. I'll do what I can, carry as much as I can, but we need to go."

She doubled over suddenly. Her vision blurred, and the world tilted on its axis. She stumbled, righting herself as quickly as she could.

Eljin was already holding on to her, ensuring she didn't fall. "What just happened?"

"Kellesha. She's in trouble," Kennara said, dread taking up residence in the pit of her stomach.

"How do you know?" Gallagher asked.

Kennara glared at him. "I don't know, but I think she's

been hit on the head or she's fainted. Something. It's not good. We need to get to the Grog Barrel and find out what's going on."

"Reilynne needs to rest. If we leave now, she risks not staying healed." Gallagher stood in front of Kennara.

The healer waved him away. He did not move.

"Gallagher, we need to move. Staying here is too risky," the healer said.

Gallagher crossed his arms over his chest, refusing to move.

"Look, I get it. Here's the deal. I just found out I have the power to heal. I'll make sure she stays healthy as we hike. I don't want to lose her any more than you do. Despite not telling me weeks ago about my powers (which could have been useful), she's my friend and mentor."

"You weren't ready," Reilynne muttered.

Kennara raised an eyebrow. "How would you know?"

"You just said it: I'm your mentor. After I couldn't heal you, part of you stopped processing. Then you were so angry at your sister, and almost everyone else. I didn't think you would believe me. If I wasn't dying, I probably would have waited longer."

"At least you're honest." Kennara couldn't help but laugh.

Her laughter changed the tone just enough. Before long, all four of them were laughing. Gallagher relented and repacked with Eljin's help. Kennara instructed them to create a pack for her. Eljin fought the idea, but in the end, she won.

Which was why the four of them were now hiking along the bottom of a mountain. Kennara had given Reilynne her cane. Eljin insisted on finding her a solid branch to use as a walking stick, which she eventually appreciated. Although what helped most was knowing she could use her magic to help her find solid footing. It didn't stop her leg from tiring out, or hurting, but it reduced her likelihood of tripping. And right now, that was a boon.

CHAPTER FORTY-FOUR

Kennara was so happy to see the Grog Barrel in front of them. Hopefully, her sister was there, safe and sound with the others, and what she had felt before had nothing to do with Kellesha at all. She didn't think her hope was reality, but it didn't stop her from wishing it was true.

She looked over at Eljin, who had walked beside her all day but had barely said two words. "Spit it out. I know you want to tell me something."

"I do, but maybe we should wait until we're sitting and other people are around. I would prefer it if you didn't light me on fire," Eljin said before rushing off to walk by Gallagher.

Like she would ever light him on fire . . . for real. What could he want to talk about though? Learning about her magic was almost more than she could handle for one day. However, it seemed like there was going to be more if she let Eljin talk to her tonight.

Who was she kidding? Of course, she was going to sit down with him tonight. She sighed. She would be happy when this was all over, even though she couldn't picture life after confronting the king. Which terrified her.

She shook her head and made her way up the steps to the public house. Straightening her shoulders, she opened the door.

Warmth and ruckus blasted her as she walked in. She longed for the quiet of the library in Wreswell. Funny . . . she hadn't thought about working in the library in such a long time. But she missed the days wandering through the stacks with all the knowledge right at her fingertips. She also missed how cozy her life was in Wreswell. The Faerie Glen had reminded her just how much she loved her and her sister's home.

"I got us a room," Eljin said.

She raised an eyebrow.

He shrugged and smiled. "I didn't think there was any need to pretend. Everyone knows about us. They've probably known longer than we have."

She couldn't help but smile at his logic. Who was she to say it wasn't true? And she would rather sleep in his arms than alone in a bed. "If you say so. Where's Reilynne? I want to check on her before I do anything else."

"Gallagher got them a room. I think he said it was room seven."

"Seems to be going around, this presumptively sharing rooms." She laughed as she found the stairs and walked up to the rooms for the overnight guests.

The narrow hallway definitely didn't have the same ambiance as the Faerie Glen, but the place looked well-tended. She looked at the brass numbers on the doors that shined even in the low light. Seven must be the one at the end of the hall with the open door.

"I . . ." She entered the room, but stopped when she saw

Reilynne and Gallagher sharing an embrace. She took a step back, waited for a bit, then knocked on the door before entering. "I wanted to make sure Reilynne was okay for the night."

They both looked at her, chagrined. She didn't give away that she knew what they had been doing, though. If they wanted to kiss, they should kiss. They were adults. And kissing made the task they had set to accomplish seem a little less burdensome—at least it had for her.

"I'm okay. I don't think I need any more healing for today. Thank you for checking on me, though."

"Of course, you're my first patient. I feel like it's my duty to make sure you're good for the night. If you are, I'll see you in the morning." She turned to leave. "Don't do anything that's going to reopen those wounds. You've told everyone I've seen you heal that it's easy to undo. So don't mess up my first time."

She shut the door as she left, giggling to herself. It was now time to find Eljin and see what he wanted to talk about.

She found him sitting in the public room holding a tankard of ale, or at least, she presumed it was ale. She hobbled through the intricate maze of tables and chairs. He looked so desolate sitting there alone. She wanted to make him smile, which was when her right foot caught on something, probably an uneven board in the wood floor, and she went flying. She tried to catch herself with her other leg, but it twisted in her skirts. The next thing she knew, she had knocked the tankard out of his hands and was sitting on the ground at his feet with her dress twisted around her legs.

He looked at her, concern in his eyes and the set of his mouth.

She looked down, her shoulders shaking.

He dropped to the floor next to her. "Are you okay?"

She looked up, gasping for air, laughing so hard tears streamed down her cheeks. "Yes." She laid her head on his shoulder. "I'm fine, just my normal clumsy self."

"I haven't seen you tumble like that for a while."

"It's the magic. I wasn't using it just now." She laughed even more.

She felt him laugh as well. Laughing felt amazing. She couldn't remember a time it had ever felt so good.

Eljin stood. "Let me help you up."

She offered him her hand; instead, he scooped her up in his arms and plopped her down onto the chair.

"So, what do you want to talk to me about?" she asked, the laughter fading away as the subject turned to something more serious. "Wait, are Abria and the others here yet? Have you seen Kellesha?"

He shook his head, taking her hand in his. "I don't think they're here yet; hopefully tomorrow."

She looked down at their hands as her eyes filled with unshed tears. "Okay then, let's talk about the other thing."

He shifted in his chair as if suddenly he couldn't get comfortable. "When we went to the Rare Quill, Zenevieve found the prophecy her mother had told her about. I have it in my pack because she wanted you to have it when you were ready."

"Why does everyone assume I'm not ready for things? It's so frustrating." It was her turn to shift in her chair.

Eljin looked up. "Because you're constantly beating yourself up, always worried you'll be the reason someone else gets hurt. And if this is an actual prophecy and you are who we think you are, those thoughts can't be clouding your mind."

She frowned. "I hate to break this to you, but those thoughts are always on my mind. They have a home there, and despite giving them notice to vacate, they refuse to leave."

"That may be, but now we don't have much time. So it's come to terms with the prophecy, or risk losing everything."

"Okay, what's in this prophecy, and why do you think it applies to me?" She gestured for a server to come over. "I think I'm going to need a drink for this."

"Come on, Kenna, take this seriously." He glared at her.

She glared right back. "I am taking this seriously. If I'm in some kind of prophecy, I need a drink."

"Fine."

He waited while she ordered two ales from the server. She hesitated, but decided she was hungry, so she ordered steak and potatoes as well. Eljin stayed silent while they waited for her order. When the server came back, Kennara felt her mouth water: she was more than a little hungry.

"Talk while I eat. I'm also in dire need of sleep." She gestured with her fork for him to talk.

His expression was so serious she wanted to laugh. She didn't think he would appreciate that, so she ate while he figured out what to say.

He cleared his throat. "The prophecy talks about a woman, a descendant of the Five Sisters, that can control all the elements."

"And."

"And what? That's you."

"Yeah, but what does she, or I, do? What's the point of the prophecy?"

Eljin sighed. He actually seemed frustrated with her. "You know, just saving humankind from an evil king intent on taking magic away from anyone who possesses it and murdering anyone who gets in his way of obtaining as much power as he can."

"Wait, are you saying I'm the only person who can stop King Sheamus? That's ridiculous. You're the one with the claim to the throne." She dropped her fork on her plate. The clattering it made should have caused people to look over at her, but the room was so loud no one noticed.

"You know, you have a tie to the throne as well. It's an ancient one, but you're a descendant of the Five Sisters. They're the reason we have magic at all."

"We don't know if that's true or not. I was just guessing." Kennara pushed her chair back.

Eljin stood. "Where are you going?"

"Away. I don't want to talk about this anymore." She took a step back, stumbling. Eljin wrapped his hand around her waist, preventing her inevitable fall. "I can't be the chosen one. I can barely walk." She pushed him away, tears streaming down her face, and left.

CHAPTER FORTY-FIVE

Abria sat at the bar, staring into a tankard of ale. She hated the taste of ale. The tankard was heavy in her hands, and she swirled the liquid in the cup then tossed it back. She coughed, the stale liquid hitting her stomach, making it burn. It was what she deserved. All of it. Kellesha was kidnapped and it was all her fault. Everything she had done, all the precautions, it wasn't enough. She had made a promise to keep Kellesha safe and she failed.

Cas sat beside her. He gestured to the barkeep for another round.

"How long do you plan to sit here and sulk?" he asked as the barkeep set down two tankards.

Abria slammed her fist on the table, anger and guilt swirling together inside her until one emotion was indistinguishable from the other. "What do you want me to say? Or do?"

Cas turned towards her, leaning on the bar. "I don't know, maybe remember that we are on a mission. And if we were to meet up with the others, we could formulate a plan to save her."

Abria took another drink of the awful liquid. "You should go without me. Clearly, I don't know how to plan anything to keep anyone safe." She took a swig of ale and grimaced.

Why did people drink this stuff? It wasn't like it got any better the more she drank it.

"No, you're terrible at keeping us safe. We've travelled for miles and you've managed to keep us safe until earlier today." Cas took her tankard away from her. "We all messed up today. I should have stayed next to Kellesha when I saw you were protecting Zenevieve. If I had . . ." Cas swiped his hand across his eyes.

Abria looked at him. She had forgotten that Cas had known the twins for years now. He loved Kellesha too; not in the same way she did, but Kellesha was still important to him. She felt terrible, thinking only of herself and her grief.

She put a hand on his shoulder. "You did what you thought you had to. How long had you trained beside her? You must have thought she could handle herself."

"I wish I had some thought of her capabilities in that moment. But no, all I could think of was Zenevieve. I was so selfish." Cas dropped his head into his hands.

Abria shook her head. "We're quite the pair right now, aren't we? Where is Zenevieve?"

"I got her a private room. I didn't want anyone coming around and feeling her magic."

Abria crossed her arms. "I didn't even think of that. I didn't think about anything but my own failure."

Cas raised his head, his eyes wet. "I want us to have time to wallow in this, but we don't. We need to meet up with the others and get inside that castle before something terrible happens to her."

"How do you know it hasn't happened already?" she

asked, wanting any reason to believe Kellesha was alive and still had her magic.

"Because she's not the one." Cas stood. "The king's not going to do anything to her because she's not the one he wants. Now, are you ready to go?"

She nodded. Now was not the time to sit around in her own guilt, as much as she wanted to do exactly that.

"We have to keep moving." Abria walked beside her friends, leading the horses behind her. "Gallagher and the others should already be at the Grog Barrel."

"We would, too, if you hadn't decided it was necessary to spend time in that awful tavern." Zenevieve shook in an exaggerated shiver of disgust.

Abria focused on putting one foot in front of the other. "I know. I shouldn't have stopped. But I did."

"So we all get to hike through the night because of it," Zenevieve complained.

Abria rolled her eyes. "Yes, that's exactly what we are going to do."

"Fine." Zenevieve huffed and walked off.

"I'll go talk to her," Cas muttered before jogging after the water woman.

Abria watched the two of them talk, Zenevieve's arms gesticulating, Cas trying to touch her shoulder, the woman having none of it. It was clear to Abria that Zenevieve had no intention of calming down. Really, why should she? It was Abria's fault that Kellesha was gone, and now it was her fault they were on the road in the dark, that they were late meeting up with the others.

A twig snapped behind them.

She stopped, spinning around, looking for the source of the noise. "Who's there?"

Cas and Zenevieve stopped walking, stopped arguing, and stared at her.

She drew her sword, waiting for an attack. "Come out, whoever you are?" she called out again when nothing happened.

There was a rustling to her left. She spun to look to see what, if anything, was there. As far as she could see, there was nothing. She moved down the trail until the three of them stood together, the horses behind them.

The sound of a sword sliding against its sheath let her know Cas drew his weapon.

"Maybe we should keep walking," Zenevieve whispered.

Abria nodded. "Let's go, but stay alert."

They continued on their way, Abria flinching every time she heard a noise. She expected the king's men to jump out of the trees. But it never happened, nothing came at them for miles upon miles. The tension followed them as if it was a fourth person.

"It's probably just animals. We are in the forest," Cas muttered.

As if on cue, an owl called out, then off in the distance, a wolf howled.

Abria tried to suppress a laugh, but it escaped, and before long she was laughing uncontrollably. Next to her, Cas started laughing, and a giggle escaped from Zenevieve. They continued like this for a few minutes, the stress of the entire day easing as the laughter subsided.

"Why are we laughing?" Zenevieve asked.

Abria almost started up again. "It was the wolf that did me in. The timing felt like I was being told not to worry about being followed."

"Maybe that's what the wolf was saying. Or maybe it was saying 'hurry up.' Can we please go faster; I'd like to get there some time tonight." Zenevieve walked faster.

"You heard her, let's move." Abria laughed.

The three of them followed the trail until night turned to day. Stars disappeared, replaced by pink clouds and light blue skies. Rays of light cut through the trees, highlighting the morning mist.

"How are we not there yet?" Zenevieve whined.

Cas shrugged. "I don't know; did we lose our way at some point during the night?"

Abria took out the map. "No, it looks like we are still on the correct path. It should be around that bend." She pointed down the road.

"Do I get to eat breakfast when we get there?" Zenevieve asked.

Cas's stomach growled in response to her question. "Apparently, I could use some food as well."

"Sounds like it. We're almost there." Abria tried to sound encouraging, but she was just as exhausted as they were.

She stumbled forward. The night of walking was catching up to her. She looked up. In front of them was their destination. The Grog Barrel.

And standing outside of it was Kennara looking extremely distressed.

CHAPTER FORTY-SIX

Kennara stood outside the Grog Barrel. She knew it was an unnecessary risk being out in the open alone, but she couldn't stand to be inside anymore. It was all too much. She needed fresh air, the feeling of freedom. She sat, thankful for the bench on the porch of the tavern. What she needed was a peaceful place to think through everything she'd learned yesterday. She stared down the road that led to the inn.

Three weary travellers leading two horses made their way up the road. She stared harder—was it her imagination or did they look familiar? She stood, grasping the porch railing as she winced, trying to see if she knew the people walking up. She swore she was looking at Cas, Abria, and Zenevieve; the horses looked like Whiskey and Shadow. It was them.

Trying to find her sister, she looked at the horses. No one was riding; instead, the horses were laden down with gear. Where was Kellesha and why was she not with them?

Her knuckles turned white as her grip tightened on the rail, her mind returning to that moment. Something had happened to Kellesha, she just knew it. She released her grip, her hands and eyes both burning.

Forgetting about everything else, she picked up her skirts and ran towards them. When she tripped and stumbled, she barely noticed it. She had to get to them, find out she was wrong, or if she was right, she needed to know what happened right now.

"Where is she?" she yelled, tears hot on her face blurring her vision. She took a step on her leg. It betrayed her, collapsing beneath her.

Cas scooped her up before she hit the ground. She pushed on his chest, trying to find her twin even though she could feel Kellesha's absence.

"Let's get to the tavern. I'll tell you everything," Abria said.

Kennara pounded her fists on Cas's chest as he cradled her in his arms. "Now, I need to know now. Is she dead?"

Cas tightened his arms around her. "We don't think so."

"You—don't—think—so?" She enunciated each word that came out of her mouth. "You don't know?"

"Please, let's get inside. We'll tell you everything." Abria's voice was tinged with guilt.

Kennara slumped down, the fight leaving her. "Fine, it's not like I can convince you otherwise. Just like I couldn't convince you that splitting up was a bad idea. She's just my twin sister, which is apparently not worth much when you want to find out why she isn't here." She couldn't stop the words, she wasn't sure she wanted to.

They walked in silence the rest of the way. Every now and then she saw Zenevieve look at her, sadness written all over her face. Whatever it was they were waiting to tell her, it wasn't good. Not that she could think of any good reason for her sister not to be here, or anything that would be more worthwhile than meeting here before continuing on to the king.

The door to the tavern swung open.

"Why are you carrying Kennara? Where is Kellesha?" Eljin sounded confused. "Here, give her to me."

"I'm fine. If you set me down, I promise you I can walk the rest of the way," she bit out.

Cas set her down. Eljin reached out to steady her, and she shrugged him off. Everything felt raw right now. She wanted answers, and then she wanted to be left alone.

"I'm going to take the horses to the stable." Zenevieve refused to make eye contact with her.

Kennara walked through the tavern door, pushing past Eljin as she did so. "I assume you want privacy to have this conversation." She glared at Abria, inundating her with orders. "I'm going to get Gallagher and Reilynne; you get a room for the night. Meet me in my room." She continued to the wooden stairway, ignoring the stares of the others.

The pain in her leg was suddenly very noticeable as she climbed the stairs. She wondered if she had the capability of reducing her almost constant pain. She didn't really understand how heart magic worked and while she had healed Reilynne, it had felt more like luck than skill.

Standing in front of their room, she knocked. "We need to talk. Can you come to my room?"

She didn't wait for an answer.

Opening the door to her room, she glanced over at the welcoming fire with scorn. She didn't want to feel comfortable or cozy while her sister was missing. She wanted to take action, go get on Whiskey and search high and low for her sister.

Eljin knocked and stuck his head in the room. "Can I come in?"

"Of course. It's your room too." She waved her acceptance.

"I wasn't sure you would want me here tonight." He walked in, closing the door behind him.

She sighed. "I'm not sure either, but—here we are." She sat on the bed's edge with a huff.

It wasn't long before the others filtered in to the room. It started with Gallagher and Reilynne, confusion written all over their faces, but Eljin held up a hand, asking them to wait.

Abria and Cas walked in a few moments later. Gallagher and Reilynne's faces lit up when they saw them. The absence of Kellesha and Zenevieve became obvious.

The looks on their faces were almost comical. She would have laughed, but she knew something was very wrong, and she didn't have it in her to find humor in the small things.

"Are you going to tell me what happened now? I've made it easy; you won't have to repeat yourself," Kennara said.

Cas looked over at Abria.

"Where are Zenevieve and Kellesha?" Reilynne asked, interrupting the uncomfortable silence.

Abria cleared her throat. Cas reached over and squeezed her shoulder. The warrior woman looked at Kennara, her eyes filled with tears, pleading for forgiveness. Kennara didn't know what she was supposed to forgive, and she couldn't even consider granting it until she knew what had happened.

"We were in Ballenburg when it happened— Wait, I should probably back up a bit." Abria paused, taking a deep breath. "I took us to Dradon to figure out why Maeryn wanted me to hand over your sister."

Kennara focused on Abria's words, surprised when the prophecy was mentioned. She wanted to look over at Eljin, but he didn't need to know she was thinking about what he had told her. Her hand shook when Abria mentioned Viggo. Kennara had never met him, but she feared him almost as much as she feared the king. The stories she'd heard were the things of nightmares. She was thankful they had run into Maeryn. Viggo would never have struck a deal with her.

Abria continued, mentioning their time on the road and their last stop in Ballenburg. Kennara knew this was where whatever had happened, had happened. The words tumbled out of Abria's mouth. How she had gone to protect Zenevieve, leaving Kellesha on her own. That's when the enemy took her sister—when she had been left to fend for herself, because she was strong enough to fend for herself. At least, everyone had thought so; but if she was, why wasn't she around?

No, Kellesha wasn't there. She hadn't been strong enough.

Silence fell over the room when Abria finished retelling the story, and Kennara looked around. They were all waiting for her to speak.

Did they expect her to say it was okay? That they were right in protecting Zenevieve, leaving her sister all on her own for that moment. That it was okay, because it was just for a moment?

Part of her wanted to offer those words to Abria and Cas. But the words would have been empty. She didn't forgive them, not in this moment. Why should she want to do something to make them feel any better? They should have been more careful. All that time spent on edge, worried about something happening, for it to be forgotten in the moment that mattered.

She shook her head before she climbed into bed. She circled through thoughts and emotions as she lay there staring at the door. The only reason she had made it as far as she had was because she knew Kellesha would be by her side soon. And now she wasn't. Kennara didn't know what to do. She didn't know how to continue on this mission without her sister.

"Let me talk to her," Reilynne said.

Eljin tried to deny her, but she insisted.

Kennara heard the woman's footsteps walk across the room to where she was curled up. The bed sank as Reilynne sat on it.

"I won't ask if you're okay. I know you're not." Reilynne placed her hand on her shoulder. "I also know it's almost impossible not to think the worst, but if we leave in the morning, we have a good chance of saving her. They got here as quickly as they could. They've done everything they could."

She sniffed.

Reilynne squeezed her shoulder. "I also know you want to spend time and wallow in all the things you're feeling right now. Unfortunately, we don't have time for that. To save your sister, we need to be at our best. Take tonight, get it all out . . . Cry, scream, whatever you need to do, but you only have tonight. Tomorrow, we need to get back on the road. There needs to be a plan, and we need to get to the castle. End this thing."

Kennara didn't move, she didn't say anything. After a bit, Reilynne got off the bed. Her footsteps retreated to the door. Kennara heard some whispering but didn't understand anything that was said.

Eljin closed the door behind Reilynne. He didn't say anything once the two of them were alone. Instead, he climbed into bed and gathered her into his arms. He dropped a kiss on the top of her head.

The slight gesture broke the floodgate, holding back her tears. Sobs racked her body as she let the news that Kellesha had been kidnapped sink in. Her tears weren't silent as Eljin held her in bed; they were loud and messy, a lot like her relationship with her sister.

But right now, she wanted her sister with her more than anything. She wanted to talk to her sister about her magical powers, powers no one else in the world had. Then there was the prophecy. She wanted Kellesha there to talk it through with her. But now, instead of having the relief of seeing her, Kellesha was another worry, a loss she couldn't handle. If they didn't find her, she wasn't going to be able to continue with this mission. She couldn't do it on her own.

She cried herself to sleep in his arms. Not once did it cross her mind that she wasn't actually alone.

CHAPTER FORTY-SEVEN

Kennara tried to open her eyes, but they felt like they were glued together and her head was pounding. She snuggled under the cover, wishing the light and pain would go away. Eljin's arms pulled her closer to him.

She bolted up. "My sister, she's been kidnapped." She rubbed her crusty, swollen eyes, trying to get them to fully open and failing. The amount she cried the night before meant puffy eyes all day.

Eljin muttered in his sleep, pulling her back into bed.

"Wake up." Kennara shook him.

He slowly came to, smiling when he opened his eyes and saw her sitting above him. His smile drifted away. She assumed the night before was coming back to him. Especially when his eyes clouded over and he raised an eyebrow.

"Are you okay?" he asked.

"Not really, but that's to be expected." She climbed out of bed. "We need to go after Kellesha. I want to leave today. They have a head start on us."

"Okay."

"I don't even want to think about what the king will do to her if he ever finds out she's not the one he's looking for."

"Okay." He got out of bed and started packing up his things.

She stopped. He was shirtless and the way his muscles moved as he moved about the room was mesmerizing. There wasn't time for that. She shook her head, somewhat appalled at herself. How could she be lusting after someone while her sister was in danger?

"Do you have the prophecy? I don't think it's about me, but if the king thinks it's Kellesha, I need to learn everything I can about it." She grabbed her stuff and shoved it into her pack.

Eljin dug around until he found the scroll and handed it to her. She took the leather-wrapped tube, untied the ties, and carefully unrolled it. She was thankful to find it written on paper that was thick, almost like fabric. It would be easy for her to read it on Whiskey's back without worrying about destroying it. She carefully rolled the scroll and secured it before putting it in the leather pouch hanging from her belt.

He picked up both their packs. "Ready?"

She nodded. They made their way downstairs. Kennara was surprised to see everyone else there, all ready to leave.

"The horses are out front. Everyone is ready to go, if you are." Abria turned to leave.

Kennara followed Abria out. She wasn't ready to talk to the woman that let her sister get kidnapped. It was too fresh, the loss too new.

Deep down, she knew it wasn't Abria's fault. She knew Kellesha would never blame anyone but herself. But Kennara needed someone to blame right now and Abria was the easiest, especially since she seemed to wear her guilt.

Whiskey whinnied at her as she walked up. She stroked her horse, offering the animal a carrot as she rested her forehead on her horse's neck. Water filled her eyes, and she tried to blink them back before the tears fell, but she couldn't stop them, overwhelmed by the emotion of being reunited with Whiskey.

Eljin was in front of her when she looked up. He folded her into his arms and held her. She stayed there for a moment, but moved away before the tears turned into something more.

"Let me help you up," he whispered next to her ear.

A quick nod gave him the permission he needed. He grabbed her waist and lifted her up, steadying her as she found her seat on Whiskey.

She looked down, offering him a weak smile. "Thank you." She held out her hand. "Why don't you ride with me? Please."

"Are you sure? I was going to give you space." His eyes questioned.

She nodded. "I don't want to feel alone right now. And I want to go through the prophecy. You can help keep us going in the right direction."

"I can help you with all of those things." He put his foot in the stirrup, took her hand, and swung himself up behind her. He took the reins from her hands.

She leaned back into his chest and sighed as she took out the scroll. She almost pulled out the journal as well, but she feared dropping something and losing it on their journey. Hopefully, she would have time to compare the two later.

She unrolled the scroll with great care and started reading. It wasn't long before she was enraptured by the words. The prophecy was fascinating. As she kept reading, it moved on from ancient history to something, not modern, but definitely more recent. It was almost like reading a history book about the Five Sisters and Awel's daughter. She read through the story of how only women ended up with magic.

If the king had this prophecy, he had to be annoyed. The Five Sisters had given magic to everyone, but over the years men stopped believing in the need for magic. They stopped using it, and eventually the magic stopped working for them. Women, however, cherished their magic. At least, most of them did. Eventually, only women had magic.

The prophecy predicted King Sheamus's rise to power —not specifically him, but the rise of a man so jealous of women having magical power that he turned against his own people to make the power his. How his need for more would overcome everything else. He would steal so much magic that only one person could stop him. A woman, the descendant of Awel and King Balor, the only person to ever possess all five magical elements.

What if the prophecy was true? She just learned she could use all five elements. Could she really be the only person in the world who could do that? How did everything work out that she was alive while King Sheamus was, well, king? And more than anything, why would anyone or anything make her responsible for saving the world? Kellesha and Abria were heroes. She wasn't; she was just normal. It was Kellesha who had always wanted to change the world. The only reason Kennara was on the journey was the need to save her magic. She wanted to be back in Wreswell in the library, reading there, not on the back of a horse.

She put the scroll back into the pouch. The prophecy only described the person who was supposed to defeat the king. It didn't say how, or even give hints as to how. There was no mysterious poem they needed to decipher that would help them form a plan to defeat the king, not even a riddle. Just the note that a woman who possessed the power of the five elements could defeat him. Not even would defeat him, *could* defeat him.

Kennara wanted to scream and throw the scroll to the ground and stomp on it. Not that any of those actions would help, but it might make her feel better.

Seriously, what was the point of a prophecy if it didn't give clues on how to save the world?

Reilynne must have seen her put the prophecy scroll away. "Did reading that help at all?"

"Have you read it?" Kennara asked.

"I have," Reilynne said with a slight shrug.

She looked down at the healer. "Did it help you at all?"

The healer looked away, shaking her head. "No, it confirmed what I thought I felt when I tried to heal your leg, but something was missing. Why have this information out for anyone to find, including King Sheamus? Which he obviously did, because he thinks your sister is the one the prophecy is talking about."

"It does seem to make us a target."

"Did you mother ever talk to you about anything?" Reilynne's words were quiet, as if she wasn't sure she should be asking the question.

Kennara shook her head. "All I know is, she made Kellesha promise to watch over me at all costs. I always thought it was because I was weaker than Kellesha, but now I wonder if it was something else. Something having to do with this."

Eljin's arm tightened around her. "I think she knew about this and the prophecy. She knew you were special," he said right by her ear.

"I have to agree with Eljin. She must have known. But how?" Reilynne looked up at her. "Did your mother ever read something to you, was there a story she told you all the time, or a song she would sing?"

"She told a story to Kellesha and me all the time. It was about two sisters and how each was special in their own way. That the world needed both of them, and they needed each other. It was important that the sisters learned to lean on each other because one day they would be called on to do something that would change the world."

"Interesting," Eljin said.

"Hmm, it sounds like your mother either knew something more or just wanted her daughters to get along. It does make me wonder how Kellesha plays into all this. It's like the prophecy is missing the fact they're twins. I wonder if that was intentional?" Reilynne's eyes looked off into the distance.

"Awel's daughter Dalanay had twins too. It's all in her journal. She even drew pictures of them. They look like Kellesha and me." Kennara reached into her pouch to grab the journal. She handed it to Reilynne. "See, there. Those could be us."

"Do you mind if I take a look at this? Maybe there's a clue in here that will help."

CHAPTER FORTY-EIGHT

Abria stared at the fire as they settled in for the night. It was cold, colder than it had been for most of the journey. The weather had changed as soon as they left the Grog Barrel, and now they were making their way into the mountains. She feared it was only going to get worse as they made their way deeper into the king's territory.

Kennara sank down next to her. "I think you need to talk to Reilynne about her bringing back your magic."

"Why are you bringing that up now?" Abria crossed her arms. "We don't have time to waste on something that's not going to happen."

She watched Kennara as they sat in silence. It was obvious the twin wanted to say more and convince her to do something.

"It could help us save Kellesha."

"You don't know that. You don't even know if it will work." Abria avoided making eye contact with her, focusing on the dancing flames.

Kennara flicked her fingers, and the flames were

suddenly twice their original size. Abria leapt up, ready to protect the twin in front of her.

Kennara also stood and grabbed her by the shoulders, forcing her to do what she was avoiding. "You don't know what will happen, either. It could work, and you using your powers could be the one thing that saves us all. How can you not try?" She dropped her arms. "You say that losing your magic destroyed your life, that an essential part of you was taken away. Why wouldn't you try to get it back? Think about that." Kennara left her, allowing her to contemplate the severity of acting, or rather not acting.

"Because if it doesn't work, it might just destroy me," she muttered to herself.

Abria thought back to those days when she could make the earth do things with a flick of her wrist. She could make rocks fall, plants grow, or make the ground rumble. Her favorite was growing flowers in the winter. The burst of color against the snow made her happy.

When the power was gone, she was lost, and it wasn't just her—there was no one for her to turn to because her mother hadn't been able to function without her power, and she was put in charge of two children that still had magic.

It was one reason why she left them. She didn't know how to protect them when she felt broken. Since then, she discovered who she was without it; she learned to live without it. If she got her magic back, would she still be the same person she was now? Would she have to learn to live all over again?

But Kennara was right, how could she not try if it could help everyone? But how could she allow herself to hope, when it was something part of her wanted so badly that if it didn't work, the disappointment might drown her.

She clenched her fists. "Reilynne!"

The healer stumbled into the clearing, her hair mussed and lips swollen. "What is it?" she asked, breathing heavily.

Abria looked up, her eyes pleading. "Can you try to heal me?"

Reilynne wiped her hands down her skirt. She looked confused, but walked over anyway. "What do you mean?"

Abria looked away. "You said— That is— Why is this so hard?" She took a deep breath. "My magic, you said you could feel it. I want to try to get it back." She looked back at the healer.

Reilynne's shock was almost comical. "Now?"

She nodded. "Before I change my mind."

Gallagher walked into the clearing. "Are you sure?"

"Eavesdropping?"

He shrugged. "I didn't want to interrupt, but I know this is a difficult thing for you. If it doesn't work— I don't want you to spiral. We don't have time for that. And you don't need any extra trauma."

Her eyes burned with tears. He had found her after she left the twins, and he'd been by her side ever since. Through all her battles, mental and physical, he'd been with her. And here he was again, proving what a good friend he was.

"I'm sure. I need to try—what if having my magic made the difference in saving Kellesha, and I didn't even try to get it back? I can't let that happen." She almost said more. That she was in love with Kellesha. But right now, that was something she wanted to hold on to, it was something just for her.

"I don't know what this is going to feel like. It could be painful," Reilynne said, looking around for the others. "If it is as painful as it was being taken, we could probably use two people to hold you down. Where's Cas?"

"You don't have to do this," Gallagher muttered. "You've been through enough pain."

"If it works, it will be worth it." She squeezed his hand.

"And if it doesn't?"

She shrugged. She didn't know what it would be like if it didn't work, but she wouldn't be any worse off than she was now. She just needed to keep that in mind.

Reilynne came back with Cas and Eljin, and Zenevieve followed them. Kennara peeked out of her tent, probably curious as to what all the commotion was about.

Abria threw up her arms. "Might as well all gather round. I'm going to see if I can get my magic back. It could be quite the show."

Zenevieve stifled a giggle. "Kennara and I can go somewhere else, leave you to it, if you don't want an audience."

Abria thought about it. "Actually, I would like to have all of you around. You're like family, and whether this works or not, I could use your support."

They all circled around her.

"This will be easier for me if you lie down."

She did as the healer requested and lay on the cold, hard earth. She tried to relax, but a chill seeped into her bones, causing her to lay there stiff, trying not to shiver. Reilynne kneeled next to her, nodding to the men, letting them know to take the necessary position to hold her down if it came to that. Kennara knelt on the other side of her and took her hand.

"I'm sorry, Kennara, you're going to have to let go. I don't want to take any of your magic away during this process. No physical contact if you have your own magic."

Abria took her hand away and placed it on her waist. The comfort would have been nice, but she understood.

Reilynne closed her eyes, her hands hovering over her.

"There it is," she said so quietly she was almost impossible to hear.

Abria felt a warmth in her chest. Unlike the pain she felt when it was taken, this sensation was pleasant; actually, it was more than pleasant. But almost impossible to describe. She imagined it was what a rose felt like as its petals unfurled and felt the sun hit them for the first time. The cold was replaced by the perfect amount of warmth, the kind that caused a person's muscles to relax. She felt like she was basking in the sun, soaking in a hot bath, and it was one of the most amazing things she had ever felt in her life. Once completely unfurled, it was like she felt whole again after walking around like a part of her was missing for what now felt like forever.

Reilynne wiped her forehead and sat back on her heels. She stood and held a hand out to Abria. Cas and Gallagher helped her to a sitting position.

"Did it work?" Kennara asked.

Abria nodded. She knew exactly what she wanted to do to prove it. She pictured pulling her magic forward and what she wanted to happen.

Everyone's eyes were on her as she flicked her wrist. A plant sprouted from the ground where there had been nothing but a patch of snow. It grew a few inches tall, then continued to fill out and grow.

A bud appeared. It opened, spreading into a beautiful coral color. It was one of the most beautiful flowers she had ever laid eyes on, and her magic had created it. Magic she hadn't felt in years.

Tears ran down her face, and for once in her life, she didn't care who saw them.

CHAPTER FORTY-NINE

Kennara shivered. The cold was almost unbearable. She was never going to travel when it was cold out again. Unless she was sleeping somewhere with a fireplace and the type of bed she could sink into. It would not be sleeping on the ground where the frigid temperatures seeped into a person's bones, making it painful to move. She threw off the covers and her teeth chattered. Searching her pack, she found the cloak from the mysterious shop owner and wrapped it around her. Finally, she stopped shaking.

She peeked outside of her tent. If the fire wasn't going, she wasn't leaving the slightly warmer feeling of her portable home. The fire was going, which almost brought tears to her eyes. She might have cried if she wasn't worried about the water freezing as it travelled down her cheeks.

"I love whoever started the fire. It's frigid," she said as she walked up and rubbed her hands in the radiating heat.

Eljin shuffled his feet and looked away.

"Did you do this?" she asked.

He grinned sheepishly. "I did. I've been watching how

you stack the wood. It took a while, but I finally got it right."

"It's so nice." She held her hands out, appreciating the warmth. She would give anything for a cup of tea. She imagined having a moonberry tart from Quade and her favorite vanilla spice tea, and she salivated.

"I figured we could use it. We're only half a day away from the king's castle, and we need a plan."

Zenevieve walked up and warmed herself by the fire. "What? You don't think we should just knock on the door?"

Cas laughed as he rubbed sleep from his eyes. "That's a strategy, probably not a good one, but it does have the element of surprise going for it."

"Not for long, it doesn't," Abria said, walking up from behind Kennara.

She watched the flames as everyone half joked about what they were heading to do. It was probably a good thing, a way for them to lessen their nerves, but it did nothing to reduce hers, which were causing her hands and knees to tremble for a completely different reason than earlier.

"Shouldn't we try to determine where Kellesha's being held first and foremost? Try to do that without alerting anyone. I want to save her first if that's an option we have." Kennara sat on the rock behind her.

Gallagher sat beside her. "I know someone in the kitchens. I can go talk to them today, find out where Kellesha is being held. Meanwhile, I've given Abria everything I know about the castle. You guys can plan how to get in while I scout."

"I don't like you going by yourself," Reilynne said as she slid her arm around his waist. "It could be dangerous."

He dropped a kiss on the top of her head.

Kennara turned to Eljin and smiled. Eljin wiggled his eyebrows back at her. She knew those two were falling for each other a long time ago. It was nice that they were no longer trying to hide it.

Gallagher turned back to the group. "I shouldn't have too much to worry about. I'm the least recognizable out of all of us."

"He's right. We can't risk sending anyone with magic, or the prince and his guard," Abria said.

Eljin and Cas nodded. Kennara hated they agreed with Abria. She didn't want to leave it to others to find her sister, to make sure she was okay, to ensure she was still alive. This was something she should be a part of, something she needed to be a part of.

She stood. "I want to go with you. What if this is the one chance to get my sister back and you can't do it on your own? I'll burn the place down if I have to."

Gallagher turned to her. "You need to stay here and come up with the plan, one that aligns with whatever all of you read in that prophecy."

She opened her mouth to argue with him, to tell him why she needed to go.

Gallagher grabbed her shoulders. "Trust me, if I think there's an immediate threat to her, I will do whatever I can to get her out. But this trip is about gathering information, not saving her. And if you come, I don't think you'll be able to stop yourself from doing just that."

She looked at him, saw the truth of what he was saying in his warm brown eyes. She didn't like it, but she could acknowledge the truth of his words.

"Go, before I decide to follow you." She waved him away.

"Good thing I was already ready to go." He hugged her,

then turned to Reilynne and wrapped his arms around her. "I'll be back as soon as I can." With those last words, he walked out of the clearing.

Kennara turned back to the group. "Well, we need a plan if this is going to work. I don't want to go in there, trying to beat the most powerful man in the realm and winging it." She sat back on the rock.

"Abria, I have an idea, and I doubt it's something Gallagher told you about," Eljin said as he looked at everyone. "There's a secret tunnel that leads out of the castle. It's how we escaped all those years ago. I don't think many people know about it. I doubt King Sheamus does. He found us on the road."

Kennara watched as he drew a map of the keep in the dirt. He sketched the way up to where the tunnel was located. She didn't like the idea of going in through the tunnel. Something about it seemed wrong. How could the king not know about it? He had grown up in the castle and lived there since he usurped the throne.

"Is there another way in? Maybe through the kitchens, or some other servants' entrance?" She twisted her hands. "I can't believe he doesn't know about the tunnel."

Eljin shrugged. "My mom didn't know about it, so I assumed my brother and I found it and no one else ever knew about it."

"That seems unlikely. How could they live there all their lives and not know?" She raised an eyebrow. "It makes sense your mother might've not known, but your father and uncle—didn't they grow up playing here just like you did?"

Abria stepped in. "Are there other options?"

Eljin was silent. He shook his head. "Not that would

keep our entrance quiet." He paused. "That's not completely true, but the other is dangerous."

"It's all dangerous," Zenevieve chimed in, stating the obvious.

Kennara looked at Eljin, tapping her foot. "What is this other way?"

"They use ropes and baskets to get the supplies into the castle. The entrance, if you want to call it that, is at the top of a sheer cliff face. The only way to get up there is in a basket. But that's reserved for supplies. Servants pull the basket up when a shipment comes in. I don't even know if it's strong enough to hold a person."

"Of course, it's strong enough to hoist up a person. They pull up cows." Zenevieve rolled her eyes.

"I think we should try that," Kennara offered.

"I don't." Cas listed all the reasons he didn't think it would work. "It feels rather exposed, just dangling in the air, hoping the person bringing you up is on your side. What if it's someone like Viggo or Maeryn? We're dead before we even get into the castle. There are too many variables."

Abria shook her head. "Cas is right: it's way too exposed, and we would have to have someone up top we could trust. We don't have time to make that happen. Maybe if there was a way to let Gallagher know it was necessary."

"Fine, we'll go in through the tunnels." Kennara pressed her hands down on her knees. "Once we're in, we'll free Kellesha and then—"

"—and then it's off to the king to end this once and for all." Eljin crossed his arms.

CHAPTER FIFTY

The day was the slowest day in the history of days; at least it was the slowest of days in her existence. Kennara prided herself on her patience at being good at waiting. But whatever skills she once had were gone. Where was Gallagher? Shouldn't he be back by now?

She turned towards the clearing where everyone else sat around the campfire. Abria was pacing. It was like she was doing anything she could to expend the nervous energy that resided in her body. Kennara wanted to pace with her, but it always made her feel more frustrated, not less.

Instead, she continually accessed her magic and released it. She went through each of the elements, calling one forward after another, then letting go. There was a part of her that didn't really believe she possessed the magic that she did. Like she would wake up one morning and it would be gone, given to someone who deserved it more. But there was another part of her that felt . . . complete. As if finding out all this magic was inside her somehow made sense.

Right now, she was leaning into that part of her. If she was going to storm the castle and the king, she needed to believe she could do what was necessary.

There was the sound of rolling rocks and snapping wood.

"I think he's back," she said to anyone listening. "Either that or we need to be prepared for an ambush."

Abria stopped walking, her gaze following where Kennara was pointing.

Gallagher burst into the clearing, out of breath. "She's there. They haven't touched her. According to Sera, she's been locked in the tower this entire time, and the king hasn't even gone to see her."

Abria ran over to Gallagher, putting her arm around his waist and taking him to the fire. "He hasn't even gone to see her? That doesn't make any sense at all."

"It has something to do with the prophecy that he has. Tomorrow is the full moon, and his scroll says something about needing the full moon." Gallagher sat on the edge of a rock near the fire.

"This seems too good to be true," she said as she used her cane to make her way through the camp.

Eljin stood as she approached, always the gentleman, even if they planned a rescue mission and putting an end to his uncle. She took the seat he was offering. He sat next to her casually, draping his arm across her shoulders.

"It does, but even if it is, does it matter?" Zenevieve asked. "I mean, we're still going to save her. Which means storming the tower."

"She's right," Cas said.

Zenevieve smiled. "Say it again. I really enjoy being told I'm right." She laughed.

Kennara leaned forward. Eljin's arm dropped to her back. There, he rubbed her neck lightly.

"Where's the tower she's being held in?" She held the stick out to Gallagher.

He stood and sketched it out. The tower was close to the supply drop off, the opposite side from the secret tunnels Eljin wanted them to use to get into the castle.

"I wonder if we should split up," Kennara offered. "Some of us could try the tunnels, and the rest could climb the rope and get the others up in the basket."

"I don't like it. We've spent too much time split up." Eljin kicked a rock with his booted foot.

"You may not like it, just like I didn't like it before, but I think it's the right thing to do." She looked around, hoping someone would agree with her. She didn't want to try to sneak in all together.

Abria was the only one who would look at her. "I hear you, and I don't disagree. We just don't have the supplies to get up there safely. I think we take advantage of the tunnels and then split up." Abria took the stick and used it to point out where everyone should go. "I'll go with Reilynne and Gallagher to get Kellesha; the rest of you need to find the king."

"I don't think it's the right move, but since I'm outvoted, I guess it's what we're doing." Kennara stood. "We leave at nightfall."

She walked back to where she was practicing earlier. Instead of practicing her magic, she went through the physical movements Abria and Reilynne taught her, focusing on her breathing, core, and balance.

Reilynne and Zenevieve joined her. The silent company was reassuring. Together they went through the moves, inhaling and exhaling with the rhythm of her steps. They were lost in the exercise when Abria came over and told them it was time to leave.

The walk to the castle wasn't that far, but it was challenging, steep. The keep was built into the side of the mountain to protect it from attack; it was a tactical nightmare to approach in secret. Thankfully, their band of renegades was small enough they shouldn't be noticed.

The underground passage was on the west side of the castle behind a waterwheel powered by a waterfall. There were steps cut into the mountain that led to the waterwheel. Eljin mentioned they had been there so long no one knew who had created them. Now they were used to maintain the waterwheel. They were going to use those stairs to get to the tunnels.

"Do you know of any servant halls? Like from the kitchen to the dining hall, or any other rooms in the keep?" Abria asked. "My mother mentioned them when she was delivering her baked goods to the manor homes."

Zenevieve clapped her hands. "My mother mentioned there were some in the castle. I didn't pay much attention at the time, but they are there."

"We need to find them and use them once we're inside." Kennara grabbed Zenevieve's arm. "What do you remember about them or what your mother said about them?"

"Not much. I was a bitter kid sick of being stuck in a cottage on the beach with no one else around."

"Think." She shook the water woman. "We need to know where some of those go."

Zenevieve shook her off. "Look, I'll try to remember."

They continued on the trail in silence, allowing Zenevieve to think. Kennara hoped the woman would remember something, anything that could help them.

The pace was steady, slow for her benefit, but it gave

them more time to think this thing through. While they had a plan, it was more of a checklist, not an actual plan. She didn't really understand how any of it was going to happen.

"Wait," Zenevieve said.

Everyone stopped.

"There's at least a servant's passage from the kitchen to the queen's chambers. And if there's one there, they have to be all over."

"I remember playing in the hidden halls with my brother," Eljin added to the conversation.

Kennara looked at him, shocked. "Why didn't you mention this before?"

"I was a kid and I blocked out a lot of what happened there. But there are servants' passages leading everywhere. We can use them to sneak in almost anywhere in the keep." He ran his hand through his hair. "When we get into the tunnels, we can split up. It's going to split, the passage to the left leads to the kitchens, the one to the right leads to the private rooms."

"This will help. At least we won't all get caught since we won't be together," Abria said.

Eljin pointed to the side of the mountain. "Here are the stairs."

Kennara looked at them. There were a lot of stairs to walk up. She rubbed her leg without thinking about it. The thoughts that went through her head were not polite.

Reilynne came up beside her. "Are you ready?"

"Ready as I'll ever be." Kennara took a deep breath. "Which means I'm not ready at all."

The healer squeezed her shoulders. "Use what you're feeling to stay aware. You can do this, we all know that you can."

Kennara rolled her shoulders back and started up the stairs. Walking up these stairs was the true meaning of trudging. If she wasn't so scared, she would definitely be complaining. Instead her stomach was tied in knots, her palms were sweating, the rest of her clammy. If she thought she could turn and run, she probably would have. But, if the prophecy was true, she was a necessity to this battle, and she couldn't be the reason this mission failed. So, she put one foot in front of the other and walked up the stairs, each step making her more and more nervous.

It felt like they had been climbing all night long when the sloshing of water interrupted her panicked thoughts. She looked up to see a waterwheel right in front of them.

Eljin pointed around the wheel. "That's the entrance to the tunnels."

"I wonder if they built these to make it easier to maintain the waterwheel?" Kennara asked.

Cas raised his eyebrow. "Is that really important right now?"

"No, but my mind is running so fast I couldn't keep the thought quiet." She gestured to the stairs. "Climbing those stairs every time you need to fix this thing—coming out of the tunnel makes much more sense."

"That's true." Gallagher pitched in to the conversation.

"Which means at least someone knows about these tunnels," Kennara said.

Eljin shrugged. "It's too late now. This is our way in."

"Let's get this over with then."

Eljin held a torch out towards Kennara. She flicked her wrist and suddenly there was light throughout the tunnel. There were stones all around them and moisture clung to the walls. She took a step and felt her foot slide out from under her. Both Cas and Gallagher grabbed her by an arm, steadying her. She was going to have to watch where she put her feet.

"How long is this tunnel," she whispered.

"It's not that long. We should be beneath the castle soon," Eljin whispered back.

They continued down the tunnel for what felt like an interminable amount of time. Kennara longed to be anywhere but where they were. Back at the Faerie Glen Inn would be nice, she really liked it there. It was warm and cozy, even romantic. She thought about it and everything that happened there. Looking up, she saw Eljin ahead of her. She caught up to him and slipped her hand into his. He looked down and squeezed it three times as they continued down the tunnel.

Cas stopped. He pointed towards a spot where the tunnel split into two other directions. "I think the one to the right is the kitchen and the one to the left takes you to the dungeons. If we keep going straight, we will end up in the main hall. I think there's another split that leads to the private chambers."

"Are you sure?" Gallagher asked. "I feel like the kitchen is on the other side of the keep."

"I'm pretty sure. But it's been a while since I've been here."

Abria tapped her teeth. "We'll head to the left. You go to the right."

And that's what they did. Kennara, Eljin, Cas, and Zenevieve went to the right. The path curved one way and then another, causing Kennara to lose all sense of direction. Eventually, they came to a large arched door made of thick planks of wood held together by metal bands. Cas pushed the door open.

They did not walk into the kitchen. The place on the other side of the door was dank and gloomy. Kennara was ready to turn around and find another place to enter.

"Looks like Gallagher was right. This isn't the kitchen," Eljin said with a shrug.

Zenevieve shivered. "Looks more like a dungeon." She sniffed the air. "Smells like one too."

"I'm pretty sure it is a dungeon. And it's creepy," Kennara said.

She looked at the stone rooms blocked off with metal bars. There was one room after another, too many to count, all of them empty. It was better than the cells being filled with people, but it still felt like an area that had been abandoned a long time ago.

"I wish we had ended up in the kitchen as planned. I could use a snack. Maybe a slice of cheese," Zenevieve muttered.

Kennara shivered. "I really don't like it down here. Can we please get out of here, now?"

"Hmm . . . Should I keep you down here, or help you out of the dungeon?" A man with a scar running down his face walked into view. "It would be easy to lock you up down here. Then again, I'm sure the king would love to know that he has guests."

Kennara stared at the fair-skinned man in front of them, her hands shaking. He must be Viggo; who else would stand in front of them and take such pleasure in the thought of locking them in the dungeon?

Zenevieve stepped forward. "You must be Viggo. I'm

sure the king would rather see us right away. No need to waste anyone's time."

He sauntered over to her and grabbed her by the chin. Cas tensed beside Kennara. She put a hand on his arm to prevent him from doing anything impulsive.

"And you must be the one in charge of . . ." He eyed each one of them up and down. "This little expedition of yours."

Zenevieve shrugged. "You could say that, if you wanted to." She picked up her skirt, preventing it from dragging on the dungeon ground, and walked past Viggo. She turned. "After you." She gestured.

Viggo laughed. "My, aren't you brazen? I like it." He pushed her hair off her cheek and behind her ear.

Kennara's grip tightened on Cas's arm. They made eye contact. She stared back, trying to tell him to let Zenevieve do this, whatever she was doing. The water woman clearly had a plan.

Viggo gestured towards the door. "Follow me, but don't get any ideas. It may not look like I have a weapon, but I'm more powerful than you think."

Three amulets appeared from inside his doublet, three magic elements he could use. Kennara pulled her cloak tighter as fear settled even deeper inside her.

The four of them followed the king's righthand man up a spiral staircase and through a few halls to another staircase. Why, she wondered, why were there so many stairs? She leaned on Cas, allowing him to help her keep pace with Viggo.

Double doors opened into the great hall. At the opposite end, King Sheamus sat on the throne, the gold-and-jeweled crown nestled in his salt-and-pepper hair. He smiled through his beard, but it didn't reach his cold, cruel eyes.

Standing behind the king was the white-haired Maeryn, and at his knees was a red-headed woman in a blue shift.

Kennara lunged forward, but Cas caught her around the waist. Somehow, her movement wasn't noticed by anyone else. She glared up at Cas, who only shook his head. He was right. She shouldn't act until they had assessed the situation, but her sister was right in front of her.

Kellesha looked like she'd been broken. Her hair was loose around her, hiding her face from Kennara. She willed her sister to look up at her, but she didn't budge. Not knowing if it would work, she called on her heart magic and sent it towards her sister, only to feel like she had hit a solid wall. Maeryn looked over at her and shook her head. Kennara didn't know if it was a warning or an admonishment.

Kennara's magic couldn't get past whatever Maeryn was doing. She didn't like the feeling of her magic not working. The feeling of helplessness was overwhelming. They were finally here, and she couldn't do anything, even though she was the one who was supposed to fix everything.

The king laughed, stealing her focus from her sister. "Did you really think you could get into my castle and I wouldn't notice?"

Eljin took a step forward. "I think you mean *my* castle." Everyone in the room turned to the young prince.

Kennara yelled out, but a hand clamped down over her mouth before any sound escaped.

"Prince Bryok, how wonderful it is to see you again. If that is, indeed, who you really are?" The king stood and walked off the dais. He walked until he stood right in front of Eljin.

"I thought I had you killed."
"You thought wrong."

CHAPTER FIFTY-ONE

Abria, Gallagher, and Reilynne worked their way through the bustling kitchen. It was so busy in there they were more in danger of being put to work than anything else. She hoped the others were in a similar position.

Gallagher took the lead since he was the most familiar with the castle. Once they left the kitchens, they tried to stick to servant halls as they creeped through the keep. Abria breathed a sigh of relief every time they made it through another room. It wasn't long before they were walking up the spiral staircase to where Kellesha was being held. Gallagher let Abria through. She stood in front of the door, afraid to knock.

"Just do it," Gallagher whispered.

His words broke the spell that held her frozen in place. She knocked on the door. There was no noise, no movement, nothing.

"Kellesha, are you there?" she loudly whispered through the door.

Again, there was nothing, just silence.

"I'm breaking down the door," she said to no one in particular. Taking a couple of steps back, she angled her shoulder to prevent damage and rammed into the door. It flew open, sending her sprawling on the floor in the middle of an empty room.

"What?" Gallagher sputtered. "My source is a good one. They wouldn't have lied to me."

Abria stood, looking around the room. She took in the small mat in the corner with a wool blanket and nothing else. The room had housed a prisoner; whether or not it was Kellesha, she couldn't be certain. But someone had been held here.

"I don't have a very good feeling about this." Reilynne's breath shuddered. "I hope the others are okay."

It felt like a giant boulder had taken up residence in the pit of Abria's stomach. Something was wrong, but she didn't want to voice those concerns out loud, as if saying it would make it real. If it stayed in her head, it wasn't real yet.

"Let's go find the others. Make sure they've stayed out of trouble."

Gallagher led them back to the servants' passages Eljin told them about. They moved through the castle without running into anyone. It would seem the only people awake were those that worked in the kitchen. They continued on until they hit a spot where they could only go up or down another set of winding stairs.

"I say we go down; up is only going to take us to the bedchambers," Reilynne stated.

They followed her down the spiral staircase until they ended in a passage next to the great hall. Abria pushed open the door ever so slightly, careful not to be seen.

What she saw before her did not put her at ease. King Sheamus was on the throne he stole, and behind him stood Viggo and Maeryn. Kellesha was at his feet. Kennara was being held by Cas. Zenevieve and Eljin stood in front of them.

It sounded like Eljin was talking to his uncle. None of which was part of the plan.

They needed to do something, but she didn't know what to do. She looked to the other side of the room, opposite the king. There was a minstrel's stage high above the great room. A plan started to form.

"We need to get up there." She pointed to the stage area.

Gallagher looked up. "Why?"

"We need a distraction, something that can save our friends, at least from this predicament."

Reilynne looked at the stage. "What's the plan?"

Abria shrugged. "I'm going to do something that distracts the king."

Reilynne wiped her hands down the front of her dress. "I think we can come up with a better plan. Maybe use magic and stay hidden."

Abria looked back through the door, but quickly pressed herself against the wall in the passageway. "Maeryn saw me. You two need to get out of here."

They didn't move. She stared at them, tried to shoo them away, but they stayed.

Which was why they all got caught standing there.

"What do we have here?" Maeryn pushed the door open.

"Just an old acquaintance coming to visit." Abria tossed her braid over her shoulder.

Maeryn laughed. "Not many people come to visit after I take their magic away from them."

"I guess you could say I'm different."

"That's for sure. Who do you have with you?" Maeryn peered into the hall. "I sense someone with magic. Tsk, tsk. Not obeying the king is sure to get you in trouble."

"It's not like you've obeyed the edict," Abria muttered.

Maeryn rolled her eyes. "He needs me to help enforce his edict. It's a win-win for both of us. Now if you'll follow me, the king is waiting." She held the door open.

Abria nodded. It wasn't the distraction she was planning, but it was a distraction. She watched as the rest of their group turned to see them enter the great hall.

Kennara raised an eyebrow. Abria shook her head imperceptibly.

"It seems I'm in the presence of someone who's devoted her life to stopping me get what I want." The king leaned forward on his throne. "If I wasn't so annoyed by you, I would be impressed."

Abria smirked. It wasn't a good idea, but at the sight of this weaselly old man sitting there staring at her with his dead eyes, she just couldn't help herself. "You should be impressed."

She watched as his face went from tan to bright red. "But you didn't make it out with your magic, did you?"

"Doesn't that mean you've been stopped by a normal woman?"

If it was possible, the king turned an even brighter shade of red. It was probably going to make things harder in the long run, but she was enjoying provoking his ire.

A breeze made its way through the great hall, causing strands of hair to come loose from her braids. Maeryn put her hand on the king's shoulder and squeezed.

Interesting, Abria thought. Maeryn has some influence over the king. She wasn't sure if it made her dislike the white-haired woman more or less.

"Viggo, take them back down to the dungeon. They seemed to like it there."

It wasn't the best place to end up, but if they were put together, they could rethink the plan now that they were inside the castle—captive, but inside the castle nonetheless.

Viggo gestured for them to follow him. Abria fell behind the scarred man; the rest of their band of renegades followed her.

She turned back to the king. "Are you going to put her in the dungeon as well?" She nodded towards Kellesha.

"I don't think so. I plan on keeping her."

"How long are we going to have to stay in here?" Kennara hit the bars on her cell.

Abria watched Kennara come undone. The stress, anxiety, worry, it was all getting to her.

"Kennara, we can come up with a good plan." Abria examined where the bars connected to the rocks. It wouldn't take much to knock them out. "And it's not like these bars can actually hold us in."

"Then let's get them out now. There's no time to plan. Did you not see her there? She looked broken. I have to go save her now."

Abria was familiar with what Kennara was feeling. She knew it was never a good time to act when it was out of extreme desperation. Which was what Kennara was feeling if she were to guess.

Reilynne leaned up against the bars. "Now's not the time to act rashly."

Kennara turned on the healer. "Now seems like the perfect time to act rashly. In fact, I think we should rip the bars out, and go burn this place to the ground, the king with it. If we do it before they suspect anything, Maeryn won't be able to do whatever she was doing to block my magic."

Eljin laughed. "While that sounds like a fantastic idea, I think Abria and Reilynne are right. We need to regroup."

Kennara sank down to the ground. Abria wished there was something she could do to make her feel better.

"The most we can do right now is plan," she said, "especially if Maeryn is blocking your magic."

"It wasn't so much as blocking, as building a wall I couldn't get through." Kennara shrugged.

"That's something we need to consider as we put together an actual plan."

"The only plan that works for me is burning this place to the ground. Until you've come to accept that as the plan, I'm going to sleep, or at least pretend to."

Zenevieve poked her head out of the bars. "I second Kennara's plan."

"You would," Cas said, lying on the ground, his hands behind his head.

"I thought the whole idea was to get the throne back for me. It's going to be hard to rule if I don't have a home," Eljin added.

"It's too cold here. You should move your castle to the coast." Cas pushed himself to a sitting position.

Eljin rubbed his chin. "I wouldn't be opposed to that. A fresh start after all the misery caused by my uncle."

CHAPTER FIFTY-TWO

This was all Kennara's fault. Her sister was broken at the king's feet. If she had fought harder to keep them together, she never would have been kidnapped.

Then yesterday, she had just stood there. She had done nothing to save her sister. Kellesha wouldn't even look at her when they were all in the great hall.

Now, Kennara was locked up, and her sister was somewhere else in the castle, who knew where.

She knew this was going to happen, that she was the reason everything was going to go wrong. Now they were all trapped by the king with zero options.

"Are you blaming yourself for everything again?" Gallagher leaned up against the bars.

Kennara shrugged. "Who else is there to blame?"

Gallagher chuckled. "Oh, I don't know, one of the other seven of us you've been on this journey with."

Zenevieve stuck her head out. "She's not in the mood for a reason. Just wallowing in her own undeserved guilt."

Reilynne joined in. "Sometimes wallowing is necessary

—but it's going to delay us, which we don't really have time for."

"You know I can hear you," Kennara said, banging her head on the bar.

"Yes, that's the point." Reilynne said. "Maybe you can find strength rereading your ancestors' words. There weren't any instructions to help us, but the connection could be a source of strength." Reilynne tossed the journal through the bars toward Kennara.

They all turned as the door creaked open.

"It seems the king wants to see you again. Not surprising, it's a full moon, after all," Maeryn announced. She flicked her wrist and all the doors unlocked. "I assume you don't mind seeing him again. It is why you're here, after all."

They followed Maeryn up to the great room. Kennara took up the rear, every step increasing her feeling of impending doom. It also made her dislike of the woman leading them grow into something much more akin to hatred. How could Maeryn do the things she did to women and not feel guilty every single moment of every single day? It outraged Kennara.

Outrage burned inside of her. Suddenly, it no longer felt like they were walking to their end. Her emotions shifted as she walked up the stairs, always using her left leg to climb the step. Maybe they didn't need a plan; maybe she just needed to go in with confidence in her own abilities.

She twisted her hands, trying to feel the magic course through her. It started as a tingle in her center. It was like there were five strands of magic weaving around each other, waiting to be used. The magic wouldn't have to wait long; she was ready to feel the power coursing through her body again.

Maeryn opened the door to the great hall, and Kennara glanced over at the woman. She still didn't understand why the woman would align herself with King Sheamus.

They made eye contact as Kennara made her way through the door. Maeryn nodded. Kennara pulled up the hood on her cloak, wondering what the nod meant.

She followed her friends as they filed into the room. King Sheamus watching their every move from the throne. Kennara wanted to wipe the smirk off his face. The fact he thought he'd already won annoyed her to no end. She felt the air shift around her, the breeze ruffling her skirts.

Reilynne looked back at her and shook her head. Kennara shrugged in response.

Kellesha was not on the dais in front of them. The king was there, as was his henchman Viggo, but her sister was nowhere to be seen. Kennara's head whipped around to Maeryn, who only raised an eyebrow as she passed to take her place behind the king. There was something going on with that woman, and Kennara wanted to know what it was.

Maybe her idea last night wasn't such a bad one. She didn't have to worry about harming her sister if she used her magic right now. Deep down it felt like that's what she was supposed to do. And for once in her life, she felt strong enough to do what needed to be done.

She stepped forward, throwing her cloak off her shoulders. The scryer in the room's eyes went wide as she felt the magic that was inside Kennara.

The king stood. "Who are you?"

"I'm the one you fear. The person you've been searching for this entire time."

He turned red. His eyes were almost white. He might have even had a little spittle come out of the side of his mouth as he opened and closed it over and over again, no words ever coming out.

Her friends stepped back. Abria, Zenevieve, and Reilynne falling in behind her. The guys moved to the doors, blocking whatever exits they could. They might not have ever come up with a plan, but they were moving in sync, as if they could read her mind.

"You know I have magic. I have at least as much as you, if not more," King Sheamus spat.

Kennara's hand shot out, and she circled her wrist around as if she was coiling something in her hand. She yanked. One of his amulets went flying across room, skidding to a halt in front of Abria. The woman looked up at the king, contempt written all over her face.

"I know exactly what to do with this." She lifted her booted foot and brought it down on the amulet, splintering the stone. Blue mist rose from it. The king's screams echoed throughout the room alongside Abria's laughter.

Kennara took a step forward. "You were saying."

She raised her arms and flicked her hands open, causing flames to ripple across her palms and up her arms. The king tried to combat her by accessing water magic, but with the help of Zenevieve, she swatted it away and grabbed another amulet from his neck and destroyed it before he could blink.

The king turned to his officers, screaming, "Do something."

Viggo ran down, but Kennara wasn't concerned. Especially when she saw Abria grab an amulet from around his neck and toss it onto the stone, where it splintered, and a tan mist filtered through the room until it completely dissipated. The scarred man fell to his knees with a sob.

Kennara gestured towards Cas to detain the man. They

didn't need him getting in their way, or more likely, her way. She would have liked to watch the scuffle behind her, but she could only stare at the king.

She took another step forward, wind and flames whipping around her, her brow furrowed with determination.

The king's guard ran into the room. She rolled her eyes in disgust at their black-and-silver uniforms as they surrounded her and her friends. With her left leg she stomped on the floor. The stone beneath her foot rumbled, and the rumbling spread to the edges of the room. The guards stumbled and fell back against the walls.

Stones fell, holding the guards to the ground. Kennara laughed. Abria must be having a little fun now that she had her magic back.

As she moved closer to the king, she could see his eyes fill with fear, his hands shaking, his breath unsteady. One more step forward and he would have nowhere to go.

A scream filled the great hall.

Kennara turned to see her sister dragged into the room. Her magic sputtered for a moment as she watched the guards toss Kellesha across the floor.

"Take her magic now," King Sheamus yelled. He pointed to her sister's body lying on the ground in nothing but a white shift. She looked broken and exposed.

The king ran by her.

Her arm shot out, grabbing him by the neck of his royal garb and three leather cords, each holding an amulet.

"Think again, Your Majesty," she whispered next to his ear, sending fire down each of the leather cords into the amulets.

She felt the moment he realized he was losing his last hold on magic. His body stiffened, his heart raced, and he tried to get away. Instead, each amulet exploded, sending fragments of stone into the ermine trim on his doublet.

"You are going to abdicate. I will leave it up to Eljin whether you rot in the dungeon or are banished from here. I personally never want to see your face, so my suggestion is sending you to the forbidden realm of the Slotuslands. But the decision isn't mine: you didn't kill my family."

Kennara tossed him aside. Flames licked at his clothes, and he tried to pat them out, eventually dropping to the ground and rolling.

Kennara turned towards Maeryn.

"What are you going to do now?" she asked the white-haired woman.

Maeryn looked at her for a moment, then dropped to her knee. "Whatever you want me to, my queen."

CHAPTER FIFTY-THREE

Every free person in the room suddenly dropped to their knees.

Well, that was unexpected, Kennara thought as she looked around to see her friends standing, looking at everyone else bowing to her.

"No, you don't understand—" She was interrupted when Eljin put a finger up against her mouth.

He leaned in so he was next to her ear. His breath tickled her neck. "You are going to be their queen."

He stood by her side with his arm around her waist.

Sheamus groaned. Eljin walked over to his uncle and squatted beside him.

"How does it feel, Uncle? To be replaced by someone you were so desperate to destroy."

The man said nothing.

"Someone get him out of my sight," Kennara said.

Gallagher stepped forward. "My pleasure." He hauled the old man on to his feet and took him to the dungeon.

Kennara looked at the woman still kneeling in front of

her. "Maeryn, we need to talk," she said as she limped over to her sister's side.

She sat on the floor beside Kellesha, knowing any one of her friends would ensure her safety.

"I always knew you could do it. As soon as Zenevieve told me about the prophecy, I knew it was you." Kellesha coughed.

Kennara felt the tears she'd been holding back fall from her eyes. "What did they do to you?"

"It wasn't that bad, other than wearing nothing but a shift. Maeryn made sure I was kept in the tower instead of the dungeon and snuck food to me when she could. I'm pretty sure she convinced the king to let me keep my magic until you all got here." Kellesha pushed herself up. "It was still dismal and cold, but it wasn't as bad as I feared it would be when I was captured."

Kennara threw her arms around her sister. She let her heart magic loose and pictured her sister hearty and healthy, as if they were still in Wreswell and she was training every day. Her magic flowed into her sister, strengthening her muscles and fixing whatever it could along the way. When she let go, Kellesha looked like the sister she remembered, no longer a broken body on stone.

"Of course you would." Kellesha laughed. "You know, I could have done that myself with a bit of exercise."

"Or you can just say thank you and let me take care of you for once."

Kellesha grabbed her sister's hand. "Thank you." Her eyes darted over to Abria.

"Apparently, our sister reunion is over. Go over and make her feel better; her guilt's been eating at her, and I'm afraid I didn't help at all."

Kennara turned back to Maeryn. "Why did you help her? I don't understand."

Maeryn shifted her weight. "When we made eye contact in the forest, I felt kinship. You felt fear, but I couldn't imagine destroying you or your sister. You're Awel's descendent, and I'm King Balor's."

To Kennara's surprise, Maeryn was crying. She wanted to reach out and comfort her, but she didn't know if she should trust her. Although, why shouldn't she? This woman had never lied to her. In fact, Maeryn had given her a chance to escape, and warned her what would happen if they met again. She had, in a way, always been honest with Kennara.

Maeryn looked away. "Then we met at the inn, and you gave some long heroic speech about me always having a choice. I blew it off at the time, but the more I thought about it, the more I questioned. I realized I died a little more inside at every Quickening." Maeryn wiped the tears from her eyes. "I knew if you made it here, I would help you. And if you won, I would vow my allegiance to you, and no one else."

"But I'm not actually a queen."

Maeryn laughed. "I've seen the way you and the prince, or should I say king, look at each other. One way or another, you'll be queen and I'll stand by your side, or let you banish me if that's what you feel is right. Either way, you don't have to worry about me ever again."

CHAPTER FIFTY-FOUR

Abria looked at the woman walking to her in nothing but a shift. She should not be staring at the curve of her hip when the fabric grazed up against it as she moved, and she definitely shouldn't be appreciating the way the muscles in her legs rippled as she took one step after another, or anything else of that nature. Because Kellesha wouldn't have been trapped here if Abria had done her job and protected her like she'd promised Kennara.

"Hi," Kellesha said, stopping in front of her.

"Hi," Abria responded, suddenly finding the stone floor fascinating.

Kellesha reached out softly, touching her chin with two fingers, pressing until they were looking at one another.

"Is that really the only greeting I get after all of this?" Kellesha asked.

Abria tried to look away; she didn't want her love to see the guilt in her eyes. "I don't know if I can do more. If it wasn't for me, you would never have gone through this ordeal."

"Darling, you can't blame yourself. Do you really think I wouldn't have charged in blindly to save Zenevieve if you hadn't? The king set a trap. It was a good one." Kellesha wrapped her arms around Abria. "I've had time to rethink every moment of that fight. I was going to be kidnapped one way or another. Now put your arms around me."

Abria did as Kellesha ordered. It was the first time she'd thought about forgiving herself. Relief swept through her body, so strong it was palpable. Tears streamed down her face and she couldn't stop herself from sobbing.

The two fell to the ground, Kellesha holding her as she let out all the emotions she'd kept pent up until this moment.

She leaned back to find Kellesha's blue eyes staring at her. She reached up to her love's face and caressed her cheek as the other hand found its way behind her neck. Abria pulled her in for a kiss, pressing their lips together softly for a moment before it turned into something much more frantic, a clash of battling tongues and teeth. She moved away from Kellesha's lips and rained kisses all over her face and neck before wrapping her arms around her for another hug.

Abria heard Zenevieve say, "I think we should follow their example, don't you?"

The strangled response from Cas made her laugh.

"What's so funny?" Kellesha asked.

Abria nodded towards Cas and Zenevieve. "I think she's going to be trouble for Cas. He's used to spending time with you and Kennara, and now there she is, in her forward, sassy way. He's not going to know how to handle it."

"I heard that," Cas muttered over his shoulders. "And I know what to do."

Zenevieve sauntered up to him, walking her fingers up his chest. "You do, do you? Well, prove it."

With little warning, Cas swept her up into his arms and threw her over his shoulder.

Abria couldn't help but burst into laughter. She laughed so hard she cried as he carried the woman around, and Zenevieve alternated between staring at his bum and pounding on his back to let her go.

"That's sweet," Kellesha said. "I think we should wrap up everything here and find somewhere a little more private."

Which was exactly what they did. Abria released the trapped guards, and they were put in the dungeon until they swore their allegiance to the new king. Abria escorted Maeryn up to a tower room, where Kennara would have to decide what to do with her. She didn't know if she could ever forgive the woman, but it wasn't up to her. And Abria learned from Kellesha that Maeryn was the only reason she still had her magic, which meant she might have to let go of her grudge, eventually.

Until then, she was going to disappear with Kellesha for a while.

CHAPTER FIFTY-FIVE

"Queen Kennara has a nice ring to it," Eljin leaned back in his chair.

"You know these books aren't going to shelve themselves," Kennara responded. She tapped the stack of books sitting next to her.

She looked around the room. It was like something from a dream, wall-to-ceiling books and scrolls. The shelves were built around windows, doors, and a great enormous fireplace. It was the room of her dreams, much like the rooms at the Faerie Glen had been, which was the reason Eljin had insisted on hiring the inn's carpenter to make all the furniture for the library and their bedroom.

Eljin smiled. "I don't know if you know this, but that's what servants are for. When you're the ruler of the land and the owner of a castle, you no longer have to shelve books."

Kennara grabbed an armful of books and her cane. "That hardly seems fair. I'm the one that pulled them down; you should be the one that has to put them back up. Especially since I was trying to learn about your job—*you* are the rightful heir to the throne."

"But *you're* the one that everyone has sworn an allegiance to. So, I believe you're stuck ruling with me. Now set those books down and come over here."

She looked at him warily. "Why?"

"Because I want to kiss you before we greet our visitors," Eljin said with a smirk.

She put the books down and hobbled over to his chair. He reached around her waist and pulled her down onto his lap. She couldn't help but laugh. He brushed his lips against hers softly, licking her bottom lip. She opened her mouth, allowing him to plunder it as she wrapped her arms around his neck, deepening the kiss even more.

"They're in the library," Kellesha called out. "Where else would you expect them to be?"

Kennara pulled away from the kiss to see her sister walk in and flop into her chair. Abria followed her in and sat on her lap. The rest of their group followed, Reilynne leading Gallagher and Cas dragging Zenevieve behind him.

"Are these our visitors? Because, to be visitors, they would have to leave the castle," Kennara said with a huge grin.

Cas, Abria, and Kellesha were in charge of the guards. Cas and Kellesha had been unwilling to give up their bodyguard roles, so Cas still was the head of Eljin's personal guards, while Kellesha was the head of Kennara's. Abria was in charge of training all the new recruits. And Gallagher, well, he decided to use his network of sources to start a clandestine portion of the guard.

Reilynne was the chief healer, and she trained others that had heart magic.

When Zayden had heard about everything, he had joined them. He and Maeryn had become friends quickly and were rarely seen apart.

And then there was Zenevieve: who knew the woman alone on the ocean would turn into such a free spirit? She loved being on the road, so she would go for quick trips, doing whatever it was she did, and come back so Cas could still guard Eljin.

What it meant was no one was ever too far from the castle they had moved to Wreswell after destroying the one in the mountains. She had fulfilled her dream of burning it to the ground—after everyone had moved out, of course. Kennara hated the mountains, and the cold made her leg hurt, so they all moved to where it started for them, well for most of them.

Kennara looked around at her family, her heart overflowing with happiness. It was hard to believe that not long ago they all had been hiding, but had somehow found each other and survived in a world that didn't want them to.

Now, together, they would thrive.

ACKNOWLEDGMENTS

I started this book back in the summer of 2022, since then I've finished and published a few other books. But for some reason this one took me a lot longer to write. There were times I didn't even look at it for months on end. Now that it's done I can see why. One of the reasons is I started it when I was angry and hurt. The U.S. Supreme Court had just overturned Roe v. Wade, and I wanted to write a book that dealt with the issues of women's rights being taken away, but I didn't want it to be a political think piece or anything else along those lines. Which is how it became the book before you. Another reason it took so long is I was just finishing up with my immunotherapy treatment for melanoma and realizing that my right leg, which has had melanoma in three different spots, multiple lymph nodes removed, and a skin graft area that's never going to look normal, will never be the same again. If you've finished the book, you might see some parallels. So there were times I don't think I wanted to sit in that space, feeling any of those feelings. And now that it's done, I kinda miss knowing it's around for me to work on. But my characters have had their Happily Ever After, and I'm always working on mine with the help of amazing people.

If you've read my other books you're definitely going to recognize these names. First, thank you to everyone I talked to and has read parts of the manuscript when I've been worried about certain tones of certain scenes. Second, thank you to my Facebook writing groups and friends who reeled me in when I wanted to make things too comical for this book. Don't worry, those missed opportunities are showing up in more appropriate books. Third, I am so thankful for the team I have around me from Clara Stone at Authortree who did all the art for this book, Jamie Dalton for looking at all the art and confirming it looked good, Catherine Anderson for reading all my panicked messages, Sarah Hawkins for being the best editor and always making me feel like my work is good, and of course, my mom, who spent two weeks reading the last draft of the book out loud to me and making sure it was the best that it could be. And finally, my dad, who spent months making book nooks for the Kickstarter.

And, thank you to everyone who backed my Kickstarter Campaign. I'm so happy that this edition of the book exists, and really it's because of you.

ALSO BY STEPHANIE K. CLEMENS

Ladies of WACK Series

A Study in Steam

A Practicum in Perjury

A History in Horticulture – Coming Soon

Ladies of WACK Prequels

The Daring Adventures of Honoria Porter: Volume 1

Wynterfell Romances

For the Love of Hot Cocoa

Villain Rehab – Coming Soon

Fantasy Books

Stripped Away

Cursed by Bandits – Coming 2024

Children's Book by S.K. Clemens

Frankie Wants to be a Sled Dog

ABOUT STEPHANIE K. CLEMENS

Stephanie K. Clemens is known for many things: an author, photographer, dog mom, instagrammer, adventurer, teacher, lawyer, and more. When she's not sitting behind her laptop she can be found on some adventure. Most of the time it's a road trip with her two doggos, but recently it has been in the pages of a book.